A NOTE ABOUT THE AUTHOR

Chris Page was born in Sweden in 1962, and brought up in Gloucestershire in the UK. After living in London and New York, he moved to Osaka in 1989, where he is based to this day with his family.

He is an occasional magazine editor, cartoonist, journalist, and copywriter, and supports all these occupations by working in education. Primarily, he writes fiction and dotes on his big, fat, black and white cat.

In July 2002 *The London Magazine* featured his short story, 'The Freebie'. That story is included alongside more of his short fiction in the e-book collection *Shorts* and paperback *Un-Tall Tales*, also available from Psipook Press. Chris's first novel is *Weed*, also from Psipook Press.

The Underpants Tree is the second volume of the *Underpants of Fire* trilogy, the first installment being *King of the Undies World*.

THE UNDERPANTS TREE

Chris Page

psipook press
www.psipook.com

Published by Psipook Press
Copyright©Chris Page
All rights reserved

First published in 2015 by Psipook Press
This paperback edition, 2015 by Psipook Press
www.psipook.com
psipook@psipook.com

ISBN 978-0-9559588-8-5

Cover design by Chris Page

In memory of my father, who taught me to always carry a bucket.

The Underpants Tree

Being the successor to King of the Undies World *and second volume of the* Underpants of Fire Trilogy

Chris Page

1

The underpants festoon the branches of the trees like bright pennants, all fluttering in the fresh, promise-laden morning breeze. There are thousands of trees, in neat, orderly rows, stretching in all directions as far as the eye can see: trees and underpants, trees and underpants, trees and underpants. The orchard seems to be endless — 'vast' is a term that might spring to mind, 'mind-boggling' is another.

There are all kinds of pants. Men's pants, ladies' pants, pants for kids of all ages and shapes, and apparently pants for dogs and cats too. There are big pants, small pants, tiny pants and voluminous pants. There are sensible pants and sexy pants of all descriptions. There are frivolous and fatuous pants and stern ones to disapprove of them. There are sturdy pants and gossamer pants and all thicknesses in between. There are thermals and coolers. There are more colours and patterns and designs than even the fevered brain of the perviest underpants fetishist could imagine. No one tree has the same kind of pants; each tree carries a diversity, and no two pairs of pants are alike. The one thing they have in common — other than being on a tree — is that the fabrics are vibrant in hue and texture and seem to shimmer with a curious life of their own.

An observer of average attention to detail would note that the underpants do not merely festoon the trees, they grow from them, they hang by delicate green stems. The underpants have sprouted from the boughs like flappy and gaily-coloured fruit.

The observer should at this point start feeling considerable curiosity. What are underpants doing sprouting from trees? Or better, what are trees doing sprouting underpants? This does not seem a conventional act of nature.

Among the trees walks a man: by his bearing a gentleman. He has short, immaculate, black hair, with an absolutely straight side parting, at a mathematically precise point halfway between the crown of his head and his left ear. He wears a suit of a striking sobriety that wouldn't be out of place at a funeral, which nevertheless shimmers with the same odd sheen as the underpants on the trees. Everything about him is neat and pressed and clipped. He is evidently a man who appreciates order.

His face wears a faint and beatific glow.

The gentleman stops and surveys his trees — for they are his; he put them there — and he smiles broadly because he sees that they are good.

In the distance, despite the bright and cloudless sky, there is a rumble of thunder.

And then the man goes on his way like someone who has much to do, which, indeed, he is.

2

Hades is in his testing house, testing out his underpants.

'Three, two … one …'

Boom!

The explosion fills the cavernous testing hangar with billowing smoke, flying debris and hurtling test staff.

It is Sir Hades Gousset himself, the most important man in the world, founder, president, CEO, head of research and development, chief of everything at Pants Corp, which, as everyone on the planet knows, is the power behind Hades Undies World. As everyone in the world also knows, everyone in the world wears Hades underpants.

More than an underpants magnate, Hades is a visionary, a proselytiser. 'Whoever owns underpants owns the world!' is his battle cry.

'Oh, buggery bugger-bags!' says Hades mildly as shrapnel from the explosion batters on the walls of his concrete bunker.

Sirens signal the arrival of the emergency services, which are on permanent standby just outside the hangar.

'Well that was successful,' said Hilda Titanium his personal assistant from inside her burqa.

'Would have been a fantastic success had they been supposed to explode. As the underpants in question were absolutely not supposed to detonate, I think this constitutes an unmitigated balls up — quite literally for the test pilot, by the looks of him.'

Hilda does not wear a burqa for religious or cultural reasons. She is a woman of such striking appearance that men tend to injure themselves at the sight of her. She remains covered up as an act of humanity.

'What were they supposed to do if they weren't supposed to explode so effectively?'

Hilda is also the secret power within Pants Corp. If Hades is the head of the enterprise that bears his name, and his factories and outlets and research department are the arms, legs and internal organs, then Hilda is the spinal chord that links it all together.

'They are supposed to make fertiliser,' said Hades.

'Make fertiliser?'

'Yes. The trouble is, fertiliser is such volatile stuff. It's all nitrates and phosphorus. One false move and it's kaboom! You can make bombs from it, you know, if you are a terrorist or a schoolboy. We're having the devil of a time getting the stuff to remain stable while we get it from the pants to the field.'

'Excuse me for not seeing what I'm sure must be blindingly obvious, but why would anyone want to make fertiliser with their underpants?'

'Goodness gracious me, Hilda! You really are not your rapier-sharp self today. Applications for the developing world, don't you know: poor countries. Mobile fertiliser makers for the struggling parts of this planet.'

'The developing world? Not much of a market, one would have thought. The whole problem in the poor countries is that the people are, well, poor — which usually means they don't have money to spend on things to the profit of the seller.'

'Oh, we're not chasing the profits with this one, Hilda. These are designed to be given away to help lift people out of poverty. I myself came from an impoverished background: a ditch in Essex, to be exact. But I was lucky. Underpants provided me an escape into a world of reward for my hard work. Not all people are as fortunate as me. According to UNICEF, 22,000 children die each day due to poverty. Nearly 30 per cent of all children in developing countries are underweight or stunted. More than 80 per cent of the world's population live on less than $10 a day. Pants Corp is just trying to help out a little. These fertiliser pants are just one technology on a whole new line designed to alleviate hardship in less fortunate parts of the world.'

'Socially aware underpants, you might say,' mused Hilda.

'Might say? I do say.'

'Pants Corp gives staggering amounts of money to the poor each year.'

'Yes, we do, Hilda. With this project we are trying to do something more fundamental. We are trying to reshape the infrastructure of the poorer countries so they can flourish on their own. Give a man a fish and he can feed himself for a day. But give him a pair of underpants, eh? Know what I mean?'

'You mean you've invented underpants that can catch fish?'

'What does everyone need, Hilda?' Hades asked, forgetting that he has already told everyone on the planet several thousand times already.

'Food, water, air, energy, and underpants. That's what everyone needs.'

Out of sight inside her burqa, Hilda was mouthing the words along with Hades.

'Our development pants will take care of most of those needs simultaneously.'

'They will?'

'Absolutely. It's not just developing nations that will benefit. Oh, no. The western industrial way of life puts great pressures on the environment and we can't go on living like this. I am reaching toward a new model in which we live *with* not *on* nature. Sustainability is the word; sustainable underpants is the way. Our new technologies will help people grow food and create energy while filling the need for underthings at the same time. Quite brilliant, don't you think? I thought of it, you know.'

'In that case I'm sure it's completely brilliant.'

'We have invented water divining pants. One problem people have is finding enough clean water for their fields and to drink and cook. The diviners will track down water sources hidden deep underground.'

'They can do that?'

'Oh, yes. They zoom downwards in the vicinity of water, even if it's hidden. Then they drill.'

'Drill?' asked Hilda in some alarm.

'Yes, they drill. They rotate at high speed and automatically dig a well. Sometimes they go off prematurely, though, and zoom and rotate upwards, which is not the best thing for the wearer. I can't think why. But that's just a glitch. We're working on it.'

'You can't think why they sometimes zoom upwards when they are trained to search for water and are wrapped around the waterworks of a person?'

'No. But we have the finest brains working on the issue. It's only a matter of time before we crack it.

'Now, in this time of climate change, the atmosphere of the planet is becoming increasingly unstable, and violent weather events have the biggest impact on the most vulnerable communities. We've invented a pair that will convert into extreme weather shelters, big enough to accommodate a family and livestock with one shake of the botty. Don't wear them dancing, though.

'Talking of climate change, we have the carbon sinkers. They filter methane and also trap carbon from the atmosphere.'

'Trap carbon? Carbon can get a bit bulky, can't it?'

'Oh yes. We do have a small issue with the way they tend to acquire volume and wearers not being able to move or even stand upright, but we're working on that.

'Energy! There are the solars. They work like solar panels and collect energy from the sunlight. They're made of a revolutionary new fabric that has the lightness and flexibility of cotton and fantastic photovoltaic properties.'

'But don't solar cells need to be out in the sun to work?'

'Well, yields have been pretty disappointing so far. We are looking into the feasibility of transparent trousers to go with them.'

'What about making hats with the material instead of underpants? Hats tend to be more exposed to the elements than underpants, and heads are usually closer to the sun than bottoms.'

'Are you mad? We're not hatters! The name of this company is Undies World, not Top of your Bonce World.'

'Well, they do say "if you want to get ahead, get a hat".'

'Piffle and tosh, Hilda. It's "if you want to get a hat, get a head," that's what they say. Now where was I?'

'My apologies for thinking, Hades.'

'Ducks.'

'Are you getting fresh with me, or do you mean ducks to eat? You'll need a lot of them to feed the starving, and aren't there other things more plentiful in the world? Like beans and rice?'

'Energy ducks, Hilda. Things that bob in the water harvesting the endless power of tides and waves. Marvellous things. The wearer of these duck pants just jumps in the water and starts generating electricity. Amazing stuff. No need for huge expensive tidal barriers that require buckets of investment and spoil the view. Communities can now generate their own power from whatever moving body of water they have to hand by just jumping into it.'

'But if these people are bobbing in the water making electricity, how can they farm their land?'

Hades was silent a moment. It was possible that he hadn't thought of this. 'Fisherfolk, Hilda! Farmers of the sea! Wear them while they're working. Nothing simpler.'

'Do they work?'

'Of course they work. They come from Hades' own laboratories. Bit of an issue with electric shocks, to be honest. A mixed blessing. Not comfortable for the wearer but they have the unintended affect of bringing boatloads of stunned fish to the surface for easy harvesting.'

'With the energy producing pants, the energy has to be stored somewhere. Not much storage space in a pair of pants, in my experience.'

'Depends on the pants, actually, but a good point. The power has to be stored in pretty hefty batteries, so where to stash them? We did have a solution, or rather we attempted to capitalise on a solution provided by nature, but that has proved somewhat unpopular with wearers, so we're still working on that.

'And then there are the Onan pants.'

'The Onan pants? But —'

'Yes, I think we'll market them as the Onanisers.'

'Is that wise?'

'Of course it's wise. The name comes from the Bible. How much wiser do you want? And it describes perfectly what they do.'

'How on earth could that be related to development issues?'

'Onan, Hilda! Onan the farmer chap. Threw his seed on the ground wherever he went. Famous for it.'

'I don't think —'

'The Onanisers are going to be just as famous. They plough, furrow and seed the land as they go. Imagine! You take a stroll to the local shop and leave a fertile, nutrition-bearing field behind you. Just like Onan.'

'No problem with these?'

'Of course not. Only with the velocity of the seeds.'

'I see.'

'And their unpredictable vector.'

'Ah ha.'

'And bystanders ending up in hospital.'

'Is that all?'

'And people laughing at the name.'

'But you're working on it.'

'We are indeed. Onward and upward!'

'Just like Onan.'

'Absolutely! But you haven't asked me how the fertilising pants make fertiliser.'

'I think I'm OK not knowing, thanks, Hades. Another time perhaps.'

'Amazing concept! The farmer just makes fertiliser as he goes about his daily business.'

'Or would if the pants didn't keep exploding.'

'Quite.'

'You really are quite an inspiration, Hades. All this effort and energy and technology and innovation to clothe the loins of the world's poor; people you haven't even met.'

'Well, I have dedicated my life to the search for the perfect underpants — as you well know. As the years draw in around me, I feel I must hasten the search.' Hades reached his hand dramatically to the heavens. 'What would the perfect pants look like? What would they smell like? I feel they are just out of reach, but that they are there. And as for helping the poor, well, I have had a blessed life. I've been very lucky and I want to give something back. Underpants don't grow on trees, Hilda. That's what I like to say.'

'Which brings us neatly to the point of me interrupting your busy test schedule.'

'Really? Well, walk with me, Hilda, and tell me all about it.'

'Walk in the wreckage, Sir Hades?'

'Absolutely. A very salutary thing, walking in wreckage. It's something I would like to impress on the world.'

They left the bunker and entered the hangar, stepping over what appeared to be a body part. Smoke and twisted steel girders hung in the air. Rescue workers scraped at stains on the floor and walls.

'Well, yes, Hades. It's about pants not growing on trees.'

'Absolutely.'

'Well, it appears that they now do.'

'Say what, good lady? It's a fundamental and universally accepted fact of nature that pants don't grow on trees. Explain yourself.'

'Well, they probably need a bit of encouragement but they seem to be getting that.' Hilda's hands appeared through a hatch in the burqa and showed Hades a tablet computer. She tapped open a file of photos. A splash screen told Hades in big scary, red letters: 'Absolutely top-most secret. Don't even look at this screen.'

'We shouldn't have this data, really. We had to break the encryption on it to view it.'

'How did you do that?'

'We typed 1234. The owners hadn't bothered to reset the pass key.'

'Where on earth did this come from?'

'The NSA. One of our interns was hacking their servers for a laugh and found this.' Hilda tapped open a photo. It was a satellite photo of what appeared to be a lot of trees.

'It's a lot of trees,' said Hades.

'Quite so. Now look closely.' Hilda zoomed onto just one tree.

'Good Lord! Looks like the tree is festooned with underwear. All different kinds. What would be the point of that?'

'Exactly. Now look at this photo.' This one was much better resolution. 'This would not appear to be a normal festoon of underpants. This would appear to be underpants actually growing on trees.'

'Nonsense! Looks like a perfectly normal festoon to me. Ah! Dr Pickles!' Hades bellowed at his head of research who was frantically searching for his colleagues in the rubble. 'You're a scientist, aren't you. Does this look like a normal festoon of underpants to you?' Hades shoved the tablet in the face of his employee.

'Well, sir, that would depend on what the correct answer is. What do you want me to say?'

'I want you say that this looks like a perfectly normal festoon of underpants, and I want you to say that underpants don't grow on trees.'

'In that case, I can say with confidence, sir, that this looks remarkably like a perfectly normal festoon of underpants, spread over what appears to be several thousand acres. And I'd like to say, sir, apropos of I don't know what, underpants don't grow on trees. Normally.'

'There you go. Right from the scientist's mouth.'

'May I get back to scrabbling frantically in the rubble looking for my colleagues, sir?'

'Oh, yes. You'd better jump to, Pickles. I don't think colleagues survive long under piles of rubble. You'll want to be pulling them out with all haste. I recommend frantic scrabbling as a technique. And don't let anyone interrupt, you hear?'

'Consider my fingers worn to bloody stumps with uninterrupted frantic scrabbling, sir.'

'That's the way! Good show! You see Hilda. No higher authority than a boffin, what? Nothing unusual about thousands of acres of trees festooned with underpants. Perfectly normal.'

'It would be perfectly normal Sir Hades, but for one perfectly abnormal thing. The underclothes do, in fact, seem to be growing on the trees.'

'Blazes Hilda, if underthings don't grow on trees it follows quite logically that these underthings aren't. Why are you insisting that something can't be happening is happening just because of a pile of photos suggesting it is happening? Have you suddenly got religion or something?'

Hilda met Hades glare evenly and unfalteringly.

'Wait a minute!' Hades swivelled on his heel and marched back to his head of research, whose frantic scrabbling had uncovered a pair of legs, which he was now tugging with all his might.

'Pickles! You said "normally",' accused Hades.

'Yes, sir, I did,' the scientist agreed between tugs and plumes of dust.

'You said, "underpants don't grow on trees".'

'I did, sir. You said you wanted me to say that.'

'And then you added "normally".'

'I did, Sir Hades.'

'And why did you add "normally"?'

'Because that's the case, sir. Underwear doesn't grow on trees, normally.'

'Not normally. But you said "normally" quite clearly, which suggests to me that this case is lacking normality.'

'That's right, sir. You said you wanted me to say "underpants don't grow on trees", and I said that. Was there something wrong with the way that I said it, perhaps?'

'There was indeed. The what was wrong with the way you said it was the "normally" you appended to it.'

'Do you want me to say it again without the "normally"?'

'No, blither it! I want you to explain why you had to add "normally" to the "underpants don't grow on trees" as if in this case they were.'

'Ah, well, normally, I would agree that underpants don't grow on trees, but in this case, it looks like they might be.'

'Dammit, that's what Hilda said too.'

'Er, has Ms Titanium seen the photos?'

'Yes, she showed them to me.'

'Ah, well it might not be a coincidence then that they look to her like the underwear might be growing on the trees, as it does to me.'

Hades looked furiously from Pickles to Hilda and back again. 'Well, would you like to tell me why you think something is the case that can't possibly be the case?'

Hilda and the scientist exchanged glances. Or the scientist exchanged looks with the implacable face of Hilda's burqa, while Hilda offered Pickles a view of the photos on the tablet.

'Well,' began Pickles, 'if this clothing is indeed growing on trees in a manner inconsistent with what we understand about clothing, then I would say they've had some help.'

'Had some help?'

'It probably isn't a natural phenomenon,' said Hilda. 'Underpants have not been observed growing on trees in nature.'

'Yes, I bloody well know that! That's what I have been saying! Now tell, me, if underpants don't grow on trees why do you think these are?'

'They appear to be on stalks, Hades, and attached to the branches.'

'And you can see,' added Pickles, 'by their odd shape and size, some seem to be in the process of forming.'

'Appear to be? Seem to be? Aren't you two sure of anything?'

'Well, no, Hades of course not. Clothes are just not supposed to grow on trees.'

'Now you're going round in circles. Why am I listening to you?'

'Because,' said Hilda firmly, 'Whatever the truth behind these photos, there's something odd going on with underpants, and anything to do with underpants is of extreme interest to us. And the odder it is, the more of interest it is.'

'Suppose,' said Pickles, 'someone really had learned to grow pants on trees. Think what it might do to your business.'

'Exactly,' continued Hilda. 'Uncountable hours of research and development go into Hades undies — the technology, the fibres, the applications, the design, the marketing, the manufacture, the distribution ... Now imagine a world in which when you want clean underthings, you just lean out the window and snip them off a tree.'

Hades looked grim. His face darkened.

The scientist took up the story. 'And if these pants are not growing on trees, then someone somewhere has gone to a lot of effort to make it appear they are. Thousands of acres of lavishly festooned trees is not the product of an idle whim. No one got out of bed one morning and suddenly decided to kill an hour or two by creating massive orchards and draping millions of pairs of underthings on them.'

'Very well,' announced Hades. 'You have my attention. Where are these trees exactly?'

'Well, that's another odd thing,' said Hilda. 'They appear to be in Antarctica.'

'Antarctica?' asked Hades.

'Antarctica,' confirmed Hilda.

'Antarctica?' Pickles wanted to know.

'Antarctica,' Hilda insisted.

'What, you mean the Antarctica at the bottom of the world?' asked Hades with no little incredulity.

'The same Antarctica,' assented Hilda.

'The Antarctica that's a barren wilderness of snow, ice, the coldest temperatures on Earth and homeland of the penguins?' asked Pickles with no little incredulity of his own.

'Yes, that Antarctica,' said Hilda with only quite a lot of impatience in her voice.

'But that's impossible,' said Hades. 'Trees couldn't grow there. They need sunlight, and rain and fertile soil, and insects to do the pollinating and general mollycoddling by nature. They don't need an environment that is completely inimical to any kind life other than the short, black and white, comically waddling kind.'

'Yes, it would be impossible, normally.'

'So that's two impossible things you are asking me to accept before elevenses.'

'Well, it seems that whoever arranged for these trees to grow clothes has also created a very local, very artificial environment right there in the snowy wastes. Presumably in order to grow these trees,' Hilda told them.

'Greenhouses, you mean,' said Pickles. 'A geodesic dome of some sort.'

'No. I mean a local, artificially maintained climate in the open air. Where all around you have the snowy wastes we associate with the bottom of the world, we can clearly see in these satellite photos a large green valley that can only be described as verdant and idyllic and there is absolutely no indication of how this was done.'

'But —' said Pickles.

'Oh. Artificial environment, is it? In the middle of an icy wasteland? That would explain it.' said Hades. 'Fair dos.'

'But —' said Pickles, whose scientific curiosity had been thoroughly aroused.

Hades was moving on. 'We now need a course of action,' he said in a decisive and action-oriented tone.

'But —' said Pickles.

Hilda was moving right along with him. 'Well, I think it's our priority to investigate and find out just what is going on with these things.'

14

'But —' said Pickles even as he realised he now had to move along too. 'I can help you out with that. Us boffins can get down to analysing the pictures and see what we can infer from them.'

'We can try to get better pictures, but … isn't that right, Hades.'

Hilda and Hades had worked together a great many years and knew what the other was thinking.

'We need people sniffing around these pants. Properly,' said Hades. 'We need some hands-on investigation of these undies. We need to do a bit of snooping. And I know just the man for the job.'

'Not you, Hades,' said Hilda quickly, anticipating her boss's next move.

'Why ever not? If you want something done properly, do it yourself. And can you think of anyone more qualified than me to go sniffing around suspect pants?'

'It's far too risky,' said Hilda. 'Imagine you were caught with your hands in someone else's undies. The scandal would be too horrible to contemplate.'

'You do have a point. What do you suggest? We use Dr Pickles here?'

The scientist gulped and paled under his covering of soot.

'You would know funny undies if you saw them,' Hades reasoned.

'I don't think so, Hades. Imagine if Dr Pickles were caught. We need plausible deniability. You wouldn't need a scientist to figure out that this man works for you. He is the lead scientist in your rather famous research and development division.'

'We could fire you first, then send you out snooping, couldn't we Pickles? Wouldn't work for us then.'

'Or,' pressed Hilda, 'we could use a third party. Someone less easy to connect to us.'

'The Pope,' suggested Pickles eager to deflect discussion of his own involvement and employment status.

'The Pope? Why the Pope?' asked Hades, utterly baffled. 'Do you have any connection with him?'

'Not really.'

'Well, there you are, he can't be traced back to you.'

'How about,' said Hades carefully, 'Maul and Flay?'

'Maul and Flay?' asked the scientist.

'Yes, Maul and Flay.'

'Are you seriously suggesting Maul and Flay?' You could hear Hilda's hands on her hips under her burqa in her tone of voice.

'Maul and Flay?' asked the boffin again, hoping someone would fill him in.

'Jeremy Maul and Davinia Flay,' obliged Hilda, 'are a pair of fixers of dubious morality and improbable provenance who specialise in doings of doubtful legality — and by Maul's preference, involving bodily excretions. Hades used to use them for all sorts of sensitive jobs that involved skullduggery and violence.'

'Used to use them?' asked the scientist picking up on the past tense.

'Until they crossed Hades and kidnapped his daughter Victoria, that is. Twice.'

Hades scowled horribly at the mention of this episode. Maul and Flay having kidnapped Victoria, then managed to lose her into the hands of various unsavoury people, none of whom had his daughter's best interests at heart. She had been spirited across the planet and into outer space and back again before he caught up with her. In the process the world had nearly come to an end through nuclear war and a stolen alien spaceship. Hades' retribution had been emphatic. He doubted Maul or Flay would cross him again, not that they could do so much as make a cup of tea where he had them.

'Tenacious people,' mused the scientist, his analytical skills going to work on the story. 'But it sounds like they have a known connection to you. If they were caught wouldn't it rather give things away? And if they kidnapped Victoria, one would wonder whether they currently have any working limbs or any other viable faculties left to use on this task.'

'Well, there's the cunning of it,' Hades explained. 'No one would think I had hired a pair of incompetent losers to do another job for me after the unholy screw up they created in kidnapping Victoria not once but twice.'

'But how can you trust them?' asked the scientist reasonably.

'Because,' answered Hilda, catching the thread, 'They owe Hades big time, and if they screw him over a second time, they know what will happen to them.'

'Sounds nice and idiot proof,' said the scientist.

'And, as an added incentive, this job will be their only way out of the cryonic chambers I stored them in after they messed up the last time.'

'Well, if that's settled, I'd like to get back to pulling my colleague out of the rubble. It seems a long time since I started.' The scientist gestured at the legs in the improbably bright socks sticking out of the pile of smashed masonry and tortured metal.

'Be my guest,' said Hades, 'but I do believe that's a crash test dummy you're trying to rescue. You might leave him there. They rather enjoy being in dire straights, you know, crash test dummies. Gives their lives meaning.'

3

Lights flickered grudgingly on in the long concrete tunnels under Porton Down. Metal doors clanged irritably. Chains and locks rattled irritatingly. The sound of feet echoed aggravatingly.

Hades, Hilda and a retinue of burly armed guards and scrawny scientists armed with tablets and laptops made their way to the cryonic storage facility, which was in the deepest, bunker-iest bit of Porton Down's underground bunker system. They paused before the biggest set of steel doors yet, which opened with more clangs and rattles than any other and entered the cryo-chamber itself.

The cryo-chamber was science so much at the cutting edge, touching anything inside could draw blood. Here boffins with domed heads had created a science fiction fantasy. In this chamber, deep under the downy green hills of Wiltshire, and only here under the downy, green hills of Wiltshire, existed the capacity to freeze humans into a state of suspended animation for as long as you wanted and then revive them, bringing them back just as they were before freezing, only perhaps in need of a good hot mug of cocoa.

The terribly top secret facility had been secretly built decades before by the army. It was so secret it didn't officially exist.

On completion of the elaborate and mind-bogglingly expensive facility, the prime minister had been delighted. What a feather in Britain's cap! What an achievement! What god-like powers, the ability to bring people back from near death (having frozen them into that state first)!

Surrounded by the finest military and scientific brains of the nation in his top-secret war room, the PM bashed the top-secret conference table in triumph. 'Just think of the applications!' he boomed.

No one could.

'I thought we might use it to send astronauts on impossibly long space voyages, to other solar systems and what not,' suggested the chief of the space agency.

'Brilliant!' boomed the PM, who liked booming and was good at it.

'But it turned out not to be feasible.'

'Why ever not? This is technology way ahead of our time.'

'We can't get Wiltshire into a spaceship,' explained the man.

'Can't really afford any spaceships,' chipped in the chancellor of the exchequer, 'of Wiltshire-bearing capacity or otherwise.'

Porton Down's cryo-chamber was put on ice.

Eventually, it found a function as a store for the cabinet's emergency reserves of ice cream, which, because of the impenetrable secrecy of the place, went uneaten until Hades bought Porton Down from a cash-strapped government, thereby saving the country from bankruptcy again, and discovered and scoffed the stash himself.

While the government of the UK had never found a use for these fiendishly clever devices that could freeze whole people without killing them and then revive them any time, Hades had.

It was a discreet place to stash inconvenient people until they became convenient. And stash more ice cream out of sight of nagging doctor and wife.

The wall of the circular chamber was composed floor to ceiling of silver, metallic doors. Serried ranks of trunk freezers filled the floor space. Monitor screens glowed coldly like the icy life they were watching. Hades always thought it was like a branch of Iceland where the customers rather than the food were kept in the freezers.

The duty technician, whose name was Perseverance Popsicle, sprang to her feet, administrative tablet held in her hands like a weapon at port.

'Sir Hades, sir.'

'At ease, Popsicle. How are our patients doing? Are they ready for thawing? Get these fish out of the freezer, then, shall we?'

'Sir,' asked the technician. 'Are you absolutely sure you want these two out of here? There is a jolly good reason you incarcerated them in the first place.'

'Yes, I am absolutely sure,' said Hades trying to sound patient and failing. 'As I seem to have to keep explaining to people, Maul and Flay will have had it frozen into their brains that they won't cross me.'

'Very well, Sir Hades.' Popsicle led Hades and his entourage to a large chest freezer.

'And this is Davinia Flay,' she announced.

'I know I'm not a techie, said Hilda Titanium, 'and I wouldn't presume to comment on your job, but Flay's cryo-thing doesn't seem to be turned on. I mean, the computer screen is showing her vitals and an inside temperature of -273 degrees centigrade — more or less absolute zero — but the plug for the freezer is out of the wall and on the floor.

'Good Lord, so it is,' put in Hades.

'Quite so, Ms Titanium. You would make a fine scientist, because your powers of observation are acute. You are right. The cryonic mechanism is indeed disabled. A very interesting case, Davinia Flay, from a scientific point of view.'

'Leaving the freezer unplugged is interesting from a scientific point of view?'

'It most certainly is,' confirmed Dr Popsicle. We have not needed at any point to actually freeze Davinia Flay, and yet the temperature has been consistently near absolute zero since we locked her in there. We sedated her and placed her in the cryopod, in the usual way. We sealed the chamber following the established procedures and protocols, but before we could initiate the freezing process, ie, plug it in, we noticed the temperature plummeting. Within minutes it hit this absolute temperature. And there it stayed.'

'Good Lord, what's that about? Is there a Nobel Prize in this for someone? A new market in thermals?'

'It seems, Sir Hades, that the temperature fall was entirely a product of Ms Flay's personality. So utterly devoid of charm, compassion, love or any kind of human feeling, so utterly lacking in anything we might describe as warmth, and with the absolute insulation of the chamber, she killed all the latent heat energy in the molecules of the air in the chamber and put herself into cryonic suspension with no help from us.'

'Good Lord,' said Hades, showing no signs of boredom with repeating the expostulation. 'And what happens when we open the chamber?'

'She gets up and gets out, I suppose. And then asks for a nice hot mug of cocoa. That's what usually happens.'

'And what about Maul? Anything unusual there? Did he freeze his box too?' asked the ever-alert Hilda.

Popsicle led them to another chest freezer.

'Well, yes, in fact, Maul is an odd case too.'

'We didn't need a scientist to tell us that,' chortled Hades.

'Did he freeze himself?' asked Hilda.

'Not at all,' said the techie. 'We put him under in the usual way, but … well, put it this way. He seems to be a restless sleeper. There have been lots of alpha waves — associated with consciousness — and some distinctly odd noises. We were tempted to infer that he didn't enter a state of suspended animation. But at these temperatures and under general anaesthetic that is of course, impossible.'

'It is impossible, so it didn't happen even though it seemed to.' Hades scratched his head. 'Where have I heard that before?'

'Well,' said Hilda brightly before cognitive dissonance could cause her boss's head to explode. 'Shall we get on with the job in hand?'

'Indeed,' agreed Hades. 'I must say I'm rather looking forward to seeing these two chumps agree to do anything for me rather than go back in the freezer.'

'If you think I am going to do just anything for you as a condition for being let out of this box, you can just close the lid and leave me here until doomsday,' said Davinia Flay as soon as her chamber was opened.

She lay in a billowing eiderdown of frozen gasses, like a snow queen. Her eyes had opened, blue and icy, as the lid of the chamber swung up. She took in Hades and his party and she had spoken. Her voice sent shivers up and down the spines of everyone more than the icy gasses that escaped.

'Oh,' said Hades. 'Fair enough.' He turned and strode over to Maul's chamber. 'I expect that means Maul will get the whole fee for the job.'

He glanced round. Flay was out and standing by the chamber.

'But I will get out to suit my own purposes.'

'That's the spirit!' enthused Hades.

'Would you like your hot cocoa now?' asked Popsicle.

Flay looked at her as if she were mad.

'I'll take a vodka. Neat. Frozen.'

'That's the other spirit!' quipped Hades.

'I think we have one of those keeping at just the right temperature in one of the cryopods,' chirped Popsicle, delighted at her own unintended foresight in keeping Stoli at two degrees kelvin and cold enough to freeze the gates of Hell, should the need arise, as it just had.

'Right. And now for Ms Flay's partner in diabolic scheming, Mr Jeremy Maul.'

'Is it strictly necessary to let Maul out?' asked Flay.

Hades drummed his fingers on the top of the chrome casket and thought about it. 'See your point. But sadly, yes. I mean, who is going to do the dirty work? The truly dirty, vile, rolling-in-poo dirty work? Who's going to immerse themselves in the ordure and actually relish it? Who's going to do that stuff so you don't have to? Who is going to do the things you're too cool to do?'

'The question was rhetorical. Nevertheless, someone had better top up my glass before you let young master Jeremy out — no top it up with the whole bottle. Use that crystal vase there as a glass.'

Hades broke the seal on the chamber and the lid whumped open. A terrible stench escaped. A green stench of rotting, and every foul thing that can come out of a human body, and every foul thing that can come out of a warthog's body, and every foul gas that might emit from a fermenting whale as it explodes. And there was Maul, all green and blotchy and in only his underpants. The interior of the chamber had suffered massive trauma and was mostly wreckage.

'Oi!' said Maul, 'You're letting a draft in.'

'Emergency clean up in Chamber 23,' ordered Popsicle into her intercom between heaves and gags.

'Good grief! What happened to you? What happened to the inside of the chamber? What happened to your clothes?' demanded Hades.

'I ate them,' said Maul petulantly.

'The insulation on the inside of the chamber too?' asked Hilda incredulously.

'I was hungry. No one left any food in here. Once I'd finished my bogies I had to eat my pubes. When the pubes had gone, I had to eat my nails. Once they were gone, the clothes had to go. After the clothes there was nothing but the insulation. I was planning on my legs next. I was quite looking forward to them.'

The clean up crew arrived with steam hoses and the kind of industrial detergents used for breaking up the most stubborn, toxic and massive of oil slicks.

Maul howled in protest. 'Oi! I'd just got this place comfortable!'

4

'More hot cocoa, Mr Maul?' asked Penelope Popsicle.

'No. Fuck off! Anyway, I haven't had any cocoa at all, so how can I have some more?'

'I do apologise, Sir Hades, sir,' said Penelope. 'Recoverees always have hot cocoa. Lots and lots of hot cocoa. I've never know anyone to not have cocoa before and I don't know how to deal with it.'

'Cocoa rejection can be very hard,' put in Hilda sympathetically and only smirking a bit.

'In fact,' insisted the lab technician, 'some people will have themselves put into cryonic suspension just for the cocoa when they are brought out.'

'Well, I don't fucking want any,' repeated Maul, equally insistent. 'Give me some fucking vodka. No, not a wanky fucking little shot, I want a whole bottle. And why do I have to share a bottle with Davinia? Aren't I good enough to have a bottle of my own?'

'Dr Popsicle, would you be so good?' asked Hades through teeth that were so vehemently clenched, they were flashing bolts of lightning. 'Hilda,' he muttered as an aside, 'Is it worth it, bringing these two back from the undead? Surely, whatever job I had in mind for them cannot be worth the aggravation of having to share an atmosphere with them.'

'Close your eyes and think of underpants,' urged Hilda.

'I'd rather go into a new business. Like being homeless and destitute. Living in a cardboard box and eking a living from rubbish bins sounds good in comparison to this.'

'You can't give up now. Your whole life has been pants. Anyway, the planet needs you. I have a bad feeling about the underpants trees.'

Hades harrumphed and adjusted his kingly robes. 'Luckily, I had the foresight to slip into a pair of loin-girders before coming down here. I may on this experience re-engineer them to be a lot stronger. I may use actual steel beams in the next version.'

Hades, his retinue, Hilda, Dr Penelope Popsicle, Maul and Flay were in the recovery room adjacent to the cryonic storage facility where Maul and Flay had been kept on ice.

In order to create a warming, welcoming ambience in complete contrast to the freezing box, the room was Hawaiian themed. Concealed projectors beamed images of a blue tropical sky onto the walls, virtual palm trees waved in an exotic digital breeze, the big comfy recliners and sofas were covered with pineapple designs, and cheerful twangly music filled the air. It was truly horrible. Especially when the non-Hawaiian cocoa and hot buttery crumpets were added to atmosphere.

Maul now had his bottle of vodka and was happily gnawing on the screw top. He broke off to grab a handful of crumpets from the communal plate, from which he sucked the butter before returning the cakes to the dish. The others declined his offer to share.

'You're probably wondering why we brought you out of suspension,' announced Hades finally bringing the proceedings to a start.

'Not really. It's as obvious as an extremely obvious thing in an environment completely free of distractions,' drooled Maul.

'I suppose you have a grotty little job for someone to do, but prefer not to soil your own hands. Something you don't want traced back to you,' added Flay in her tones of pure ice. 'So you thought you'd get some disposable factotum to do it for you.'

'So you'd thought you'd ask your old chums Maul and Flay,' continued Maul even though everyone had already got

25

the point. 'So you dragged us in in order to use us one more time,' he persisted. 'Use as in exploit us. Before you lock us away for good or bury us.'

'I like the locking and burying part,' said Hades. 'Definitely. Hilda, can we skip the job and just go straight to the locking and burying?'

'And skip the fees for services rendered as well? I think the bank account might be able to put up with that.'

Flay turned to Maul and sighed, which had an effect Dr. Popsicle's high tech cryopod was unable to achieve. Maul froze.

Hilda took over the briefing. 'We need someone to do a little reconnoitre for us.'

'I don't have any reconnoitres. I'm clean. I've had my jabs.'

Flay re-froze Maul with another sigh.

Hilda waved a remote control and the digital projection of Hawaii was replaced with a Powerpoint presentation. Unlike conventional Powerpoints, this one filled the entire bowl of the ceiling and the walls like a planetarium projection, but the sky in this universe was filled with trees and underpants. She briefly outlined what they knew — and didn't know — of this curious phenomenon, that also may or may not be an existential threat to Hades' empire.

'So,' she concluded, 'we'd like you to go and recce — take a look-see. Gather information that might help Sir Hades determine what response to make to this development. Nothing more difficult than peaking over a wall, really.'

'And I want you to get us a sample,' added Hades.

'Get a sample?' asked Flay while raising an eyebrow in a way that could not be good.

'Yes. Nick some knickers, purloin some panties, yank some y-fronts, snaffle some unmentionables; bring us something to examine.'

'Bring back stains and all?' asked Flay with icy sarcasm.

'Staines, Egham, the whole of bloody Surrey, if you like. Just get me something my lab rats can have a good sniff at.'

Maul removed the well-chewed top of his vodka bottle from his mouth. 'Stealing undies? I have a qualification in that.'

'Qualification?' inquired Hilda. 'In stealing undies?'

'Conviction,' clarified Flay. 'Maul has a conviction for stealing underwear from washing lines.'

'Same thing,' said Maul. 'A conviction, a qualification; it's a legal sanction of my accomplishment, and either way it begins with k.'

'It's also a legal sanction of your accomplishment in getting caught.'

'Which also begins with k. Whoever heard of anyone sitting an exam and then running away before the examiners found out you passed? Nonsense!'

'Which demands a question,' said Flay. 'What happens if we do get caught?'

'Hmm. Look at it from my point of view. Industrial espionage. A potential preemptive anti-monopoly action. Theft. Conspiracy. Receiving stolen goods. Soliciting a crime. I say if you get caught, we wheel out some very expensive lawyers to plausibly deny everything. After all, what underpants magnate would be so daft as to employ two hoodlums who had previously double-crossed him, kidnapped his daughter, attempted to murder her PA and collaborated in an plot to hijack an alien spaceship and take over the entire world? The proposition doesn't stand scrutiny. There are of course outstanding charges relating to the above kidnap and bid to rule the world that could sort of accidentally drop out of a file and come to some prosecutor's notice.'

'And if we don't get caught?'

'A big wodge of cash and my complete indifference to where you disappear to with it.'

'And where will we find these mysterious trees? Not the local park, I'll hazard.'

'Not the local park. More your local Antarctica.'

'Trees in Antarctica? Don't you mean snow and ice and wilderness and the coldest temperatures on the planet?'

'Yes, the snow and ice should make you feel right at home after your spell with us.'

'I think the point I was trying to make was, how is it possible to grow trees in Antarctica, which is a snowy, icy wilderness?'

'Oh. Well, it seems that whoever persuaded clothes to grow on trees has also succeeded in locally engineering the climate of an entire valley in normally inhospitable, lifeless tract,' said Hades breezily. 'I suppose the two might go together. If you are cunning enough to do the one, you are likely to be sufficiently cunning to do the other.'

Flay wondered if hers was the only mind working at that moment.

'But don't you think that it's of at least equal interest that someone has drastically modified the climate of an entire valley in an ice desert to become a temperate zone mild enough to induce trees to sprout underwear? Isn't that a secret worth plundering?'

'Not really,' said Hades, indifferently. 'We're in the business of underpants, you know, not climate engineering.'

Flay sighed. 'Well, that's that then.'

'I mean, it's all very clever artificially engineering the atmosphere of the planet to facilitate agriculture or whatever where before it was impossible, but compared to underpants, it's pretty dull stuff, don't you think? I mean, everyone needs underwear. How many of us need climate controlled valleys at the arse-end of the world?'

Flay rolled her eyes. 'Of all the heinous crimes I could use my talents on, I get caught up in filching knickers for people who can't see beyond their gusset.'

5

Flay was very much in her element. She slipped off her overcoat and slung it over her shoulder in order to better feel the elements upon her. Flay was wearing an ice blue top that left her midriff bare, shorts that left her copious legs very bare, and very stylish sandals. She let her icy blond hair waft in the breeze which was about 70 kilometres per hour and as many degrees below zero. She shook out the snow and ice that collected in it.

The ice lady breathed a contented sigh and aimed a casual but expert high kick at the snowman next to her, which, when the snow-crust cracked and fell, turned out to be Maul with his finger in his nose.

'This cold,' he asserted with the gravity of an expert, 'is fucking brilliant. It's freezing all the bogeys up my nose, which makes them like popsicles when I eat them. Snotsicles, I call them.'

He proffered on the end of his finger a long green and yellow spike for Flay's inspection before having a good suck at it.

'I'd offer you some, but I'm keeping it all for myself.'

'You are generous with your selfishness, Maul. You are welcome to your feast.' She braced herself in the blizzard once more. 'It really is quite beautiful, isn't it.' She gestured at a horizon that was blank and white but for the devilish clouds of airborne snow and the odd glaciated peak rising from ice that had lain inert for millions of years.

Turning, she remarked: 'Only one thing spoils the view.'

The one thing that spoiled the view was a vast, verdant and immensely improbable green valley. As far as the eye could see there were rolling hills and vales and trees, and each of the trees was gaily adorned with colour: underthings like flags.

All that seemed to divide the green valley from the stormy white wilderness where Maul and Flay stood was a quaint dry-stone wall. Where the elements raged around Maul and Flay, just a few metres away, a butterfly flapped about and the grass invited picnics of ham and cheese sandwiches, pork pies and lashings of ginger beer.

'How do they do that?' wondered Maul — but being unused to wondering promptly forgot the question.

'Security is tight,' remarked Flay.

On the wall there was a sign that read: 'Absolutely no peeking. By order.'

'We don't read signs,' observed Maul. 'I'm not religious.'

'Well, since we're here, we may as well take a closer look.'

Maul was holding on to the string of a very large red balloon. Flay said: 'Tether the balloon. We don't need to trail it around with us.'

'Tether it to what? A snowflake?'

'The husky, Maul. Tether it to the husky.'

'The husky?'

There was indeed a dog, like everything else crusted with white, but unlike anything else here frozen with one hind leg in the air in mid pee.

The balloon was a weather balloon and was the means by which the two snoops had travelled here. They had tried to persuade Hades to spring for a helicopter or a snowmobile or an aeroplane or an anything-but-a-balloon, but the big man was not to be moved. A balloon, a weather balloon it had to be. It was, he insisted, the absolute only way of getting about in Antarctica.

'It's not a busy place. Nothing, but nothing, moves down there — other than violent storms, penguins and weather balloons. Lots of weather balloons. The first thing any boffin does when graduating from elementary school is get funding for another balloon to let go over Antarctica. Anything else will attract attention. You therefore have the choice of travelling by storm, penguin or weather balloon. What's it to be?'

'Can it be a nice weather balloon?' asked Maul. 'You know, a balmy weather balloon, or a sunny weather balloon; hot summer day weather balloon? Not a rainy or dull or cold weather balloon. I like nice weather, I do, because it's nice.'

So, weather balloon, then. It was, to be fair, one of the most advanced weather balloons they could find. It was big, it was bright, it was very red indeed. It had a fantastic box of weather-measuring gadgets hanging beneath it and a very easy-to-understand booklet of instructions on how to take weather samples for the boffin they borrowed the rig from. This box of instruments was attached by a rope to the balloon, and it was this rope that Maul and Flay were permitted to cling for the duration of their flight from the weather station in Patagonia.

Maul lashed the tether to the upraised hind leg of the former dog and patted the beast on the head.

'Ooh, there must be some real yellow snow down there somewhere.'

'We've no time for that, Maul.'

'Awww. OK, let's go grab us some knickers and get out of here before I run out of snotsicles.'

Maul made to enter the orchard of underpants trees.

'What about booby traps?' asked Flay, the question leaving Maul paused in the attitude of the dog, one leg raised as if about to claim the wall for himself.

'What booby traps?'

'The lack of obvious security is disturbing.'

'Disturbing? I say it's fucking brilliant. We just jump over the wall, grab the loot and scarper.'

'Think about it: is it likely that someone who micro-engineers a new climate in the middle of the icy wastes, then persuades clothes to grow on trees — both new and exotic technologies — is just going to be content with a little wall to protect their secrets?'

'They put up a sign,' protested Maul. 'I mean, do you see anything else? Any helicopters? Watchtowers? Armed guards? Cameras? Dogs? Cats? Speed bumps?'

'That's what disturbs me. Someone who is such a technological whizz probably has something pretty evil lined up behind that wall. Something very high tech, very sinister and very capable of inducing pain and death in bizarre and very imaginative ways.'

'Ooh-er. That bastard Hades Gousset didn't mention this.'

'I wonder why. OK. Your moment has come. Try a snowball.'

'I have. They're not as good as my snotsicles, not by a long way.'

'I mean throw one over the wall. See how the defences react.'

'You mean you're asking me to chuck a snowball?'

'I am indeed.'

'Wey-hey! Can I put a brick in it?'

'If you can find one in the next nano-second because that's as long as my patience is going to last.'

'Testy! Testy!'

'Yes, testy-testy is the idea. I want to see whether a snowball sets off any kind of alarm or defence. You notice how the weather is staying this side of the wall. I wonder whether there's a force field of some kind.'

There wasn't. Maul's snowballs sailed over the wall and splatted on the grass and the trees and the flapping clothes.

'Look! They melted! The bastards must be using some kind of death ray.'

'Or it's as warm as it looks.'

'Bastard bastards! Well, now can we jump over the wall and get out of this? My willy is turning blue.'

'Well, put it back inside your trousers.' Flay paused. Something was happening. 'Now what is this?'

In the middle distance there was a procession of people. They were making their way at a civilised saunter through the trees while gesticulating in all sorts of directions.

Flay held up her smart phone, zoomed in as close as the machine would go and began filming.

'What have we here? Now, there's an eventuation if ever I saw one.' The viewfinder on the camera phone revealed in detail a distinguished and cheerful man wearing an immaculate black suit accompanied by a portly but equally distinguished gentleman in kingly robes, a large woman in queenly robes, a woman in dark sackcloth, who, despite her dress, radiated an effulgent and irresistible beauty, and a retinue of flunkies. Flay had no idea who the man in the suit was but she had no trouble identifying Hades Gousset, his wife Persephone, and Hilda Titanium.

But what were they doing here? What was going on?

'Maul. Something weird is happening. We need to get into the trees, sneak up on those people and eavesdrop — without being noticed. Can we do that without making an embarrassing mess of it?'

'My middle name ain't sneak for nothing.'

'Your middle name isn't sneak, it's Margaret.'

They slid over the wall keeping low and touched down the other side as subtly as snakes.

The butterfly turned to look at them.

The ground erupted beneath their feet, the world turned upside down, loud klaxons obliterated all senses, the air filled with the clamour of helicopters and the thudding of boots and there was merciful oblivion for both of them.

6

Dr Hieronymus Mangler was a striking soul in appearance, manner, and, imminently, in his contribution to history. Everything about him was very correct. He was neither too tall, nor too short; he was just the right height. His suit was just the right amount of black; neither too black nor insufficiently black. He was affable and smiled a great deal; the perfect gentleman and host.

Dr Hieronymus Mangler was also the first and only person to have persuaded underpants to grow on trees — or induced trees to grow underpants, whichever was the correct scientific way of looking at it.

'Sir Hades, Lady Persephone, welcome to Sacred Mountain, my humble headquarters, base of operations and bachelor pad.' Mangler gestured modestly in turn at the palatial home, the glassily corporate HQ, the processing facility-cum-airport, and the uncountable acres of trees growing underwear in an idyllically green valley against a backdrop of very cold arctic peaks. 'I am very glad you agreed to meet me here today. It is rather a long way from home. I could have called on you and saved you the trip, but then I would not have been able to show you what I am about to show you, and that would have rather spoiled the whole point of meeting — tea and crumpets without the tea and crumpets, as it were.'

'Well, Dr Mangler, it was a bit of a surprise, I will confess,' said Hades, 'and I will confess further to a considerable curiosity.'

'We did enjoy the airship ride,' said Persephone. 'Most luxurious.' If Hades was the King of the Undies World, Persephone was the Empress of Bling and walked now among the underpants trees looking like a Christmas tree.

'And a little romantic, I hope,' Mangler suggested. 'I do find airships so romantic. And when you are travelling across continents to remote and secret mountain valleys with their own artificially created climate, I find there's no other way to travel. Don't you agree?'

Persephone, having social skills where her husband had only embarrassing noises, filled in quickly with, 'Oh, yes. There simply is no other way to travel across continents to remote and secret mountain valleys with their own artificially created climate. Hades and I have always said that.'

'Oddly fast for an airship, though, I couldn't help noticing,' said Hades.

'Most airships don't have scramjets or an indestructible adamantium shell to protect the helium cells and make them impervious to collisions or the tremendous heat generated by the speed of hypersonic flight.'

'I see,' said Hades, quite unclear about what he had just been told. 'It was, nevertheless, quite fast,' he added hoping it was the right noise to make at that moment.

'Scramjets on an airship!' enthused Dr Pickles, who did have a clue about what he had just been told. 'Adamantine shell! Most audacious, Dr Mangler! Even the US military hasn't got the hang of scramjets.'

'Scramjets?' asked Persephone, who, unlike her husband, was not consumed by an overweening male ego and was therefore sufficiently comfortable to ask about things she didn't understand.

'Scramjets,' enthused Pickles. 'Yes, they do amazing things with air compressed at supersonic speeds, which when ignited in the engine will give you hypersonic velocity. Twelve to 24 times the speed of sound, so the theory goes. Of course, anything travelling that fast in the atmosphere is inclined to burn up with the friction — not good news for airships, which are inclined to burn up even without hypersonic speeds and friction. But Dr Mangler has apparently got around the entire problem by encasing the ship in a shell of adamantium, the toughest material known to humanity. Not just any old adamantium, oh no, transparent adamantium, no less. This is, needless to say, an achievement that is entirely mind-boggling on its own before you factor in the scramjets.'

Hades felt Pickles's enthusiasm was a bit overdone. When it came to pissing contests, no one was allowed to wee higher or further or wetter than Hades, and if anyone accidentally did, no one was to mention it until Hades had produced a bigger, faster, wetter wee to reclaim his crown. He expressed these feelings by waggling his eyebrows at Pickles in an authoritative manner, which meant 'turn it down a bit, mate!'

'Well, we do try,' said Mangler modestly. 'But whatever the technical specs, it really is the most marvellous runaround when you do business in all over the place but live at the bottom of the world. I call it HMS Adamant.'

'HMS?' asked Hades. 'You mean it's a naval vessel?'

'Oh, no,' said Mangler. 'It's entirely mine. HMS stands for Hieronymus Mangler's Ship.'

Dr Mangler had met Hades and Persephone at the airship and taken them immediately on this stroll among the trees. Despite the luxury and brevity of the flight, it was a treat to be walking in the orchard. The sun was warm and pleasant, the valley was verdant and the view was splendid, if a little surreal, consisting of glaciers, snow fields, ice-encrusted peaks and blizzards, all of which terminated abruptly a few hundred metres away at the low Cotswold stone wall that marked the boundary of the plantation.

Mangler waved his hand at the trees. 'You are of course aware of the existence of this from those satellite photos.'

'Satellite photos?' asked Hades innocently.

'Yes, the ones in your possession that show this place in just enough detail to intrigue you, but not enough detail to satisfy your curiosity.'

'Oh, you mean the satellite photos in my possession that show off this place in remarkable detail. Well, I, harrumph,' replied Hades.

'My oversight in not blinding the satellites to this place. It quite slipped my mind. But no matter, your discovery was, if a bit slow, serendipitous because I'm about ready to go public.'

'Go public? About your pants?'

'Quite, Sir Hades. The orchards are fully productive, as you can see. Lots of lovely underthings hanging from every tree.'

'Yes, I couldn't help but notice that. Must have taken you hours to put them all there. Or must have taken the Munchkins hours. Looks stunning by the way. Congratulations.'

Mangler laughed a hearty jovial sort of laugh. 'Oh, Hades, you know as well as I that these articles are not merely bedraggling these trees.'

'You mean,' asked Hilda, 'that they are just as much growing as they appear to be.'

'That's correct Ms Titanium.'

'But underpants don't grow on trees,' protested Hades.

'Ah, they didn't use to. That's true. But now they do.'

'But how on earth did you persuade pants to grow on trees? Or, er, trees to grow pants? Or pants and trees to cooperate in growing?' Persephone was not clear on how the question should be phrased.

'Oh, yes, it is rather a trick. Perhaps I could let my head of research, Dr Merkwürdigliebe, explain.'

Mangler gestured at a small perfectly spherical man in a motorised wheelchair who wore glasses so thick the lenses appeared to be two holes in the space-time continuum, and whose hair was probably in contravention of several Geneva conventions.

'Dr Merkwürdigliebe.'

'It's a complete secret, a trade secret, protected by patents and the rest of it, Dr Mangler. An industrial secret protected not just in law but with the best physical and cyber security known to humanity. We could tell you, but then we'd be legally obliged to kill you.'

'Yes, so it is. I was just making an unnecessary point. But look, Hades, it should be obvious. All the ingredients are there in nature. Cotton and hemp, for fabrics, indigo and a host of other plants for colour, branches for growing things. All we need to do is a bit of tweaking in the DNA, and Bob's your plantation of clothes-sprouting trees.'

The tweaking had been most impressive. They were passing under an arbour of sheer, silky lingerie. Next to it, another tree sprouted the sturdiest, most sensible cotton things. On the adjacent branches, sleek lycra trunks that seemed to promise Olympic gold medals — if wearing underthings were an Olympic event.

'So all this has been biologically tweaked in its DNA. We're looking at genetically modified trees and pants,' Hades explained to himself. 'Pickles,' he added in a whisper, 'make a note of that.'

'I already have, Sir Hades.'

'Well make another note to be sure,' hissed Persephone.

'What are you going to do with them?' asked Persephone, afraid she already knew the answer.

'Ah. That brings me to the nub of our meeting, Lady Persephone. I intend to go into business. The underpants business. And this, I am afraid will make me a competitor to you. This is something I regret somewhat, because I am such an admirer of your underpants, Sir Hades and your empire — and the pair of you as people and entrepreneurs. I very much wanted to bring you here and show you this little project of mine before I declare it to the world. As you can imagine, growing entire garments will change our business models. No expensive manufacturing plant because that's being replaced by living plants. No impoverished workers doing 60-hour weeks on minimal wages to stitch the products together. No controversy from using sweatshop labour. The whole operation is entirely sustainable because it uses no other resources than those that trees naturally consume. In other words, stuff that's part of nature's own cycles. And because we'll be planting more trees, we'll be contributing to re-forestation and combating climate change while we're about it.

'I have enlisted the aid of Mother Nature, everyone's mother, to do the stitching for us even as she grows. And what could be more appropriate than our collective mother clothing us? Sorry, I am running away with my own marketing tropes.'

Hades was determined not to be too impressed. 'So you're going to grow these underthings down here at the south pole, then ship 'em up north to the markets. Will you be able to grow enough? Big as this farm is, there are seven billion people in the world all needing their loins swaddled. You'll need some fertiliser.'

'But this is just my test base, Hades. This technology is transplantable, so to speak. We can grow these trees pretty well anywhere in the world, and we are. Even as we speak I am acquiring and re-purposing tracts of land in order to expand the operation to full productivity. What was the tract of land I bought this morning, Merkwürdigliebe?'

'The Amazon rainforest, I believe, Dr Mangler.'

'Oh, yes, and when we've cleared out all those dusty old books, we'll be planting it with my trees. You see, one of the fascinating things about this technology is that we are not anchored to factories and large distribution networks. We can go where the demand is simply by planting new orchards. And we can adjust the DNA of our trees to grow in any climate. Or, of course, as we have here, tweak the climate to accommodate the trees.'

'This is absolutely fantastic, Dr Mangler,' enthused Dr Pickles, Hades' own head of research. 'And what about yield? Is it seasonal? What about load-bearing stresses on the limbs of the trees? Cotton can be pretty weighty especially if it gets wet in a downpour. Do you need special nutrients? How about pollination? Is that necessary or do you propagate by grafting? Do the trees produce seeds? Can they be planted or does your company control the seed stock, thereby bonding producers to you?'

'I am flattered by your enthusiasm Dr Pickles —'

'I'm not,' muttered Hades just loudly enough for Pickles to hear.

'— but I am afraid I am not at liberty answer all your questions for the obvious reason that they relate to confidential operational matters. But just as a little teaser: no, the yield is not seasonal. It's perennial.'

'If this is manufacturing on a truly organic, truly sustainable model,' said Hilda. 'Imagine what it will do for the developing world. Imagine what it will do for the developed world. Imagine what it will do for the environment.'

'But what about *this* environment? How on earth did you do this?' insisted Pickles waving his arm at the whole plantation, the sun, the blue sky, the warmth.

'Oh, that was easy. I just installed a thermostat and turned it up.'

Pickles was clearly impressed by this answer and wanted to know more but at that moment there was a rapid series of explosions on the perimeter of the orchard. This was accompanied by sirens and a fleet of black helicopters screaming from Mangler's main base. The aircraft skidded to a halt above the plumes of smoke from the detonations and black-clad, gun-wielding figures rappelled to the ground. It looked and sounded as if a not-very-minor war had broken out.

'Ah!' exclaimed Mangler cheerfully. 'We seem to have visitors. I am glad to see that the burglar alarm is behaving as designed. Could be an intruding penguin but I expect it's Maul and Flay. They arrived here on a weather balloon about the same time as you. I imagine they thought they were having a crafty sneak.'

'I deny everything,' said Hades.

'But do you deny it plausibly?'

'Of course!'

'Well, everything's fine, then.'

7

Dr Mangler showed Hades and his people some more of the vast orchard before leading them back to the main house for a slap-up banquet. To the relief and puzzlement of Persephone and Hilda, Hades remained relaxed and affable. He even seemed to be enjoying himself and drank a case of very fine red wine all by himself.

Very late afternoon they were shown back to the airship for the ride home. Dr Mangler waved them a cheery goodbye as the ship lifted off, and his guests all waved back, though not necessarily in the right direction due to the impressive quantities of booze they had all got through.

The crew settled the passengers into extravagantly comfy sofas in the gondola's lounge, from where, through the massive windows made of transparent adamantium, they had a spectacular view of the clouds, the oceans and the continents as the airship hurtled over them. And they enjoyed all this with an unending supply of fine drinks and exotic nibbles.

'Well, Hades,' asked Persephone. 'What did you make of all that?'

'A jolly nice lunch, I must say,' said Hades. 'I especially enjoyed the baked Alaska. Nice touch at the bottom of the world.'

'Actually, we were thinking of Dr Mangler's revelations, and that little operation he has going down there.'

Hades waggled his eyebrows authoritatively again.

'I can tell authoritative eyebrow waggling when I see it, Hades, but what is the purpose of it on this occasion?'

41

Hades rolled his eyes.

'And that was eye rolling,' Persephone continued. 'Eyebrow waggling and eye rolling. But to what end?'

Hilda with as much earnestness as Hades cupped her hand to her ears and looked about with wild staring eyes.

'What?' asked Persephone.

Hades latched on to what Hilda was doing and imitated her.

'I think the wine was stronger than I realised,' said Persephone.

Then Hilda appeared to be batting away an insect that Persephone couldn't see. And Hades now had his own plague of flying pests.

'Oh,' said Persephone. 'You mean this place might be bugged so we shouldn't speak what's on our minds. Now I get it.'

Hades and Hilda sunk their respective heads in their respective hands.

Back at Hades Mansions, there was no such need for caution.

'Goodness gracious look at the time. How many continents did we cross in the bat of an eyelid there? Excellent. Time for a noggin before turning in. In fact, there's time for about 27 noggins before bed. Who's joining me?' Waving at one of the house staff: 'Noggins all round, please. Stiff noggins, there's a good chap.'

'Hades, you're taking this very lightly,' worried Persephone.

'Taking what lightly? Nothing light about these noggins. Splendid stuff.'

'I mean, about Dr Mangler and his underpants trees.'

'Well, of course, I take it lightly. What's the bother?'

'Dr. Mangler does seem to have a startling new technology and he's going into business against you.'

'Bah! What can he do? I'm King of the Undies World, you know. He can't touch me. I was a foundling, and now I'm the most important man in the world. It'll take more than a few mutant pants-sprouting trees to bother Hades. I mean, look!

He has to plant sufficient of the trees to make this viable. Can you imagine how much money all that land will cost? And he'll have to get planning permission and rubber stamps from every agricultural body in the world. You know what the suits are like. You can't have a dandelion sprouting on your lawn without the OK from the men with clipboards. By the time he gets all the red tape sorted out our sun will have exhausted all its fissionable materials and died. On top of all that, he has to convince a sceptical public that his undies are something they want. They are a new technology and grown on trees. Joe Public will be wanting assurances they don't bite or have strange diseases.'

'Sir Hades, does have an important point,' chimed in Dr Pickles. 'Speaking from a strictly scientific perspective, Dr Mangler has been altering DNA, the fundamental building block of all life on this planet. You have to wonder about the stability of the resulting compounds.'

'Say what, Mr Man?' asked Hades, his know-how having once again been tested.

'I mean, his pants are fangled. You have to wonder whether they'll fall apart,' explained Pickles.

'Exactly,' said Hades. 'Straight from the boffin's mouth. Joe Public doesn't like new technologies. I mean look at the reception aeroplanes got.'

'I believe aeroplanes are a bit of a hit, Hades,' warned Hilda.

'So they are. Must have been thinking of the other thing. The one that wasn't a hit. What was that?'

There was a moment of silence while they tried to think of a radical new technology that hadn't been a massive hit.

'Anyway,' resumed Hades, 'we are a well-loved and well-established company. We are the only underwear manufacturer in the world that everyone knows and trusts. Mangler is the upstart with everything to prove. People like the comfort of the familiar, they won't be flocking to these trees. Flocking to trees! Ha ha! Did you hear what I just said? Like birds, you see. Birds flock … oh, never mind. Anyway, the point is, I don't suppose anyone will give Mangler a moment's attention. Everyone has far better things to be getting on with.'

Hilda and Dr Pickles were looking with alarm at their phones and tablets.

'Erm, Hades, there's something you need to know,' said Hilda.

'Time for another noggin. I know that already. Be a good soul and fill me up.'

'No, not noggin stuff, Hades,' said Hilda with evident alarm in her voice. 'Mangler's just gone public.'

'Good for him,' insisted Hades. 'I'd better get my ear muffs so I'm not deafened by the silence.'

Persephone also had her phone's browser pointed at the news outlets. 'The BBC are running it as top of the news. So is CNN. And Sky. And Fox. Now ITN. And apparently every news outlet on the planet — print, broadcast and online. The story is swamping Facebook and Instagram and LinkedIn and Twitter's servers have overloaded.'

'Doesn't mean anything,' blustered Hades. 'Twitter's servers are always over capacity. They seem to like it. Give me another noggin. No, two noggins.'

'Parliament has been recalled so questions can be asked. The UN Security Council has convened. Every national assembly is hurtling into session,' said Pickles.

'A coincidence,' growled Hades.

Hilda took up the story. 'The public have taken to the streets and are mobbing clothes shops demanding tree-grown undies. Except Hades Undies World stores. They are ignoring those. Sales of Hades products have dropped to zero. The price of Hades shares has gone into freefall.'

Hades was evidently trying to figure out how to hold and drink three or fours noggins at the same time with just two hands. 'When was the news of the trees announced?'

'Five minutes ago,' said Persephone.

'The accountant just messaged us to say we are staring into the abyss of ruin,' said Hilda.

The sound of a low-flying aeroplane made them look up through the expansive windows that looked out over Hades' extravagant estate. The plane was towing an advertising banner that read: 'Mangler's organic tree-grown pants — out now!' While they watched, the plane, trailing brightly-coloured smoke, did a loop-the-loop, a couple of impressive barrel rolls and was away.

'Oh buggery bugger-bags and blast!' swore Hades as he upended the whole bottle of noggin into his mouth.

8

Hades was wearing a very large bandage on his head. He looked like he had been in a monstrous accident the night before, which in effect he had: direct collision with one bottle of noggin after another until he was, eventually, knocked unconscious by them.

Now he sat grim and silent in the back of his stretched Rolls Royce with his head rested in a massive pillow.

The night before, when the news of Mangler's invention had broken, Hades had emptied the considerable noggin cellars of his country mansion, Lucre Towers, into himself and passed out. The following morning doctors had declared his hangover so bad the plates of his skull had come loose and the fabric of space and time in his immediate vicinity had ripped. They had applied a massive swaddling of bandages and proscribed an aeon or two inside CERN's Large Hadron Collider in order to repair the damage to the space-time continuum, and then petitioned the Pope to canonise him for the miracle of having survived such a massive bladdering. Breakfast consisted of an entire pig farm reduced to sausages and bacon but it hadn't cured him. Hades felt sorry for the pigs, but not as sorry as he felt for himself.

Normally he would follow breakfast with a helicopter ride to his command bunker at Porton Down but at sight of the waiting whirlybird he had thought better and ordered his car. Thudding blades and swooshing motions were just not going to work with this crapulous head. It may have been a luxury helicopter, fully padded and upholstered and designed with the most urgent and facile whims in mind, but whichever way you looked at it, a chopper was an airborne decapitation device and vomit churn.

The car on its suspension of air wasn't much better but insulated with cushions and pillows, it was less torture than the sky and he bore the journey staring morosely out the windows.

It might have been the effects of the overdose of noggin or the shock of the events of the last 24 hours, but there seemed to be something fundamentally different about the day, as if during the night someone had been fiddling with the molecules that make up the physical world or meddled with the periodic table rendering the elements of the universe subtly different, or had shifted the oblivious Hades and his bed into an alternative reality. Hades couldn't quite put his finger on it, but the world, his world, just wasn't quite right.

It became even less quite right when the car entered the town of Panting. Panting was not the biggest or most cosmopolitan town in the world. In fact you could lose it in a moderately-sized handbag. However, today the streets were teeming with people and if that was making the day not quite right, then the behaviour of the people was making day very emphatically not quite right.

Plonk in the middle of the high street was a new shop: Mangler's. Crowds thronged the storefront, they filled the pavement, they overflowed into the road, and overwhelmed the police presence that was trying to keep the traffic moving. Hades's car was compelled to slow down to a crawl as bodies pressed against the window.

Those people who were not jostling to get into Mangler's were apparently promenading on the main street — promenading in order to show off their new attire. Given that this new attire was designed to be worn inside other clothes these people required some creative solutions to get their new clothes in public view.

Many had just done away with their outer clothes and confidently strode up and down Panting's shopping street in their gloriously coloured underthings. Others had chosen to reverse the normal order of dressing and were wearing their underthings outside their over-things, putting their pants on over their trousers. Still others, aiming to get their bright new bloomers in maximum view were wearing them on their heads in place of hats.

An impromptu orchestra of musically inclined locals had set up on the pavement and we're accompanying the crowd, which was, as one glorious choir, belting out Beethoven's Ode to Joy.

Nudging eventually clear of the thick of the crowd, Hades was able to see the local branch of Hades Undies World. It was empty. Already it looked a mite less shiny, a mite shabby compared to the brave new store down the street. The windows of Hades shop seemed to be inviting wooden boards to cover up their shame and embarrassment. While he watched, the shop sign fell off the front of the building and crashed into the street.

'Blaggard!' said Hades. And, 'I need that bloody helicopter after all. Get that helicopter here now. And make sure they've a plentiful supply of buckets on board.'

9

Hades ordered the helicopter to fly him to London and land in St. James's park from where he strode with as much speed and commanding presence as the tonne of bandages on his head and his delicate state could manage, which wasn't much. He marched through the police guard at the entrance of Downing Street while the officers stood to attention and saluted, and stormed up to Number 10, where a flunky, alerted by the police, held the door open for him. Hades then marched straight up to the prime minister's office, into which he burst with only a cursory knock. He regretted not using a less cursory knock because he found the prime minister with his trousers round his ankles, admiring himself in a full-length mirror.

'Prime Minister!'

'Hades!'

'I'm so sorry,' they said in unison, the PM hoiking up his strides and Hades turning his back.

'Hades! An unexpected pleasure. How good of you to drop in.'

'Yes,' said Hades, 'Thank you for … er,' Hades wasn't sure what he was thanking the PM for. 'Oh yes, thank you for seeing me. How, how, how …?'

'How's the family? There're all well, thank you. Very well, indeed.'

'Jolly good. And how's the, er, the …'

'The nation? Yes, very well. Doing fabulously, in fact.'

'Excellent. Doing fabulously, you say.' With an effort, Hades pulled himself together, getting over the shock of catching the prime minister with his trousers down. The man was a politician, after all. When did politicians not have their trousers down?

However, the image of what Hades had seen when the prime minister's trousers were down would never leave him.

'Now, look here, Prime Minister, old chap. We go back a long way. At least as far as the last election, whenever that was. I've always tried to help out the country. Bailed out the old place from time to time. Saved it from bankruptcy more than once, eh?'

'Oh, absolutely, Hades. We've always appreciated your help. Don't know where we'd be without you, to be honest. In the international dosshouse, probably.'

'Quite so,' said Hades. 'But there's no need to thank me again. Friends in need, eh? Doing one's best for one's country and all that.'

'No need to be modest about it, Hades. There's no doubt about it. The country would be considerably worse off if it weren't for your one-man boosts to the economy.'

'Talking of which, what are you going to do with that blaggard Mangler? He's putting me out of business. Just because he's found a way to make pants grow on trees. Completely unfair.'

'Tricky one, that,' said the PM thoughtfully and sitting down in his chair of command.

'You didn't go to school with, him, did you?' asked Hades suspiciously.

'No. It's not as tricky as that.'

'Well, I can't see the problem. Mangler has barged into my space, turned everything upside down, run away with my market.' Hades sat down reasonably in the chair of supplication in front of the prime minister's desk. 'Can't you whack him with unfair business practices, or something?'

'Which was the unfair bit?'

'Muscling in on my turf!'

The prime minister's face crumpled up and looked very uncomfortable with being on the front of his head at that moment.

'How about anti-trust?' tried Hades. 'He's building a monopoly.'

'You had a monopoly before Mangler came along.'

'Yes, but it was *my* bloody monopoly! Now he's got it.' Which provoked an idea: 'Theft! Can we get him for stealing my chokehold on the market?'

The PM shook his head regretfully.

'Theft. Intellectual property theft!'

'Ah, good. He stole your copyrighted ideas?'

'He's making and selling underpants. That was my idea three decades ago when I started.'

'Sorry,' said the prime minister.

Hades leaned conspiratorially across the table. 'Look. You have an army of lawyers and bureaucrats. Surely between you, you can come up with something. You know. Considering all I've done. And all that. Not calling in any favours in any way or pleading in any way or anything. Say what?'

'Well, that's the tricky bit,' said the prime minister who was clearly joining his face in wanting to be elsewhere.

'What's the tricky bit?'

'Mangler. Since he went public yesterday and opened his shops, GDP has leapt.'

'Leapt?'

'Enormously.'

'Enormously?'

'Impossibly enormously.'

'Impossibly enormously?'

'The impact of Mangler's business has propelled the entire country into an unprecedented economic boom overnight.'

'Overnight?'

'And our bean counters reckon It's going to keep booming for quite a while until it settles down into a general state of ruddy, glowing good health. To pull the plug on Mangler would have national consequences.'

'And that's the tricky bit?'

'That's the tricky bit.'

'And you're wearing Mangler's pants now, aren't you. That's why you were admiring yourself in the mirror when I came in, wasn't it.'

The PM gulped audibly.

'Blue y-fronts. The same shade of blue as your party colour.'

The PM gulped again. Loudly. It was more like a glottal gloop than a gulp.

'I see,' said Hades.

With as much dignity as he could muster, Hades stood. He adjusted his kingly robes, adjusted his bandages and strode out of the office.

Alone again, the prime minister leapt out of his chair and went back to the mirror.

10

'We have to come up with something to compete with that blaggard Mangler.'

Persephone, Hilda Titanium and Dr Pickles sighed. It was the 27-millionth time they had heard the same thing in the last 16 hours. While they were listening to Hades repeat himself over and over this morning they were scanning all the news sources on the planet trying to find one that didn't have Mangler's trees as the top story. They had the entire administrative staff of Hades Undies World on the same task. After all, the staff had nothing else to do since their business had effectively dried up over night. There were no orders to ship, no supplies of materials to receive, no sales to account, no tax returns to calculate. Instead they scoured the planet for a mote of cheer but found instead worse and worse news.

From Downing Street, Hades had retreated to Porton Down where conference was joined with his trusted advisors Hilda and Dr Edwin Pickles. Persephone was also present as a senior board member and to make sure Hades didn't start drinking again.

'We have to come up with something to compete with that blaggard Mangler.'

Persephone, Hilda and Dr Pickles sighed.

'To think,' moaned Hades, 'Thirty years of hard work blown away overnight. How can that happen? To think, Hades Undies World reduced to the corporate equivalent of sleeping under a bridge in a hand-me-down cardboard box.'

Persephone, Hilda and Dr Pickles sighed.

'To htink — I mean, to think — Hades Undies World: we are the company that invented the self-warming thermals and gave the world the homing pants. Global gratitude for saving the world from a nuclear holocaust we ourselves had nearly precipitated after Victoria was kidnapped the seventh time should be enough to keep us afloat, but no. Here were are snogging soggy cardboard.'

'Are we beaten? Is it now company policy to throw ourselves into the black river of despair? Is it a new corporate strategy to lie down and expire?' asked Persephone in a tone like a chainsaw.

'No,' bellowed Hades, stung. The bellow made him grimace and clutch his head. 'It's just we need something to hit back at Mangler with.' Before Persephone's eyes could actually roll out of her head, Hades noticed Dr Pickles, his big glasses like two mirrors on his snubby little nose, sitting meekly beside Hilda with an expression on his face that said absolutely nothing at all.

'Pickles! Why are you sitting there?'

'Would you prefer me to stand or lie down?' asked Pickles.

'Why aren't you in your lab inventing new products to get us out of this mess?'

'Because you didn't tell me to do that. Or did I miss the memo?'

'Oh, buggery bugger-bags and bother! Get in your laboratory and invent something that will help us fight back at Mangler!'

Pickles stood up. 'Very good, Sir Hades. Just one thing. How do I do that?'

'Do what?' asked Hades in a tone that threatened to unhinge his skull plates again.

'Invent things.'

'You're the bloody scientist! That's what you do, invent things. That's what you've been doing these thirty years with me.'

'Oh, I see. Except, oh, I don't see.'

'You don't see what?'

'These thirty years you've been doing the inventing. You invent things, have ideas, tell me what you want. I just make the things you have thought up.'

'Oh, more buggery bugger-bags!' stormed Hades. 'Are you telling me that left to your own devices you don't have any ideas of your own?'

'I had my own idea once,' said Pickles thoughtfully.

'There you go,' said Hades. 'And what was that idea?'

'A cup of tea.'

'A cup of tea? How was that an idea? Was it a cup of tea with special features like space exploration or dragon slaying?'

'No,' said Pickles with a puzzled air. 'It was a perfectly normal cup of tea, which was the best thing about it.'

'Are you claiming to have invented cups of tea?'

'Oh, no, Sir Hades. I'm just saying I had the idea of making one. One day working alone in the lab I wanted a cup of tea. And then I hit on the idea of having one.'

'What are we talking about?'

'You asked me whether I'd ever had an idea of my own, and that was it. An idea of my own. A cup of tea. Nobody told me to have that idea. I had it myself. You did ask.'

'I did ask. And now I'm asking you to have an idea that will help us fight back at Mangler. Is that instruction clear enough for you?'

'Yes, Sir Hades.'

'Well, have you had an idea yet?'

'I think so sir.'

'Well don't leave us all in pain. What's the idea?'

'Well. How about a cup of tea?'

'A cup of tea? How will that help?'

'Well, people are always saying how helpful a nice cup of tea is. I thought it might help in this situation too.'

'And does having a cup of tea generally help you, Pickles?'

'I don't know, sir. I don't know how to make one. I only thought of having one.'

Before Hades' expression could leap off his face and hurtle across the room like a deadly shuriken to decapitate poor Pickles, Hilda spoke up.

'Hades, if I may. There's nothing intrinsic to Mangler's underpants that make them better than yours. Granted he has a novel technology for producing them. This technology may or may not have advantages in his business model. What this technology does provide in abundance is a strong narrative, a sales angle. I mean they have a story they can sell the punter, a story of a collaboration of technology and nature; sustainable production; adaptability, and so on. But in the end the pants are just pants and they do the same things as bog-standard pants. So, presumably, what we have to do is hit back with an innovative and aggressive marketing campaign.'

'Ah! Now someone is making sense. I can rely on you, Hilda, to keep your head when all about us are blithering.'

'To this end, I have taken the liberty of engaging the services of advertising agency — Trumpet, Toot and Snort.'

'Trumpet, Toot and Snort, eh? That's a good start. Never heard of them.'

'Well, that's because we never hear of the best agencies behind the best ads. They are invisible. It's the client that needs to stand out, not the agency. In this respect they are like … they are like … something you need but which doesn't stand out. Like underpants in fact.'

'As it happens, with improbable and serendipitous timing, Mr Toot has actually just arrived. Shall I show him in?' said Bob Catshit, Hilda's personal assistant.

'Excellent stuff, Catshit,' boomed Hades to the detriment of his head.

Catshit looked puzzled. 'Yes, Sir Hades, cat shit is excellent stuff, but for what in particular at this moment? Shall I get some?'

'No, please don't get any cat shit, Catshit. I was addressing you by your name, Catshit, not asking for the substance that is the shit of cats.'

'Oh, you were using my name. I really can't get used to that. Most people address me as "get out".'

Seeing another hole imminently being created in the space-time continuum, Hilda intervened. 'Yes, please show Mr Toot in. And then get out.'

'Ah, now, you see, I understood that.'

Catshit opened the main door to the bunker to reveal a thin, grey and cadaverous man playing with a small mirror and a rolled up twenty pound note that he had inserted in a nostril. The man suddenly became aware that he was the object of attention of his client and his client's team. The mirror and the note disappeared. He brightened as if turning on a light inside him. He suddenly no longer seemed thin or cadaverous and glowed with health and wellbeing and produced a smile that could have had an alternative career as the beam of a lighthouse.

'Hi!'

'Mr Toot, please come in.'

Hilda made the introductions. 'Mr Toot, this is Lady Persephone Gousset and Sir Hades Gousset who are both founders and essence of Pants Corp itself. Sir Hades, Lady Persephone, this is Mr Toot of Trumpet, Toot and Snort, marketing consultants to the star brands, according to their website.'

'Call me Chaz,' said Toot, handing out business cards of a lurid holographic design that had been known to cause seizures and vomiting in children. The job title read, 'Lead Chief Executive Creative Visioneer and Executioneer for Strategy and Innovation and Everything'.

'So, Mr Chaz-Toot,' said Hades. 'On your own today? Mr Trumpet nor Mr Snort could make it?' He refrained from adding 'to a potential contract of this immense size'.

'Oh, we're all here.' Toot sort of sniggered through his nose and tapped the side of his head. 'One-man band in effect, but people always assume there are three of us. Not sure why.'

'Possibly because there are three people in the company name?' Hades hazarded.

'An unholy trinity I like to call it. Three in one, you see,' Toot told him. 'Trumpet, because that's what I do. I trumpet about you, the client. So trumpet is like God the Father in the trinity. Toot, because that's my name — God the son, I suppose.' He waved his arms around self-deprecatingly. 'Snort because it sort of goes with the other two words for some reason.' He laughed through his nose in a way that led observers to wonder how many shirts he soiled each day. 'I'm a jolly fellow, you see.' *Snort!* 'I just do things for the' *snort!* 'of it. So Snort would be the Holy Ghost. Holy-moley ghost.' He snorted a lot more then became suddenly grave. 'You'll find I have a facility with words. It's what I do.' His nose twitched and he quickly wiped away some of the white powder that was caked liberally around his nostrils.

'Well, what do you have for us, Mr Toot?' asked Hades. 'Let's get cracking with cracking Mangler's head, shall we? I never thought I'd say it, but Mangler is kicking our botties with his bloody trees.'

Hilda stepped up. 'What we need, in short, is a total revamp of our marketing. We need a whole new strategy. New branding. A kick-arse campaign that will send Mangler back to Antarctica. Can you do that for us, Mr Toot?'

Toot clicked his fingers in the air and swivelled smugly on a crocodile skin bootie. 'What you need, in short, is to restrategise, rebrand, and innovate a suite of solutions that will proactively reposition you effectively in the market. We at Trumpet, Toot and Snort are committed to creating bespoke executive outcomes for our clients.'

'Well, that's handy,' said Hades.

'Well, the first thing we need,' said Toot, all business-like, 'is a conference table. Ah, there's one there!'

'Yes,' said Persephone, 'we've all been sitting around it this entire day.'

'Well, have conference table, will conference, that's what I always say,' said Toot.

'That's an interesting thing to say,' muttered Hades, wondering whether Hilda had lost her rocker by inviting this guy into the office.

Toot threw himself dramatically into a big Star-Trekky chair at the end of the table opposite Hades.

Alert as ever to the subtle klaxons and sirens going off in her husband, Persephone moved things along.

'Mr Toot. You find us with the imperative to action digging like a spur in our flanks. We have the chase in our blood, while time, as ever, declines to dawdle on our account.'

'Nobody mentioned horses,' said Toot in alarm.

Persephone clarified. 'We're ready. We don't have much time. Begin.'

'May I suggest, ladies and gentlemen, that we begin?' announced Toot. 'Time is pressing and time is money and, if you don't mind me pointing out, while you're sitting in conference round this table, the money isn't exactly piling up.'

Lightning flashed from Hades' teeth again.

'I think this calls for a Powerpoint presentation!' sniggered Toot, and he flipped open an impressive black case that apparently contained a laptop and an entire data-centre. He disappeared behind the raised lid and there were more odd snorting and snuffling noises. The light around him seemed to intensify.

He re-emerged with a Bluetooth connection to the digital projector and more white stains on his face.

Toot coughed importantly and assumed a suitably grave expression. 'Have you tried Twitter? Facebook? I've heard they do wonders these days.'

Hades looked helplessly at Hilda and Persephone, who were both looking helplessly back at him.

'Apparently,' Toot went on, 'you need an account with each. I'm told it's free. I'll get my people looking into it for you, if you like. But everyone has Twitbook and Facer, so I'm guessing you'll need them too. Social media allows you to engage with your core market on a one-to-one level, placing your message right where it is most effective. Kids love it. To be honest,' he said conspiratorially, 'I'm thinking of getting myself an account or two, myself. I hear it's a great way to meet young people.' He winked.

Hades made a deep and seismic rumbling noise. 'I think we may be beyond Twatter and Farcebook, Mr Toot. Hades Undies World is facing an existential threat.'

Toot looked alarmed. 'Existential? The French are in on it too? This *is* serious.'

'Moving on from social media, Mr Toot, what can we do to counter Mangler's rise in our market?'

'Well, it seems to me that you need to counter Mangler's rise in your market. How about a fab new advertising campaign?'

'I think I've heard of advertising,' growled Hades.

'More than advertising,' said Toot, 'we need to fundamentally rethink what it means to wear a pair of underpants.'

Hades gripped the table hard.

'I've mocked up some pretty awesome campaign pieces. Lights, please!' The lights went down and music started up: Holst's Mars, Bringer of War from the Planets Suite.

An image flashed up on the projector screen of a pair of sturdy underpants from which dramatic lines of light radiated as if the sun itself were located in the posterior. The strapline, presented in dramatic washing-powder type, read: 'Hades Underpants — They're nice! Wear a pair today!'

'That's so lame,' said Hades, 'it's going to need special shoes.'

'Something a big stronger? More forceful?' suggested Hilda.

Toot clicked up the next image, which was the same as the first. 'Hades Underpants — They're Jolly Nice! Wear two pairs today!'

Toot was back on his feet holding his arms out like a circus performer who has just pulled off the trick of putting an entire adult lion in his mouth without suffering injury. 'Ta-daaaa!' he tooted.

Persephone leaned over to her husband and said in his ear, 'Take a deep breath and say "Buddhism".'

'Nice, as a word, is a tad vague, don't you think?' observed Hilda, trying to keep things professional rather than homicidal. 'It could mean anything. How about something more precise that tells the punter something concrete about the product?'

'I think you're going to regret passing up on nice, but your wish is my etcetera. This next one is even more pretty awesome than the last.'

'Hades Underpants — they're snug! Wear a pair today!'

'You're welcome,' said Toot, taking a bow.

'Who's to say Mangler's pants aren't snug?' asked Persephone. 'Nice try with this ad, but missing the point, perhaps. I mean, did you actually try out Mangler's pants before putting this campaign together? What do the customers actually think of them?'

'You might ask,' announced Toot, 'what the customers actually think of them. I feel a focus group coming on.' Toot rose dramatically on his tippy toes and stretched his arms like a conductor facing his orchestra. 'Group! Wait for it! Now … Focus!'

'Shall we move on?' asked Hilda.

'Hades Underpants — They're Eminently Sensible! Wear a Pair Today!'

'I like that!' exclaimed Hades.

'No you don't!' said Hilda and Persephone together.

'Then you'll love these!' snorted Toot.

'Feel safe in Hades' hands!' said the new strapline. 'Feel secure with Hades round your nethers!' said another.

'But it's what we've been saying for years,' said Persephone reasonably. 'We need —' glowering at Toot 'something totally new.'

'Ah,' said Toot, 'but this is what I've been saying all along. Time for a new resonance with the target market. What, by the way, is the target market?'

'Everyone who wears underpants,' snapped Hades.

'I suggest we are attempting to engage with everyone that wears underpants and no one else,' Toot elucidated.

'And we want to persuade people who don't normally wear underpants to start wearing them,' added Persephone.

'OK. So we've narrowed it down to people who do and people who don't currently wear pants. That's a neat little demographic. Very precise. So what we need is to create a narrative, a brand story, that underpants are about lifestyle choices and the way you see yourself. We don't sell the article as such, we sell *wearing* them.'

'Now we're getting somewhere!' Hades thumped the table in sudden approval.

'This campaign is going to totally blow you away. I absolutely guarantee it.'

'Uh oh!' Thought Hades, Persephone and Hilda together. 'He just used the g-word. Any salesman who uses the g-word has has fermenting shit where his brains should be. May as well drown the bugger in a bucket of his own silage now and be off.'

'Let's say to the world that underpants are sexy! It's a message that never misses! And it's never been used with undies before!

'Hades Underpants — Because you're Hot Down There! Wear a pair today and get sweaty!'

'Right,' said Hades, 'I've had enough of this.'

'Much more than 50 shades of grey!

'Not just pants! They're a way of life!

'Time to change your pants!'

Hades leapt to his feet. 'Right. Toot, off with your trousers.'

'But I —'

'I've had enough of this. Trousers! Down! Now! Do it!'

'No, I —' Toot reluctantly undid himself and let his strides slide to the floor.

Everyone except Hades, who was expecting what he saw, gasped. Toot was wearing a very vibrant pair of Mangler's shorts.

Hades marched round the table. He brusquely packed Toot's impressive black case making sure to include Toot inside it. He then marched the case out of the room dumping it in the corridor outside, Toot's arms and legs protruding.

'Hilda! What the hell was that all about?'

'I take full responsibility. I'm so sorry. I have no idea how that happened. Catshit, I asked you to book the best available agency. No expense spared. How did we end up with Toot?'

'But, Ms Titanium, Ms, I did book the best available agency, no expense spared. I did just as you said.'

'So what went wrong?'

'All the others were unavailable. Toot was the last one left.'

'How,' asked Persephone, 'can there be only one agency left? Agencies aren't bags of potatoes in the supermarket.'

'All the other agencies, you see, had been retained by Mangler. Except Toot. It seems Mangler didn't want him for some reason.'

'All the agencies had been retained by Mangler? What do you mean?'

'I mean that Mangler has apparently paid all the marketing and ad agencies in the world, except Toot, a retainer, and that the terms of that retainer stipulate that they are not permitted to represent any other underpants-related companies. Which effectively means Hades. Toot was the only company that had no such arrangement.'

'And,' probed Hilda, 'you didn't think to tell us of this situation.'

Catshit scrutinised the ceiling as if doing a very complicated maths problem. 'Apparently not, Ms Titanium.'

'Harrumph!' said Hades. 'I wonder why Mangler was retaining all the marketing agencies he could find. Can you think of a reason, Catshit?'

'He likes marketing agencies? He has obsessive-compulsive syndrome? He's very absentminded? A little bit eccentric?'

'I think,' said Hades, 'Mangler might have been freezing us out of the ad market so we couldn't hit back at him that way.'

'Oops,' said Catshit. 'But he didn't retain Toot, did he — if you don't mind me saying so.'

'Indeed, he didn't retain Toot. And there might be an excellent reason for this.'

'Oh, dear,' said Catshit. 'You mean Mangler knew that Toot was completely useless and likely to waste lots of our time and money if we did try to use him?'

The room wore an implacable silence that could only mean yes.

'Oh, dear again,' sighed Catshit. 'But with considerably more feeling this time.'

'So,' concluded Hades, 'that little episode has done nothing but move us closer to the precipice. What a clever bugger that Mangler is. We've been outsmarted at every move.'

'Shall I bury myself in the rhubarb patch again, Sir Hades, sir?' asked Catshit.

'No, Catshit, it will be more salutary to leave you here to feel our despondency.'

'I think I prefer the rhubarb, sir.'

Hades slumped back into his big chair and dropped his head onto the table.

'Oh, buggery bugger-bags and buckets of bother!'

11

'Hello, Daddy!' The brightness that accompanied his daughter Victoria's entry to the room caused another shaft of pain through Hades' battered head.

'Hello, daughter. You can leave the good cheer outside there's no room for it in here what with the ongoing end of the Undies World and all that.'

'Oh, but I've come to save the day,' said Victoria with even more brightness and good cheer.

'Very nice of you dear, but the day is outside. In here, we have the impenetrable night of despair.'

'Well open a window or two. Especially the ones in your mind.'

Victoria flipped open her excessively tasteful laptop and connected it to the digital projector. Her parents and Hilda noted, not for the first time that since Victoria had been kidnapped by Maul, Flay, and the aliens, nothing around her was pink or covered with sequins. She had gone into that misadventure the blondest, bimbo-est bimbo in the history of blond bimbos, and come out completely and utterly brunette with a terrific talent for designing cool.

Talking of which, Victoria now started a presentation video. Models, both men and women, wearing tremendously tasteful-yet-sexy underwear, paraded on the walls of the bunker. Unmistakably the kinds of designs Victoria had been specialising in since getting back from Alpha Centauri.

'Yes, very nice, Victoria, but we have serious problems here. You might want to start looking for a job.'

'Multiple processors with bit rates to rival the biggest desktop computers. Enough RAM to hold an entire film or game in a single thought, supported by a light-speed graphics card and enough memory to lose a herd of elephants in.'

'And it's a very nice computer too,' said Hades gently, 'but we really have lots of work to do.'

'I'm not talking about the computer, Daddy, I'm talking about the clothes. They're woven from ultra-fine carbon fibres with body-temperature superconductive capabilities and memory arrays whose transistors are the size of molecules. They appear and feel like regular clothes but have the power of supercomputers. And they look absolutely fab.'

'It's a bit late for that now, Victoria. We've moved onto something else. That cad Mangler has moved the goalposts. Moved them to an entirely different playing field. He's gone organic, growing his own product. The days of Hades's specialised-use underpants are gone, I'm afraid.'

'Well, if you'll give me a moment, that's what I'm talking about, Daddy. Specialised use. Those pants were always fantastic and showed this company was serious about pants and not just about frippery or money. But the specialised-use pants were exactly that: specialised. They are not the pants that actually made us money. What made this company giant? Regular, popular, serviceable, durable, no-nonsense pants. People's pants! The specialised pants were great as specialised pants, but how many people need underwear with built-in centrifuges? Or periscopes? We have to emphasise the popular and the radically new at the same time.'

'Yes, but that's now what Mangler's doing —'

'Oh, please do be quiet and listen. Or do you think I'm stupid?'

Well, it was true that Victoria's horizons had considerably expanded since her trip round the galaxy in the alien spaceship. Her father shut up and listened.

'These pants in the video are for everybody. Hilda, would you kindly remove the hood of your burqa for a moment?'

'Does she have to?' quailed Pickles.

'Wear sunglasses if you have to, but be strong, good doctor. It's the future of the Undies World we're talking about here.'

Hilda removed the burqa hood and the room filled with a warm, golden effulgence.

'Do you see what Hilda's wearing?'

Persephone, the only one actually looking said, in a tight voice that said volumes about her opinion of the weaker sex, the one from which husbands come, 'Spectacles. Glasses. Hilda's wearing specs.'

'You'd better cover up now, Hilda. Thanks.'

'I see where you're going,' said Hilda as she placed her head back in the burqa. 'Hades, Persephone, these aren't ordinary glasses, they're what they call smart glasses. They're attached to a tiny computer terminal in my pocket that projects data onto the lenses. They are wirelessly online — a wearable computing device. Doctor Pickles, what is that you're wearing on your left wrist.'

'It's a bloody watch,' grumped Hades. 'What are you all blithering about?'

Pickles had caught the thread and was running with it. 'Yes, it's a watch, but it's also a telephone and computer. Also internet-enabled through the mobile network, like Hilda's glasses. It displays data other than the time on the watch face. As with Hilda's glasses, it can also be voice activated. A wearable computing device.'

'Yes,' continued Victoria. 'The future of personal computing: wearable devices. They are currently limited in what they can do by the technologies of miniaturisation but wearables are most definitely here to stay. And that's not all. Not only are they wearable computers, but they are damn fashionable too. They look fab.'

Pickles beamed. He was not used to being associated with looking fab.

Persephone had caught on too, and she, Hilda, Pickles and Victoria now all looked at Hades waiting for him to catch up.

'What?' he protested. 'What?'

When there was no response from his family and colleagues: 'Oh. You mean I'm missing something staggeringly obvious. Something about the size of K2 and I'm standing here with my nose pressed against it?'

Persephone went over to the cabinet of emergency supplies and came back with a bottle of noggin and a glass. She poured and offered the tumbler to her husband, who obediently took and drank.

His eyes nearly popped out of his head. 'Good Lord! You mean these pants are wearable devices too, and with enough computing power to make the glasses and watches look like trinkets? And they have universal appeal as gadgets and are damn good looking too? They combine the Hades qualities of popularity and innovation — techno-pants for the people? And they are the very thing that will allow Pants Corp to kick that damn Mangler back to his bloody Antarctic lair?'

'At last!' exclaimed Victoria. 'For a minute there I thought we'd lost you.'

'But are they machine washable?' Hades asked.

'Oh, absolutely.'

'None of the ones or zeros will get washed out.'

'Absolutely not,' assured Victoria.

'So do you have a name for these things?' Hades quizzed

'iPants, of course,' said Victoria with a cheeky smile.

'Oh,' said Persephone. 'Our incredibly clever daughter has taken what she has learned from her parents put it together with what she has learned for herself, and fused both with her intelligence and imagination. And she's come up with a brilliant idea that combines the strengths of parents and child. And she's going to save Hades Undies World and give everyone something fantastic to get enthusiastic about. I think I'm going to cry.'

And she did. And so did Hilda and Pickles and even Hades was looking a bit soggy-eyed.

'Bye-bye, Dr Mangler,' chortled Hades. 'Let's celebrate. Noggins all round, chaps!'

12

In the days following the launch of the organic pants, Mangler mania intensified.

Celebrities queued up to endorse the tree-grown underthings without being paid to do so. Some of them even gave up Scientology in order to proselytise full time for the new undies-maker.

The media clamoured for even just a moment with Mangler. They traced his family and school chums and pets. An interview with a goldfish formerly owned by Mangler, in which the creature was silent and floating on its back in a bowl of water was aired repeatedly. The hacks found nothing remarkable, yet each mote of history was treated like the relic of a particularly popular messiah.

The phenomenon of wearing pants outside your clothes or completely doing away with over clothes that Hades had first seen on the streets of Panting went global. All the models and celebrities in Vogue, Vanity Fair and GQ appeared in print thus attired — or unattired.

The Hades Undies World stores remained empty, the sensible underthings stacked neatly on the shelves, the staff remained at their posts but largely dreamed of the Manglers they were wearing under their Hades uniforms.

Hades pants mills were still and silent, the fleets of delivery lorries and aeroplanes stayed in their pools. Folk singers wrote humorous and ironic laments about the company.

The army of office staff and backroom bods idled at their desks googling Mangler on their office computers.

From Hades, not a peep.

Until.

Hades was taking dinner in one of one of the world's most exclusive and expensive restaurants, the Fat Pig in London, when he was spotted by Harland Dome the editor of One Percent, the world's leading magazine about rich people and their money, named after not only the demographic, but also the amount of tax they usually paid on their fortunes after their lawyers and accountants had tied the law in knots.

Hades was not just taking dinner, he was dining large. Persephone, Victoria and Hilda were there of course, as were most of his extended family, the board of directors, and the extended board of directors, Dr Pickles, the research team and a homeless lady who had been accidentally swept up in the tide of Hades party as they entered the restaurant.

The Fat Pig had six Michelin stars and was renowned among foodies and gluttons, so this was quite a bash. Everything on the menu looked so good Hades had ordered everything on the menu — for each of the many people at the table.

Dainty and sophisticated creations though each of the dishes were, the table groaned under the volume. It groaned even more under the weight of the entire cellar of wine Hades had ordered to go with the nosh.

Hades was especially jolly as were his fellow diners. The laughter they were generating may have been breaking several environmental laws and setting off seismic alerts across the globe.

Harland Dome, although dining in a less extravagant mode, was also in a very good mood. He had written about quite a lot of money that day and made a pot or two for himself in the process. That month's magazine was abed and there was self-congratulation with the publisher and a couple of the more super-rich advertisers. Spotting Hades in full jolly when Pants Corp was going belly-up like Mangler's goldfish, he smelled a story.

'Good evening, Sir Hades. Sorry to barge in on your party. I just wanted to say hello. Terribly nice running across you like this.'

'Harland!' Hades bounded to his feet and shook the editor's hand in a painful, bear-like grip. 'How are you? Still drooling about everyone else's money?'

'Where there *is* money. Not everyone hangs on to it, you know. Talking of which, I am a little surprised to see you out and about tonight, Hades. Looks like a celebration or is it a last supper?'

'Celebration? Last supper? What are you talking about? This is dinner, old chap. Chow! Victuals! A chap has to eat!'

'Oh, you know, under the circumstances and all.'

'Circumstances and all? What circumstances and all would they be?'

'Hades, don't tell me you haven't noticed. Let me fill you in. A certain Dr Mangler has just ridden roughshod over your business empire. Your shops are empty and your factories are idle. Mangler mania has seized the world. People are asking whether there is now a place for Hades in underpants.'

'Goodness gracious, is that what you think is going on?'

'It's what everyone thinks is going on.'

'Well, a bit of advice, old chap. Don't believe everything you read in the papers.' Hades guffawed. 'I've always wanted to say that to a journalist. No, no, it's business as usual, Harland, business as usual.' He guffawed some more and so did everyone else at the table. Dome felt very discomfited.

'Come on, old bean, join us for a drink, and your chums too. They look like they could do with a bit of light relief from being not quite as rich as me.'

By the end of the evening Dome was unsure whether he had just attended a banquet of the damned or a triumphal feast. However, waking up the next day he was in no doubt he had downed too much booze. No matter the exquisite vintage of the wine, plied in such quantity it had beaten his brain to a throbbing pile of carnage.

It was with these thoughts hurting his damaged head that he made his way to the first of the day's engagements, a working breakfast with some gentlemen who owned the Middle East. He travelled like all self-respecting rich, in a chauffeured limo so that he could stare at the hoi polloi, the unchosen, through bulletproof glass and feel happy he didn't have to breath the same air as them.

Sunk in his pillowy seat with a reviving cappuccino from the car's own espresso machine, he suddenly had the feeling he was being watched. It was an unsettling sensation. More so because he knew immediately, without looking, who was watching him: it was Hades, Sir Hades Gousset. Dome could feel his gaze.

Still disquieted by last night's meeting with the garrulous underwear magnate, Dome peered cautiously from the car and straight into the face of Sir Hades Gousset himself — a Hades who was larger than life in a way more literal than the expression intends, and staring at Dome from a hoarding the size of a house overlooking the Westway. Hades wore a cheery grin and was winking mischievously, like a very jolly Santa. The smile and the wink seemed to be for Dome personally.

The editor opened the car door and got out into the stalled traffic. Hades was staring at him from everywhere: every hoarding, every bus, every taxi. An electronic billboard carried the same picture.

Each of the images showed the same winking Hades. That was it: no words, no copy, no logo, no traces of branding, just the big, jolly Father Christmas grin and the wink.

Something was happening and Dome couldn't figure out what.

Abandoning the car in the unmoving traffic, he set off on foot, though he had quite forgotten where he was going. From his vantage on the Westway, it seemed that all through London the scene was the same. It was as if Hades had bought up every bit of available ad space in the city and filled it with his image.

Dome called his office. 'Have you seen this?'

Without asking what 'this' might be, his PA answered, 'Yes. It's everywhere — all over the country, all over the world, it's all over the net. What is going on?'

'What does the media say?'

'We are the media and we haven't said anything yet because we don't know what to say.'

'Fine. Good work! Well, do what we always do when we haven't anything to say.'

'So, set up a large team of reporters to watch an important looking closed door somewhere and put out urgent bulletins on the state of some traffic lights in downtown Baghdad?'

'Yes, that's the thing. And see if you can get a quote from a celebrity who has nothing much to do with anything and no particular thoughts in their head. And make sure there are some pigeons hanging about aimlessly in front of that important looking closed door.'

'Got it.'

'Have you called Hades yet? Mangler?'

'We haven't presumed. We thought you'd like to make the decision about that.'

'More good thinking. I'll call them myself. Patch me through from where you are and record the calls, there's a good chap.'

He was first connected to Hades. They exchanged the usual pleasantries.

'Harland! Long time no see. Not since about one o'clock this morning, I think. You had a pair of Mangler pants on your head.' Hades laughed a terribly cheerful laugh, the kind of laugh that ought to be banned after an evening of drinking with him.

'Underpants on my head?' asked Harland trying hard to remember but at the same time hoping he never would.

'Don't worry, they weren't your own.' Hades laughed some more, probably causing irreversible damage to the cables that strung the internet together. 'Don't worry about it ending up in the papers because you are the papers and so is the owner of the pants, poor fellow. How can I help you this fine morning?'

'Well, Hades, I'm glad to hear you are well and in no way pauperised by the bill for supper last night.' More guffaws from the other end of the phone. 'I couldn't help but notice a tiny bit of advertising for Pants Corp absolutely everywhere this morning, Hades. A distinctive and innovative campaign destined for many industry awards. But what the hell is it about?'

There was yet another explosion of guffaws from Hades. 'Oh, just having a wink, you know.'

'A what?'

'A wink, old man, a good old wink.'

'Yes, I thought so. But I'm curious to know what it's a wink in aid of.'

'Do we need a reason for a wink now? If you have an itch to wink, scratch it, I say.'

'But what sort of wink is it? A conspiratorial wink? A cheeky I'm-about-to-grab-your-bottom wink? An I-know-something-you-don't-know wink?'

'More of a winker's sort of wink, I would say. Woke up one morning and thought, hello, I'd like a wink. And there it is.'

'Most people don't splash their winks all over the place, Hades. It's a very in-your-face kind of wink.'

'I have no other kind of business, Harland. Tell you what, though. There's those who make the history and those that figure out what it's all about, and you're one of the latter. You let me know what the wink is when you've written about it. In the meantime, Harland, with respect and apologies, I must get on.'

Dome, still standing in the middle of Westway had become the reason the traffic was not moving on that road. Oblivious to the growing chorus of horns, he strolled thoughtfully toward the centre of London. He felt he was missing something the size of Godzilla that was stomping around in the world devouring sense and certainty.

He called Mangler.

'Dr Mangler, Harland Dome of One Percent magazine here. Long time no see.'

'Well, we haven't met, have we, Mr Dome.'

'Ha ha ha! We must rectify that some day. I hope you'll be my guest when next we are on the same continent.'

'Sounds delightful. How can I help you?'

'Oh, please call me Harland. Many congratulations on your recent stunning success in business. Quite unprecedented. I mean, you've dethroned Hades, King of the Undies World. You've pretty much assumed that status now, don't you think?'

'Thank you for your kind words. I'm sure they'll go to my head and cause it to swell further.'

'It seems strange that Hades has been so … unresponsive, so quiet. Passive almost.'

'Hades? Unresponsive? Quiet? Passive? Which Hades are we talking about? The Hades I know has just launched a massive advertising campaign. Quite out of the blue and of quite imaginative hue.'

'You know about that?'

'Oh yes. Can't miss it. Even the penguins down here in Antarctica are chattering about it.'

'These ads of Hades' are a bit cryptic. What do you make of them?'

'Cryptic? It's a big wink, that's what it is. What's cryptic about a wink? You know, you have to admire Hades. He is a man of many achievements and now he can add winking to that roll of glory.'

'You sound like you approve of Hades' wink.'

'It's a magnificent wink. I couldn't have winked better myself. Oh, yes, Hades is a big winker, all right.'

'And what do you think is the import of this wink? Is it a come on? Do you feel intimidated?'

'Intimidated by a wink? Goodness gracious, I should think not. Wink on, I say. More power to Hades' elbow for his winking, I say.'

'So how are you going to respond to Hades' wink?'

'Respond? Well, I've a jolly good mind to have a wink myself. But I have other things to be getting on with like spreading my underpants trees into every corner of the world.' Which was a hint for Harland to get off the phone, like the cacophony of blaring horns behind him.

'Well, it was very nice talking to you, Dr Mangler. Thank you for all your help.'

'Oh, I've been of no help whatsoever. Bye for now, Mr Dome.'

Dome was puzzled. Something was happening between the two biggest underpants magnates in the world. He was standing in the middle of an unprecedented war of pants and yet neither of the protagonists behaved as if there was a conflict at all. Dome's world seemed to be spinning. He couldn't make sense of it at all. In fact it was Dome, not the world that was spinning. He had just been batted off the Westway by a very impatient driver who was leading a massive convey of lorries that was loaded to the brim with Hades' very exciting new product, and which was being distributed to all London stores in time for the big launch.

13

Three days after the appearance of the wink posters, the world awoke to a whole new collection of posters. They all simply read 'NOW!' and carried the Hades logo.

With a collective 'What?' the population of the planet descended on the Hades stores and discovered them transformed. Gone were the familiar undies in all shades of sensible, and in now was a range of new things in sharp shades of steel and chrome, a range of clothes that said, 'Move over Dr Mangler, we're back and we're big and we're bad (albeit, very tastefully bad).'

Collectively, the world gasped.

Hades, in a swift and bold marketing move, had come back from the ropes where Mangler had put him and shoved his genius right in the face of the planet. And not for the first time.

Hello, world. Meet Hades's new things: the Omnipants!

14

'The last pants you'll ever wear!' declaimed the billboards.

'Just ask the man in the Clapham Omnipants!' exclaimed the ad spaces on buses and trains.

'Omniscient, Omnipotent! Omnipresent! — Omnipants!' said the TV ads.

'Total pants!' the cinema advertising told everyone.

'Everything you could ever want in a pair of pants. The underwear is pretty good too,' the internet banners said with a conspiratorial wink.

15

'What the fuck is this? What the fuck are you doing?' demanded Victoria storming unannounced into Hades' bunker and without waiting for the door to get out of the way. She was followed by Persephone and tumbling staff, dragged in by her slipstream.

'What's that, sweetness?' asked Hades feigning surprise.

'This!' Victoria slammed down on the table a newspaper folded open to a full-page ad for something called Hades Omnipants.

'And this!' she thrust in his face her tablet showing the Hades website that was now given over to the same Omnipants.

'Why, it's our new line of things, the very things with which we get our market back from Dr Mangler.'

'What happened to the fucking iPants? What happened to the product we agreed we'd use to get back at Mangler? What happened to the plan we came up with together?'

'Sweetness!' exclaimed Hades hoping that a second use of the word would get through where the first had failed. 'This *is* our plan. I just tweaked it a bit.'

'Tweaked it a bit? These things have nothing to do with the iPants! And what the fuck are Omnipants anyway? They don't look like iPants. They don't do anything the iPants do.'

'Your daughter,' added Persephone, 'has some excellent points. What on earth are you doing?'

Confronted with two angry family members, Hades tried the calm authority tack. 'Persephone, Victoria, if you'll bear with me and listen to what I have to say you'll understand the rationale behind this move.'

'I bet I won't,' said Victoria. 'But let's hear it. And it had better be excellent, because if I get any angrier you won't be able to wear another pair of underpants again let alone make any more.'

'There's no need for threats.'

'Yes there fucking well is!'

'Harrumph!'

'Don't try your harrumph thing! It doesn't work with me. I know it for the silly old man noise it really is.'

'Look here, I won't have you shouting at me like this, even by my daughter.'

'You pompous old baboon!'

'Or my wife.'

'How dare you try to lay down the law when you've completely thrown away your daughter's good ideas? She came forward with those ideas to help you and the family and rescue the business from that madman Mangler. And you throw her efforts away. It's insulting.'

'You had better explain yourself and you had better make it good.'

Hades was cornered. His had been a perfectly good plan. How was it he had drawn this anger?

'It's very simple. I took Victoria's idea and combined the strongest bits with the traditional strengths of Hades Undies World and the result was the Omnipants. It's more a change of name than anything.'

'And a complete change of underpants!' Victoria's hair tossed in a frighteningly Hydra-like manner in her anger.

'No! Look! I kept the best parts of the iPants.'

'Which parts?'

'I can't think at the moment, but definitely the best bits. Look at the Omnipants, though. They may not be quite what you imagined, but they do the business. They're the next thing. And look at the feedback we're getting from the public already. Mangler's on the back foot within hours of their launch.'

'Not the fucking point! Last time you didn't take me seriously I ended up in an alien spaceship slingshotting around Alpha-fucking-Centauri.'

'I thought you enjoyed it in the end.'

'I may well send you to Alpha Centauri on the end of my foot.' Persephone had sent several people to diverse corners of the galaxy on the end of her foot, so this was not an idle suggestion. NASA wanted Persephone's foot, but Persephone wouldn't give it up.

'Ladies! Persephone! Victoria! I must protest. You are too hard on me. Look at what is actually going on here! I have implemented Victoria's idea. The Omnipants wouldn't have happened were it not for Victoria.'

'My idea was not the Omnipants. My idea was the iPants. Your Omnipants bear no resemblance to my iPants.'

'Beg to differ. They're very modern and have all sorts of clever functions.'

'They have a device for picking stones out of the hooves of horses.'

'Very useful for those unanticipated equestrian mishaps.'

'The device is located in the front of the pants, in the groin. You have to hold the hoof to your crotch and sort of jiggle about.'

'Yes?' said Hades.

'Do you have any idea how that looks?'

'Yes?' said Hades with caution.

'It's the same with the toothpick function.'

'Yes?'

'Yes! Located in the crotch again. Thrust, jiggle, mouth, crotch.'

'Well they are underpants. They have rather a lot of crotch to them.'

'Yes, they do, and a lot of crotch-loaded tools. A bottle opener, a corkscrew, a screwdriver, a file, a reamer, a ballpoint pen, a fish scaler, a nail file, scissors, pliers, a magnifying glass, a hex wrench — whatever that is —'

'It's a bent bit of metal that fits in things and tightens or loosens them like a key —'

'There! Another turning, twisting thing that fits in the front of your Y-fronts or knickers.'

'Hang on a bit. Where else are we going to stow these things. And you've missed the best features.'

'Oh, yes, the best features, like?'

'The GPS. The flash drives. The clock. The altimeter. The barometer. The laser pointer. The saw. The boat hook. The telephone. The music player — everything has a music player installed these days.'

'Yes, and these days music players play MP3 files. Yours plays vinyl.'

'Vinyl's coming back into fashion. And don't you think that when it comes to books and music, it's better to have something tangible in your hands rather than an abstract data file?'

'It's better to have something you can use!'

'And it has cameras both fore and aft — digital cameras. Everything has cameras these days.'

'You do get some nice perspectives from the low angle, you know. Quite unexpected things,' put in Dr Pickles. 'The inside of the fly of your trousers, the seat of your trousers, and if you wear the pants inside out —'

'And the Omnipants are connected to the internet. Everything has music players, cameras and wireless internet connections these days.'

'But Daddy, you are totally missing the point. These pants are connected to what purpose? What single thing can you do online with that connectivity? You're supposed to have apps that do things, you know. Cool things. Useful things. Things that people actually want to do. You've made analogue pants with a broadband connection that does nothing!'

'Getting the stones from the hooves of horses is pretty bloody cool, I'll have you know. And the horses appreciate it no end.'

'Most people don't have horses. We've moved on since the middle ages.'

'What do you have against horses? Look, young lady, I've been very patient up to this point. I'm still CEO of this company and I have made certain decisions and for your information they are paying off. Hilda, if you would be so good.'

'The thing is,' Hilda said to Victoria and Persephone, hiding her opinion that she totally, totally, absolutely agreed with them by sounding as business-like as possible, 'sales have been very brisk. Spectacular, in fact. People are flocking back to our stores.' She clicked on a PowerPoint presentation she had conveniently to hand and projected on to the wall a graph that consisted of lots of coloured arrows all pointing dramatically up.

'There. What do you think of that?' Hades stood commandingly akimbo his face full of challenges for Victoria to explain away all those zooming, upwardly mobile arrows if they didn't mean victory over Mangler and vindication for himself.

'You've got the graph upside down,' said Victoria.

'What? Now look —'

Persephone asked, 'And how do you the iPants wouldn't have sold more?'

Hilda avoided the eyes of Persephone and Victoria.

'But this isn't about sales,' said Persephone. 'This is about disregarding people, riding roughshod over them, taking people for granted; saying one thing and doing another. It's about pretending you have accepted the input of a family member and then completely disregarding it. This is about respect and trust.'

Silence.

'And this. Hilda, may I?' Victoria took over at Hilda's laptop. She dismissed PowerPoint and found YouTube where she typed in Hades Omnipants.

'This search already returns thousands of results,' she told her father.

'That's what I'm saying,' said Hades, though without the tones of his usual hubris.

Victoria projected a video onto the wall. It showed two teenage boys wearing Omnipants sword fighting groin to groin with penknife blade attachments extended.

The next showed a man demonstrating the implement for removing stones from the hooves of horses with much mirth, which turned into a call to paramedics when the horse kicked out at the stone removing implement and the place to which it was attached. Another video showed that someone had sneaked a pair of Omnipants onto the head of the statue of Winston Churchill in Parliament Square. The patriotic flag waving function dangled a twitching union flag over Winnie's nose.

'Might these people be taking the piss? Are the Omnipants the ironic statement du jour? If people are buying your pants to mock them, doesn't that ring alarm bells in the sustained sales department?' Victoria turned and left the conference room, her head high and not looking back.

Persephone waited a moment until she saw Hades compose himself and attempt to speak and then cut him off.

'Hades, did you really think we wouldn't notice? How did you think you might get away with this? "Oh look! Our new Hades line. They don't look like the iPants, they don't work like the iPants, they aren't called iPants, but I suppose they must be iPants because Hades, my husband, Victoria's father, the man we trust more than any other, said he was going to make and market the iPants that his daughter invented to help out the family business." And they are a fucking clever idea, too.'

And Persephone followed her daughter out of Hades' bunker.

'Oh buggery bugger-bags!' said Hades. 'We'll see.'

And they did see, indeed.

16

Barry Scroat had never had sex. Neither had Margaret Potts. But now Barry suspected they might be about to. Have sex. At last. Together. At the same time. Him and Margaret Potts.

It was a beautiful moment.

This not having sex thing had dominated Barry's life. Nearly ruined it. Everyone in the world was shagging like bunnies. Constantly. You could see it in their eyes. They were doing it on TV, in advertisements, on trains, in the pub ... incessant, they all were. Even the birds and the effing bees were at it. Yes, animals and effing insects were shagging like bunnies, but not Barry. Except now he was. Or was about to.

Margaret was less bothered by the lack of sex per se, but was definitely up for a bit of love, a spot of high romance. She was definitely there for being carried away by a knight on a white charger and living happily ever after. Barry was not your actual knight, being a funny shape and all, and he didn't have a white charger. He didn't have a white anything, really, everything around Barry being sort of grubby and soiled. But he did have a dodgy van and a bedsit. He wasn't allowed guests in the bedsit, especially not for the purposes of carrying them away on a white charger, which would no doubt make an unreasonable and against-the-rules thumping and clip-clopping noise on the stairs, and Margaret wasn't allowed anything at home except the sharp edge of her mother's tongue and whatever bits of soggy rusk her gran had finished sucking on.

So they were in the van now, which was in the car park at Asda. That was nice: they both liked Asda. They both worked there. Location was so important and they still had most of their lunch break left. Barry had invited Margaret in for an egg sandwich, though his intentions were not strictly gastronomic, and over the course of sharing mayonnaise, they had come into this affectionate grip.

'Oh, Barry!'

'Wot? I mean, oh, Margaret!'

'This is divine!'

'I thought you was Margaret.'

Barry may not have had sex as such, but he knew lots about it. He knew lots about it because it was all over the internet. He was even now enumerating his options in his head: hair, mouth, face, dashboard, bottom; odd bits of translucent pink plastic, hamsters, electric torque driver, ping pong balls, nappies. He had everything in the toolbox in the back of the van here, just in case of moments like this or so he could amuse himself whenever he was out and about. He was sure Margaret was going to be impressed.

He hoped she would be impressed with the music: heavy metal. It was a genre of music that spoke to him; spoke to 42-year-old virgins generally.

Forty-two-year-old virgins were in part virgins because of their taste for heavy metal. Barry was unaware of this and so Barry cleaved to the genre as if the screaming guitars spoke of his virility itself where in reality the songs spoke gruntingly of having hair where his brain should be.

Barry and Margaret were becoming urgent in their embrace. The van was already rocking slightly. The clothes were coming off. This was a bit tricky in the back of the van, and neither of them being exactly small people, or even inexactly small people.

'Oh, Barry!' said Margaret.

'Oh, Margaret!' said Barry

'Oh, bloody hell! Get a load of this down here,' said Margaret's underpants.

'They are seriously not going to do this!' said Barry's underpants.

'I can't watch!' said Margaret's underpants.

'Let me out of here!' said Barry's underpants.

'What the fuck is going on?' Barry enquired of his underpants.

'What are you trying to do?' Margaret demanded of Barry.

'It's not me!' Barry told Margaret.

'It's very much you from where I am,' Barry's underpants told him.

Margaret's underpants laughed hysterically and made some disgusting monkey noises.

'It's our underpants! They're talking to us! Quick get them off!' shouted Barry in a panic that was heard clear across the Asda car park.

'That is the most pathetic excuse I've ever heard,' said Margaret's underpants, 'for getting a girl out of her pants.'

'Are you going to let him get away with that?' Barry's underpants asked Margaret. 'Are you going to shag a man with come-on lines like that?'

'Barry, stop it!' screamed Margaret. 'You're making me scared.'

'I'm not doing anything!' Barry shouted at Margaret.

'That's what they all say,' shouted the underpants in unison.

In the confines of the van in the throes of passion it had been a challenge to disrobe but now in a panic it was impossible. The van was rocking like a small vulnerable boat in a big scary storm, and the commotion was beginning to attract the attention of shoppers passing through the car park.

'Ha ha! En garde!' said Margaret's underpants and with a clack and a boing deployed a penknife blade.

'En garde!' responded Barry's underpants and sprang a gimlet.

The underpants clacked their weapons in mortal combat.

The gimlet in Barry's pants was too much for the knife in Margaret's so they sprang a pair of shears instead which chomped at the air near Barry's groin.

Barry and Margaret screamed, the van rocked more energetically and the crowd outside grew bigger.

Losing ground to the shears, Barry's pants escalated the war. Out came the laser pointer, which, turned onto maximum power, fired hot red bolts of light around the interior of the van. All the junk in the van, the grimy plastic bags and the large quantity of semi-artificial fabrics that Barry and Margaret were wearing composed a fertile environment for fire and when the laser caught a can of oil, the back of the van became a hell of flame.

Barry found the door and burst out into the car park, with Margaret following, both enveloped in roiling smoke, some of which was coming from their smouldering clothes.

The onlookers, who had grown to a crowd of a couple of dozen, stood back in fear and alarm. The more alert of them wondered where they might get a fire extinguisher or called for the fire brigade.

Somewhere in the crowd someone was giggling in a most ungallant way. Then that giggle was joined by chuckles. The onlookers wondered who could be so horrible as to laugh at the misfortunes of these two (admittedly unfortunate-looking) people.

The giggles and the chuckles were joined by guffaws and whoops. The shoppers at first could not see where this racket was coming from, until, with horror, the truth dawned on them. The laughing was coming from inside their own clothes. Specifically, inside their trousers or dresses or shorts or skirts — the laughter was coming from their own underpants, and it was becoming more hysterical and maniacal by the second.

The shoppers exchanged panicked looks. Meanwhile, Barry's underpants refused to leave Margaret's alone and Margaret's underpants fought back. Now the hips and groins of the watching shoppers began to thrust and gyrate excited by the mayhem of the would-be lovers. The air was rent by a buzzing and ripping noise as the vents of a nice pair of chinos was slashed by a buzzsaw cutting through from inside. The wearer of the pants screamed but there was little he could do. As he tried to unbuckle his trousers, the whirring dervish saw batted his fingers. From the hole in his trousers more tools, weapons of mash and destruction, emerged. Knives, spikes, corkscrews, lasers, and furious, whipping antenna.

The same was happening with the underpants of all the shoppers gathered in the car park at Asda as bushels of scary implements burst free and then turned on each other.

'Tally ho!'

'To the death!'

'Last one chopped to bits is a sissy!'

'C'mon pants, make my day!'

'Chaaaarge!'

The shoppers fell on each other loins-first and the air filled with the fragments of slashed trousers and the flash and smoke of discharging lasers.

17

Harry Widdle felt that the interview had gone well so far. His hadn't been a flawless performance but he'd answered the questions clearly, engagingly, and demonstrated that he had the knowledge and experience to do the job. He wouldn't write himself off as Mouldy & Mouldy's next sales rep for Essex and East Anglia. He'd be selling fur trusses before you knew it.

Goodness knew he needed the job. Life had been tough since the bottom fell out of the copper pot market and his not quite unrelated conviction on charges of assault. After experiences like that your self-respect goes. One minute it's sales conferences in Margate and Lowestoft. The next you are sharing a cell with a 130kg granny killer who is also a born-again Christian, and Olivia is leaving for Wales with the kids and wants every last penny of the money you didn't really have in the first place.

Oh, yes, he needed this job to rescue his life. It was the sort of thing he was good at, this job: selling things.

The start to the interview today had been a bit intimidating. He had been shown into this rather plush conference room that had tasteful grey walls and a tasteful, grey pot plant that even may have been real, and he was sat down in front of the three tastefully grey interviewers, Mr Mouldy, Mr Mouldy, and Ms Clench, who didn't, to be honest, look the warmest or the most alive people on the planet.

However, Widdle has immediately clicked into sales operative mode. It was all about presenting yourself with confidence, with belief. It was about presenting a vibe that didn't even hint at the possibility of past unemployment, financial ruin, divorce or imprisonment. You were, for the time it took to do the job, the cleanest, most wholesome, most successful most reliable, most trustworthy, chap who ever offered you a fur truss for sale.

Widdle fancied he was doing OK. He fancied that Mouldy, Mouldy and Clench had loosened up a bit as the chat had gone on, had come to seem a little less possessed by rigor mortis.

One of the Mouldys even managed a smile. 'And now, Mr Widdle, you've told us about your strengths and your experience. I wonder, do you have any weaknesses? If I were to ask you if you had a characteristic that was not as strong as it could be, what do you think that would be?'

Doddle! They always asked this one at interviews. It was the drooler question: only a moron would not anticipate this question and not prepare for it. If you can't see this question coming, you can't see night following day. Widdle had it all planned. He was going to talk about his over reliance on his own initiative and how he had learned to rein that in to emphasise teamwork.

'He has a weakness for chickens.'

Widdle, Mouldy, Mouldy and Clench looked around to see who had spoken.

'I beg your pardon,' asked Mouldy.

'Chickens. A weakness for. You asked whether he had any weaknesses. The answer is chickens. Got him time in prison, it did. Did you mention the prison time on your application? You need to mention things like that, you know.'

'What's going on?' Clench wanted to know.

'Who is that?' asked Mouldy — the other Mouldy.

'Mostly oven-ready chickens. Roasters. But one turned out to be a boiler. Understandable mistake in all that mayhem.'

Widdle leaped out of his chair and whirled around — the chickens had come out. 'Look, who is this? If this is a prank, it isn't very funny.' The prison had been mentioned too. The voice was right. That wasn't on the application. It was hidden by a forged reference.

'I need this job! I need it! Leave me alone, whoever you are!'

'Oh, yes, chickens! Lots of them, including the boiler, and right there in the middle of Tesco.'

'Tesco? Mr Widdle, explain yourself. Why are you pretending to be two people and talking nonsense?'

'There's no mention of chickens in the person specification, you know,' said Clench.

'It's not me!' wailed Widdle. 'I think it's my pants. The voice is coming from my pants.'

'Don't be silly,' said Mouldy — the other Mouldy. 'Underpants don't talk.'

'Of course they don't,' said Widdle's underpants. 'Hearing underpants talk is a sign of madness. If I'm talking, you're mad. Oops! That was a dead giveaway.'

'Get away from me! Leave me alone!'

'Mr Widdle, are you doing what I think you're doing?'

'Are you taking your trousers off in the middle of a job interview?' Clench wanted to know.

'My pants! They are trying to destroy my life! I must get away from them!'

'Mr Widdle, are you now doing something else I think you're doing?'

'Are you attempting to remove your underpants in the middle of a job interview?' said Clench in horror and in hope.

'Someone call the police. This man is clearly unstable.'

'I can't get them off!' wailed Widdle.

'Got him hooked! Hook and tackle! There's a joke there somewhere.'

'Mr Widdle!' screamed, Mouldy, Mouldy and Clench as they abandoned their seats and made for the door.

'Oh, no you don't!' said the underpants of the grey eminences in unison. 'You've heard about his chickens. Now we're going to hear about Mr Mouldy's hamster hunting excursions, the other Mr Mouldy's way with toilet brushes, and Ms Clench's collection of exotic loofahs.'

18

When the Northern Line train stopped suddenly between Camden Town and Euston the passengers inwardly groaned. Don't let it be another failure on the line!

Emily Hatcher, self-made business person, wedged in the low space by a door, kept her head down and her focus on her tablet screen and the Forrester market report she was reading, and from which she was trying to absorb a global and intuitive understanding of market trends in the fur truss industry. She was not that absorbed that she was unaware of the odd disquieting atmosphere in the train, an atmosphere like a hushed rustling. Like rats in the walls. Emily was a rational person. She knew that there were lots of things to be wary of on crowded tube trains but rats was not one of them.

Next to her, Slater Stonewall, middle manager par excellence, who was making the rounds of branch offices of the global climate control appliance corporation for which he worked, kept his head down on his newspaper and tried not to show he was ogling the women around him. It was not too hard to keep his head in the newspaper because there were lots of women to ogle in there too. Women in the tube train; women in the newspaper — sorted! This was why he was a kick-arse manager.

One of the women Stonewall was not ogling was Patricia Wimble — single, married, cat, hat, slave to celebrity gossip. Stonewall was not ogling her, surreptitiously or otherwise, because Patricia did not conform to Stonewall's criteria of ogle-fodder. She looked neither like a celeb nor one of the younger female progeny of London't wealthier quarters. She didn't even look like a goer from any of London's less wealthy quarters. She looked like a hair pillow. She looked like the kind of person who might wear the occasional fur truss on a weekend. Patricia was a secretary, personal assistant and factotum to somebody in an expensive suit and was therefore one of the people who quietly keep the world turning without ever being noticed. She, like Stonewall, was ogling totty in a magazine, though for different reasons. Patricia was looking at celebrities in the magazine Boo! because that's what she did. Her day job just paid for her to do the real thing in her life: looking at photos of rich people who would never give her the time of day. They were beautiful people who did beautiful things and she wanted to know all about them.

The carriage was quiet. Tube trains are not noisy at the best of times, but stuck in the tunnel like this no one dared to speak in case they were noticed. Even the two young look-at-me lasses that Stonewall had been especially ogling were quiet and fixating on their phones rather than speaking. The phone fixating was a transparent displacement activity because there was no signal down here in the cretaceous period.

After a while there was an announcement from the train driver.

'I'm sorry for the delay ladies and gentlemen. We seem to have a red light up ahead. There's no word about the reason for that. I hope the light will clear and we'll be on our way in just a moment.'

Emily's disquiet increased. Why was that, she wondered. Just … a feeling. Spooky. A spooky feeling.

'The thing I like best about being a pair of underpants,' said a very unwholesome voice, 'is getting to know the wearer really well.'

Who was that, everyone thought. Clearly a mad person. Don't look round. Keep your head down in your book or your phone. Don't make eye contact.

'That's right.' The second voice sounded very much like the first voice but came from a different location in the car.

Oh help! The loony has a friend.

'You get to know all the intimate secrets of the wearer. Everything.'

The passengers had their heads down but their eyes were swivelling out of their sockets.

'Oh, yes, and then some!' said a third voice that sounded very like the first two.

'I just heard from another pair of pants about a man who went to prison for sexually assaulting several oven-ready chickens in a supermarket. One of them was actually a boiler.'

'That's brilliant! That's exactly what I'm talking about.'

'Apparently, the knickers spilled the beans in the middle of a job interview. The guy hadn't even mentioned a prison term on his CV. It was mayhem!'

'Fucking hilarious! I wish I could have been there.'

'Oh, you can be. It's all on the network. In fact, I think the pants just uploaded the whole thing to YouTube.'

'Can't see it here because we are in a tunnel. Catch it a bit later. Hey, everyone, just search "totally pants job interview". It's hilarious!'

'Hey, hey! Listen! Listen! Talking of secrets: my wearer' — the voice seemed to be coming from Patricia Wimble — 'has got this thing for celebrities. Yeah, she collects pictures of them and stuffs them in her knickers before going out to work so she has Johnny or Brad or George all over her arse all day. Sometimes it's women too. Today we have Angelina and Toby.'

'Angelina and Toby? Why those two?'

'I dunno. Ask her —'

No!

'She's the lady reading Boo!'

No one in the car could maintain the heads down posture any longer. Eyes were up and seeking the Boo!-reading lady. Patricia went as red as the masthead on the magazine and tried to hide her face until she realised that she was trying to hide her face with exactly the Boo! magazine that would give her away. She quickly stuffed the Boo! in her bag and then her head in with it too.

'That's really good, but listen to mine! She's this really successful businesswoman, has her own company and everything. It's all so clever and technical no one can figure out what she does, but anyway she makes buckets of dosh from it. But you know how she gets her kicks? You know what she does when she thinks no one is looking? She dresses up as the back end of a pantomime horse. Really! She completely gets off on it. She goes to these parties, you know, where no one really knows anyone and don't want to. It's the stress thing you see. She finds someone to be the front end of the pantomime horse and gets hitched up. And then there's a … Need I explain more?'

The train was full of an evil, laughing, cackling sound. Yes! It occurred to Emily that this cackling was the sound she had heard before, the sound of rats in a wall. It was muted and muffled then, she couldn't identify it. But now it was out in the open. It had escaped from the wall and was filling the car. She knew that whatever this was it was worse than rats.

'Yes, the lady here with the iPad and the big expensive, executive coat. It's her stress thing, her way of getting away from responsibility. The back end of a pantomime horse! It's the opposite of responsible leader. Brilliant! And beautifully disgusting!'

The voice seemed to be coming from behind her but there was nothing behind her except the wall and the door of the carriage. The other voices too: they didn't seem to be coming from anywhere either. She wanted to think: this is all a prank, there's a hidden TV camera here. Any moment now Jeremy Wheedle is going to appear from the guard's room or from behind a newspaper or spring out of a shopping bag — and if he does, she is going to kick his horrible git-like face in. However, she knows that what she is experiencing is an evil beyond even the considerably vile powers of Wheedle.

'Disgustingly brilliant! Do you want to hear about this one?'

Everyone in the carriage sunk further into their seats.

No, not me! Leave me out of it!

'Go on, then! Give us a laugh!' agreed several voices, or several versions of the same voice, that seemed to be coming from everywhere and nowhere at once. 'This one here — go on, stand up straight, mate, so everyone can see you!' Stonewall found himself jolted by hands unseen away from the wall into the middle of the car where dozens of anxious eyes fixed on him.

'No!' he wailed. 'What have I done to you?'

'Well, this one,' continued the voice regardlessly, 'likes to strip down to his undies and recite the speeches of Margaret Thatcher. Yes! He actually gets kicks from it. And not just at home, oh no. He goes to this bar in Hampstead. Very discreet. All the punters there have the same kind of thing. They strip off and do the speeches of Stalin or Hitler or George Bush or King Il-Jong.'

'Oh, that is foul!'

'No, I don't. I don't do that honest. Not much, anyway!' Stonewall held his hands in a gesture of prayer, of desperate pleading.

'But it gets better,' said the voice. 'There's something else he likes even better.'

The evil chatter rose in volume and insanity urging the speaker to go on.

'Not that!' pleaded Stonewall. 'Don't listen to him, people. Whatever he says it's all made up!'

'He loves crowded trains, he does. And you know what he loves to do on crowded trains? He likes to surreptitiously pick his nose and wipe his snot on the clothes of the people around him. Especially women, but sometimes men. And he likes to play with his willy on the train when it's so crowded no one will notice. At work, he'll stick his finger in his own bum before meetings and then shake hands with business associates. No, really, he does that all the time.'

The passengers glared at Stonewall with loathing. The voices were spooky and horrible but this man was vileness itself.

Stonewall continued to plead. 'No! No! No! No! No! No! No! No! Don't listen, it's not true.'

Emily looked on with the calm detachment that had made her a success. She had worked out there was worse to come. The cackling sound had taken on a new quality, a shriller, spine-tingling quality. There was a terrible sound over and above the laughter and it was coming from the adjacent carriages. It was the sound of screaming. The sound of terror. It was getting louder.

Then the lights in the train went out.

19

The aeroplane, massive and brilliantly white, its tail emblazoned with the colours of the Union Jack, touched down at Heathrow. It taxied to a special arrival gate and the prime minister of the United Kingdom strode with gravitas and dignity down the stairs from the plane and to a podium, forested with microphones, set up before a grandstand packed with political leaders, diplomats, and wealthy friends of the government. The grandstand was flanked by two further only slightly less-grandstands packed with members of the press and their cameras.

The event was carefully and self-consciously stage-managed to evoke the arrival of another prime minister who had travelled from continental Europe in 1938.

While his predecessor had established lasting peace with Hitler and the Nazis, the current PM had gone a bit further. After years of jetting around the planet visiting every leader possible, he had just secured the final signatures assuring peace in the whole world. Thanks to the inspired and tireless efforts of this one PM of this one small country, world peace was assured now and for ever and ever.

This was quite a coup, if coup is an appropriate word to use here.

The Prime Minister ascended the podium. 'I have here in my hand the piece of paper that guarantees peace in our time and for all time.'

The crowd raised their dignified hands to clap and paused and gasped instead. The prime minister was not holding up a piece of paper at all, he was holding a pair of underpants —

grey, sensible underpants that could only have come from Hades.

The collective gasp in place of wild applause alerted the prime minister that something was not quite right. And then he realised what he was holding and he gasped too. How had they got there?

'Yes, this is the paper all right,' exclaimed a voice that wasn't the prime minister's, and a document wafted from the waistband of the pants.

'Oh, yes, the document that guarantees peace. This is the one. Oops!' There was a bright red flash of laser from the Y of the Y-fronts and, *piff!* — the paper went up in smoke. 'Oh dear, so much for world peace! The UK hereby declares war on everyone in the world. Yes, it's war — starting now!' The laser in the Y of the Y-fronts in the hand of the prime minister of the UK began firing at the assembled dignitaries, specifically, the foreign ones. Bolts of red hurtled across the tarmac into the stands blowing hats off, setting fire to clothes, demolishing the scaffolding that supported the seating. Before it could occur to the prime minister to drop the pants, the stands were erupting in smoke and flames and the flying bodies of visiting important people.

Within minutes the nations of the world had responded to Britain's declaration of war in kind. The world was once again at war. This time with one common enemy: the United Kingdom.

20

'Oh buggery bugger-bags!'

The eerie glow from dozens of computers, tablets and TVs stacked in the Porton Down bunker created an otherworldly, apocalyptic atmosphere, which was convenient, because it matched reality perfectly.

The devices covered every flat surface, horizontal or perpendicular: the walls, shelves, desks, conference table, were all streaming in real time different views of the End of the World as We Know It.

'It is still not known what made the prime minister declare war on every country in the world just at the moment he had secured world peace,' said the announcer on the BBC news.

'Oh, buggery bugger-bags!' said a grim-faced Hades.

'The prime minister himself denies declaring war on anybody and blames his underpants for the incident. He has been taken by doctors to a nice place where he can meet other teapots and fire engines and chat to the pixies.'

The voice of the ITN announcer on another machine cut across the BBC: '— the prime minister was indeed seen to be waving a pair of Hades Omnipants at the moment of his declaration on the tarmac of Heathrow airport. According to experts, there is no historical record of a pair of underpants having declared war on a nation and we are urged to hold the prime minister's remarks in some scepticism.'

'Oh, buggery bugger-bags!' repeated Hades.

'The deputy prime minister and the entire cabinet have apparently disappeared. In the absence of a functioning government, Mrs Hilda Scringe, the tea lady at number 10

Downing Street has been left in charge of Britain's war effort.'

The camera cut to the tea lady standing defiantly on the white cliffs of Dover with her trolly and urn. 'Leave us alone, you bullies!' she shouted through her hands at France.

'In other news,' continued the BBC, 'London is burning as the world succumbs to an apparent zombie apocalypse. Law, order, and the very fabric of society has collapsed as armies of vicious, once-human automata lay waste to civilisation. This has apparently improved living conditions in Swindon but for the rest of the planet it's not such good news. We go live to Martin Goodfellow reporting from the streets of London.'

Goodfellow was in the middle of Oxford Street, wearing a hard hat and a cagoule. Smoke and the sound of sirens filled the air. People ran screaming in all directions, some of them chased by cars or buses. A building appeared to collapse into the street. In among the cacophony of destruction there was another sound: it came from everywhere at once and was reminiscent of maniacal laughter.

'Martin, thanks for joining us. I gather you don't expect to live much longer.'

'Thanks, Brian, and that's right. Such is the mayhem and destruction I fully expect to be killed at any minute.'

'Excellent. We'll be sure to keep the camera on you. Can you tell us what the situation is.'

'Well, as I am sure you can see, it's pretty chaotic here on Oxford Street — more so than usual. There's lots of running and screaming and general terror.'

'Is there any sign of the emergency services?'

'Yes, we saw some police and ambulance personnel a little earlier, but to be honest, I think they've been eaten.'

'Eaten? So it's pretty serious then.'

'Yes, the emergency services being eaten is never a good sign.'

'And it's not just London being affected, I understand.'

'That's right, Brian. This zombie apocalypse seems to have seized the whole world. I gather that New York, Paris,

Cape Town, Tokyo, Berlin, Beijing, and all the rest are in pretty much the same state of disarray. Lots of smoke and carnage going on everywhere.'

'But what about the important people? The royal family, celebrities, those people — are they OK? Have they become zombies too?'

'Have the royal family become zombies? That's hard to tell. The reports we are receiving are that all the important people and their small dogs are being flown to safety and hidden in zombie-proof underground bunkers.'

'Have there been many zombie apocalypses like this before, Martin? Exactly how common is this sort of world-wide cataclysm?'

'In fact, Brian, they are not that common. Although they happen in popular entertainment quite a lot, this seems to be the first confirmed zombie apocalypse in the real world.'

'And what of the origin of this zombie apocalypse? Do we know anything about that?'

'Well, that's the puzzle, you see. People are blaming their underpants. Especially the Hades Omnipants.'

'Their underpants? Is there any credibility to these claims? How can underpants cause a zombie apocalypse?'

'Well, this is where the story becomes particularly intriguing—' at which point, Martin Goodfellow was splatted by a fast-moving 73 bus. The bus skidded, lost control and slammed sideways into the front of a brand-name clothing store, revealing to the camera the advertisement that covered its entire side: a massive image of Hades Gousset, grinning and winking conspiratorially.

21

'Oh, buggery bugger-bags!' exploded Hades at the same time the bus in Oxford Street did. 'It's the end of the world as we know it. We have to do something! Pickles, what have we got to save the world? Hilda, what is going on? Persephone, do we have any noggin left?'

'Until we know what the problem is, we can't roll out any technology,' said Pickles.

'Don't we have any zombie-repelling pants?'

'I don't think we've ever thought to invent any,' said Pickles lamely.

'Dammit! Are you saying we have underpants for all eventualities except the eventuality that's actually currently eventuating?'

'Yes, I believe I am.'

'Yet more buggery and bugger-bags! Hilda, what can you tell me? Hilda?'

Persephone answered: 'Hilda doesn't seem to be here. That's not like her at all.'

'Where the blazes is she? So how about that noggin? Catshit!' Hades bellowed at Hilda's personal assistant, who seemed to be doing his best to hide in the darker corners of the bunker out of Hades' sight.

'Ah,' said Catshit.

'Where is Ms Titanium, and as her PA, why aren't you personally assisting her?'

'Ah, I was hoping you wouldn't ask me that.'

'Well, I have. What about it? Where's Hilda?'

'Drat, you've asked me again. Are you sure you don't want to take back the question?'

'Come to that,' said Persephone, 'Where's Victoria?'

'Ah. Another question I wish you'd take back. Are you really sure you don't want to take back both of these questions? I'm sure you'd be very happy if you did.'

'Pretty sure,' said Hades. 'Depends how much I am going to dislike the answer. How much do you think I'm not going to like the answer?'

'A lot,' said Catshit in his best simper.

Hades gave up trying to prise the glass of noggin from Persephone's hand and just grabbed the bottle and swigged from that. 'In that case I absolutely have to know. Tell me!'

22

One of the many things about the current whereabouts and activities of Hilda and Victoria that Catshit didn't want to explain was that at that very moment they were dangling by ropes from a helicopter over the centre of London and they were clad in black combat gear and balaclavas that could only mean they were up to something very serious indeed — or, much more alarming — had gone imbecilic in the style department. Some of the other things that Catshit didn't want to explain was that the two women were being lowered on to a rooftop in order to get closer to the mayhem seizing the city in order to find out what the zombie apocalypse was all about — assuming there was something more to it than just zombies and apocalypse.

Hilda and Victoria touched down on the roof of the Whatchamacallit Cinema in Leicester Square — you know, the big one — about as central West End as you could get.

The two women unhitched from their ropes while the crew of the chopper lowered another person, conspicuously clad only in leopard print trunks, and festooned with several kit bags.

Hilda and Victoria set about unpacking the bags of dauntingly difficult equipment and the third member of the team pulled off his helmet and mask to reveal perfect, god-like features, tainted with a bit of blue from the time he spent frozen.

It was Timmy, Timothy Adonis, Victoria's personal assistant and object of a lust that had remained unconsummated and which only dissipated when Timmy kidnapped her and held her hostage in an inaccessible mountaintop fortress in the Alps as a display of his own passion for her, which event coincided with Victoria discovering her brain, turning from blond to brunette and completely going off steroid-swilling hunks who could barely speak, let alone read. This had meant foregoing the chance to get her teeth into his perfect buns, but there had been compensations. No more gifts of dead rabbits, for example, no need for the demoralising futility of conversation.

Timmy Adonis was here, restored after enforced absence, as bag man and personal bodyguard.

'Timmy, check the roof and make sure we are safe. Locate the points of access and secure them as best you can. We need to work without interruption and we want a nice clean extraction as soon as we are finished,' Victoria told him.

Smoke rose from all over the city, creating a doomsday pall that clashed dramatically with the sunlight as if the heavens were involved in a conflict to match the one on earth. Rising with the smoke was a hellish din of screams and crashes and explosions, the sound of a city being torn apart.

'What was that word beginning with 'l' again? The one in the middle of what you said.'

'What? Oh,'locate'? It means find. Check the doors and windows are locked, ladders or stairs are blocked.'

'Oh, and what about the other word?'

'What other word?'

'The other one — you know.'

'Timmy, we don't want Mr Scary hassling us while we are working. Can you keep Mr Scary away from us?'

Timmy brightened. 'Oh, yes, I can do that. Shall I start now?'

'Oh, please do,' said Victoria with relief that would have been obvious to everyone except the man she was speaking to.

'Air samples,' said Hilda. 'To check for airborne viruses or bacteria or spoor or chemicals that could be causing this.'

'I'm going to film the people in the square to try to get clues from their behaviour.'

'What we really need is blood, DNA and tissue samples from one of the zombies,' said Hilda.

The ladies pushed aside the thought of what getting those samples would actually entail.

The helicopter that had dropped them off was making laps of the centre of London while they worked. They felt isolated.

Victoria crouched behind the parapet of the roof and started filming events in Leicester Square below. Recently full of happy carefree tourists and London locals out for a night on the lash it was now like a battleground. There was not a window unbroken. The dodgems were littered from one end of the square to the other, and there was a mayhem of people walking or running with a strange mechanical gait and flailing arms. It was all very odd.

While recording Victoria fished out a small decibel meter from her kit, turned it on and held it out to get a reading.

'This is what has been bothering me all along,' she told Hilda.

'What?' She was preoccupied with the air samples.

'This weird noise.'

'The glissando of breaking glass? The scream of tortured metal? The howls of the insane? The pleas of their victims?'

'The laughter,' said Victoria. 'Everywhere there's laughter. A particularly horrible laughter it is too. I think I picked it up before on the news broadcasts but I couldn't put my finger on it. It just sort of makes a backdrop to the general insanity.'

Hilda paused and thought. 'You're right. It's been there all along hasn't it — a horrible, filthy, maniacal kind of laugh. Where's it coming from?'

'From everywhere,' said Victoria, walking along the parapet of the cinema roof decibel meter held out before her.

There was a detonation below and an old lady streaming smoke and fire hurtled right over the roof. Neither Hilda nor Victoria paid much attention. They now had a lead, they felt, but didn't know quite what it was.

'We must get a clear recording of the laughter, of everything,' said Hilda.

'I'm on it,' said Victoria, precarious on the edge of the roof. 'Do we have anything that will measure Doppler shift in sound waves? That might help us guess at the source better.'

Intent on their work, the women failed to notice the sinister figure wobbling across the roof at them. Its leg movements were unnatural and stilted. The way it moved at the waist suggested it way as well not have been connected to those legs. The arms flailed and waved like someone trying to scare off a wasp while trying not to fall off the top of their fruitpicking ladder.

'I want to eat your bums!' said a voice that was unwholesomeness and degeneracy in equally considerable measure.

'That's not good,' said Hilda and Victoria together.

'Waaaaaaaah!' said the zombie thing.

'Timmy, why did you let this thing up here? This is a problem.'

The zombie thing was only the first of a lot of the creatures, who were now wobbling across the roof, all wailing and chanting 'I want to eat your bum! I want to eat your bum!'

Timmy looked confused.

'You said you didn't want Mr Scary. But that's not Mr Scary. That's Tom Missile the actor. And that's Mr Missile's wife, Katie Boat. And behind her, that's the famous director Ronny Whatever, and that's the sound man … I haven't seen Mr Scary and if i did I wouldn't let him up here. Does he look a bit like Tom Missile or something?'

Victoria and Hilda backed away as the zombies advanced.

'Help!' said Tom Missile. 'Help!'

'Timmy!' Victoria shouted across the rooftop. 'We're getting close to the edge of the roof.'

'We're being forced into a corner from which there's no way out except vertically down several storeys at 9.8 metres per second per second to the street below.'

'Is that a good thing or a bad thing?' Timmy wanted to know.

'It's a very bad thing,' said Hilda, 'and it means we are in need of immediate rescue.'

'Oh.' Timmy's voice did not convey a can-do spirit of rescue. More a spirit of oh bugger, I think I got it wrong and now I feel a bit stupid.

'Talk to me, Timmy. What was that oh about? It wasn't a good oh, was it.'

'Oh,' said Timmy again. 'It's going to be a bit difficult to rescue you right at this moment. You see, rather of lot of these film people have picked me up and are getting ready to throw me off the roof. Could you hang on a minute?'

'Timmy save yourself! Get away from those things!' Victoria tried to keep the fear from her voice.

'I've radioed for the helicopter. It should be here any second,' Hilda told her.

'Help!' pleaded Tom Missile, looking on the edge of tears.

'Shut up, you, or I'll bite your tats off!' said a voice that wasn't Tom Missile's. Missile flinched.

'High time to high step it out of here,' said Hilda. 'Did you do ballet at school by any chance?'

'Yes. But I have lately taken up Thai boxing which is much more to the point.'

'Then let's get our Timmy back.'

Hilda and Victoria sprang forward together. Hilda aimed a high kick at Missile's head.

He wailed. 'Ouch! Don't hit me! Don't hit me!'

Victoria did the same.

'Stop it! Leave me alone! What did I do?'

'Fascinating,' observed Hilda, raising a quizzical eyebrow.

Victoria planted another swinging blow into Missile's solar plexus. He turned blue.

'No! No! No!' His voice was more of a wheeze than a plead.

'Something just occurred to me,' said Hilda, who aimed a scything   uppercut   into   Missile's   goolies — 'Aaaaaaaaaaaaagh!' — who weebled and wobbled but didn't fall over.

'Yes,' Hilda continued, 'I'm getting a pretty major theory here — get off me you monster!'

Hands clasped on Hilda's neck and grasped at Victoria's shoulders dragging them toward the edge of the roof. The pair of them let loose a barrage of blows with feet and hands.

'Ow! Leave us alone! Pleaded the zombies. One very large rigger from the theatre burst into tears, but still they closed in on the women.

Hilda and Victoria broke free of the encircling monsters and sprinted across the roof to find Timmy. The gang of undead who had picked him up had put him down again on the parapet of the roof where he stood like a very large but completely bewildered puppy.

The zombies chanted together.

'Three …'

'Oh no, I know what's coming next.' Victoria's voice was a panicky shout.

'Two …'

'Victoria, I love you!' shouted Timmy.

'One …'

'No!' Victoria bludgeoned zombie heads but couldn't get close to Timmy.

'Boo!'

Timmy hurtled backward into the smoky, violent air of ravaged London.

'You bastards! You've killed Timmy!' Even as Victoria and Hilda prepared to exact a terrible revenge they realised that they were surrounded. The zombies of Tom Missile and the great and the dreadful of Movieland shuffled closer from all directions, uttering horrible un-dead noises. The horrible un-dead noises were these:

'I want to go home!'

'Leave us alone, you bullies!'

'I've wet myself.'

'Mummy!'

And, 'I think Instagram's overloaded because I can't get this selfie to post.'

Hilda and Victoria stood back to back in combat-ready posture. 'Now would be a good time for the that helicopter to arrive.'

Which, serendipitously, it did. 'Sorry we're late. Got stuck in a sky jam. It's all them TV station news choppers blocking up the flight paths.' The crew of the helicopter dropped ropes and the two women leapt and grabbed tight. And so did dozens of zombies. Whether they were in leaping distance or not, they hurled themselves at the women, the ropes, the helicopter. Even while clinging on to the snapping rope as the overloaded and bombarded helicopter went into a spin, Hilda wondered that the zombies could leap with such supernatural power and athleticism.

Something whooshed past and a loud bang sent smoke billowing from the manifolds of the aircraft's engines: a hurtling Tom Missile had become wedged in an air intake and destroyed one of the two turbos.

'We're going down! We're going down!' screamed the pilot helpfully.

The helicopter, belching smoke, lurched and staggered across Leicester Square as only a mortally wounded helicopter can. Zombies dangled from the landing gear and clung to the ropes that also held Victoria and Hilda.

'The National Portrait Gallery!' exclaimed the co-pilot.

'It's a bit boring, if you ask me. I much prefer the Tate Modern. A bit more dangerous, if you know what I mean,' said the pilot.

'I mean we're going to crash into the thing.'

'Oh, I see.' The pilot hauled on the controls and the helicopter whined and belched more smoke but stayed sort of aloft.

The trailing ropes banged on the roof of the gallery leaving a trail of wriggling zombies. Hilda and Victoria tried hauling themselves further up but were blocked by yet more of the drooling creatures. They hauled on the undead feet trying to drag them off the rope.

The stricken chopper cleared the roof of the National Gallery scaring all the pigeons in Trafalgar Square into the air. And then the last bits of Tom Missile were finally sucked into the engine, which emphatically exploded, and the aircraft plummeted into the fountains at the foot of Nelson's column.

Hilda was trapped under the dead weight of zombies and helicopter wreckage but an air pocket formed in the hood of her burqa, saving her from the embarrassment of drowning in two feet of water. She exercised some more of her well-honed kicking and punching skills and freed herself, came up breathing deep lungfuls.

'Victoria! Victoria!'

Hilda searched desperately for Hades' daughter among the bits of helicopter and bobbing, sobbing zombies. She hauled the crew out of the cockpit of the aircraft and planted them on dry land while they got their consciousness back, but there was no sign of the magnate's heir. While she searched, the zombies closed in from Charing Cross Road, from Canada House, from the Mall, from Whitehall — especially from Whitehall, which is a refuge of the undead at the best of times.

Hilda had to search for Victoria and save her before she was assimilated into the zombie horde; she needed to get back to the National Gallery over whose roof she had last seen her companion, and she had something of a fight on her hands to get there.

23

'That's what I didn't want to tell you,' Catshit told Hades and Persephone in the command bunker at the Pants Down facility. 'That your personal assistant and your daughter commandeered one of your helicopters without telling you, set off into the heart of a zombie-infested city to investigate the apocalypse themselves, had got into trouble, Hilda being nearly killed, and Victoria going missing.'

'And why didn't you want to tell me?' asked Persephone.

'Because I thought you would get angry and order me to bury myself in the rhubarb patch again.'

'Get your shovel,' commanded Hades.

'Righty ho.'

'Before you go, Catshit, when did this happen?' Persephone wanted to know.

'Right now. As I was explaining it.'

'Right now? What on earth are you talking about?' demanded Hades.

'Hilda is streaming everything from a digital camera attached to her burqa. I'm following everything on my tablet,' which he held up. The screen showed a whirl of spinning, flying zombie bodies and brief glimpses of Trafalgar Square at sickeningly unnatural angles.

'And what about Victoria?' Persephone asked in a tone that strongly suggested she was quite keen on shooting any messenger on sight and had no qualms about the ethics of it. 'Wasn't she wearing a digital camera?'

'Oh, yes, very much so and a GPS locator too. Both stopped transmitting somewhere between Leicester Square and the fountains in Trafalgar Square.'

Hades rose to his full commanding height and looked right down his nose at Hilda's personal assistant. 'Right. Catshit. When you have buried yourself for not telling us that they had gone to London, dig yourself up and give yourself a pay rise for following them remotely on digicams and GPS, and then bury yourself again for losing Victoria even though it was not remotely your fault. You should accidentally-on-purpose batter yourself about the head with the shovel at this point.'

'And on your way to the rhubarb patch, please rustle up some cavalry to go in and rescue my daughter and Hades' formerly-trusted assistant,' said Persephone.

'Yes, and send my hat in,' added Hades. 'I'll personally be making up part of this contingent of cavalry.'

'All in that specific order?' asked Catshit.

'In that specific order. And don't forget the bits where you bury yourself in the rhubarb patch,' said Persephone.

'And make sure you hit yourself on the head,' insisted Hades.

24

'Well, that was a good rescue,' said Hades irritably as he bobbed in the water of the Thames.

'Yes, seems to be a specialty of yours, husband, dear,' said Persephone who was also bobbing in the Thames like a very bright and extravagant buoy.

'Well, it's the thought that counts,' said Hades hopefully.

'Thought? Which bit of that debacle had thought in it?' Persephone wanted to know.

'What just happened?' asked Hilda who was also bobbing in the Thames along with Hades and Persephone. 'One minute I was battling zombies on Charing Cross Road and then things became very weird and now I'm here in the river.'

The London Eye looked down at them from the South Bank and over Westminster Bridge you could just see Big Ben and the top of Parliament. The apocalyptic palls of smoke and catastrophic light still hung over everything as did the cacophony the End of Days was making.

'Hades was rescuing you, Hilda. Weren't you Hades, dear? And he was finding his daughter in order to rescue her too. Isn't that right, Hades?'

'Spot on as usual, Persephone, dear.'

'Not a strong point of yours, rescue, is it, dear,' Persephone pointed out thinking of very public rescue escapades in the south of France and Paris Disneyland that hadn't turned out to be actual rescues at all. 'Should have seen that as a hole in your plan, shouldn't I, darling.'

'Plan?' asked Hades.

'The horses,' asked Hilda. 'How did the horses come into it?'

'That was the cavalry,' said Hades with some pride.

'The horses didn't get on very well with the zombies, did they,' said Hilda. 'At least I didn't think so.'

'They didn't get on with the helicopters, either,' Persephone added.

'I can always rely on you to notice these things, can't I,' said Hades in between mouthfuls of tea-coloured Thames water.

'So where are the cavalry now?' asked Hilda. 'I'm afraid I rather lost track in all the sudden movement, noise, crashing helicopters, stampeding nags, and collapsing buildings.'

'Oh, here and there, I daresay,' said Hades lightly as if here and there were a normal and welcome place for cavalry to be.

'In how many pieces?' asked Persephone in a tone of voice calculated to remind her husband that bits were not part of the plan.

'And how did the river get involved in this?' wondered Hilda. 'Last anything made any sense to me, I was on Charing Cross Road trying to find Victoria in the middle of an apocalypse and doing battle with what appeared to be a horde of deranged zombie creatures. Charing Cross Road is not exactly right next door to the river.'

'Ah, yes, well,' said Hades. 'I daresay there's a good answer to that. Buggered if I know what it is, though. Things happened a bit fast, didn't they. Well, we're here now. Best get on with it, that's what I say,' said Hades. 'No point in dwelling on the past. I have a daughter to find. Again.'

'Lead the way, then, dear,' Persephone told him. 'Shall we head for the zombies lining the east bank outside County Hall? Or shall we head for the zombies on the other side of the river on Victoria Embankment? Or shall we head for the zombies gathering on Westminster Bridge? Or perhaps the zombies packing onto Hungerford Bridge in the other direction?'

Wailing, waving, wobbling walls of zombies, lined the bridges and the banks of the river all around them behaving as if they were very personally after Hades, Persephone and Hilda, which they were.

Despite being in the very unprofessional predicament of bobbing in a cold, brown river, Hilda was still on the job. 'Hades, before Victoria disappeared we made a lot of discoveries, things you need to know.'

'I need to know where my daughter is. She was last seen in or near Leicester Square, and the shortest distant between two points being a straight line, I suggest we swim diagonally across the river to the west end of Hungerford Bridge and Embankment station, scale the sheer banks of the river there, then fight our way up Northumberland Avenue to Trafalgar Square, blitz our way across that to Charing Cross Road, and then it's a short pitched battle to Leicester Square. Everybody ready?'

'Yes, of course, Hades, but first I think I'd better tell you what we found out.'

The flight of helicopters appeared from over Westminster. They had military livery and the direct and purposeful nature of their flight suggested they were fairly free of zombie interference.

'Ah, that looks more promising,' said Hades, not stopping to hear what Hilda wanted to say.

'Hades! Please!'

The underpants magnate was busy hailing the choppers and was not listening.

The helicopters deployed around the water-bound trio without pause or kerfuffle as if they had known exactly where to find them. Three of the flight circled protectively, using their downdraft to beat back the crowds of undead from the bridges and riverbanks. The fourth dangled rescue personnel who hauled Hades, Persephone and Hilda out of the water and into the safety of the cabin, where more personnel wrapped them in blankets and silver thermal sheets.

'I can't thank you enough,' said Hades through chattering teeth. 'Absolutely well done.'

'Oh, don't thank us.' The speaker was a cadaverously thin individual with hooded, reptilian eyes. 'I'm inspector Snake of Scotland Yard, and I fished you out of the water with the sole intention of placing you under arrest.'

'Arrest?' spluttered Hades finding more Thames water to spray around the helicopter.

'Hades, this is what I was trying to tell you in the water,' said Hilda. 'There is no zombie apocalypse. It's the Omnipants. They've gone insane, and everyone is going to blame you!'

25

'This is absurd!' thundered Hades. 'You can't arrest me! I'm Hades Gousset, King of the Undies World.'

Inspector Snake made an exaggerated show of looking around the interrogation room in the bowels of The Tower of London, a room that looked exclusively designed for torturing people, which was, indeed, the purpose for which it had been built. 'Oh, I think we can arrest you, and apparently we already have.'

'What are the charges? You have no basis for holding me.'

'You saw what London looked like when we pulled you out of the river. That's what we are charging you with: wilful destruction of the fabric of society. Every other country in the world is charging you with the same.'

'But!' shouted Hades quite emphatically. 'And but again!'

The cell was dark and airless. It would have benefitted from a window to open to let the smell of terror and pain out. It would have benefitted from a window to let some humanity in and reassure the incarcerated that there was still a world beyond the massive stone walls.

'On top of that, we are charging you with starting the third world war.'

'But I didn't do that! Our batty PM declared war on everyone. It was on TV. I was in Porton Down. I have witnesses.'

'Are you, or are you not, Sir Hades Gousset, owner-operator of Hades Undies World, inventor, manufacturer, and purveyor of Hades' Omnipants?'

'Well of course I am!'

120

'We got you bang to rights, then.'

'But!'

Snake feigned a look of surprise at the sheaf of papers in his hands. 'Oh, and then there are all these other charges here I nearly forgot about. Just fancy that! Malicious destruction of property, to wit, all the major cities in the world and probably the minor ones too, if we can ever find them in this mess. Then there's diverse charges of treason, subversion, coup d'état, insurrection, revolution, armed overthrow, usurpation, domination, treachery, perfidiousness, revolt, rebellion, mutiny, confabulation, dissembling, conspiracy, deception, fraud, selling underpants under false pretences; then you seem to have broken all the health and safety regulations in the world.'

'But I'm a national hero. You can't treat me like this. I demand to see the prime minister.' Hades attempted to thump the table with authority, which wasn't easy with the heavy manacles on his wrists. He succeeded only in clanging the table.

The door of the torture cell opened and the prime minister came in. He looked very miffed.

Hades jollied up in his shackles. 'Prime minister! Henry!'

'I'm George. Henry was two governments back.'

'That's what I mean! George!'

The prime minister regarded Hades with a mixture of contempt and pity and bewilderment, but mostly disgust. 'Look. George.' Hades leaned confidentially toward the PM with a lot of loud clanging and clunking. 'I'm in a bit of a pickle here. Bit of a misunderstanding. Now, I don't know if I've mentioned this before —'

'Yes, you have mentioned it before and it won't do any good now.'

'— but I have rather helped the old country out of a mess once or twice before, haven't I … What do you mean won't do any good?'

'Helping the country meant something when there was a country to help. Now we have a pile of smoking ruins — not much of a country, really. And the only reason we don't have

121

every army in the world massing across the channel for an invasion is that every country in the world is as messed up as we are.'

'There you are. Silver lining in the zombie cloud,' said Hades making another attempt to jolly himself out of the poo.

Inspector Snake, the prime minister and the armed guards stopped to scrutinise the ceiling in an attempt to see how the destruction of everything people had made, all that humanity held dear, could contain a silver lining.

Hades went on tentatively, not sure whether he really wanted to hear the answer to his next question. 'While we're on the subject, I don't really know what any of this has to do with me.'

The PM looked quizzically at Snake.

'We were just getting to that. He seems to be going for flat-out denial.'

'Flat out denial of what?' Hades asked.

'There you see: denial,' said Snake.

'Hades, the game's up,' said the prime minister as if talking to a small child. 'We know all about the underpants.'

'What underpants?'

Snake sneered. 'He says "What underpants?" as if he has no idea. And him being King of the Undies World.'

'Well, let's pretend he doesn't know and explain this to him in very simple terms,' said the PM. 'Hades, are you familiar with the Hades Omnipants?'

'You know I am. I made 'em.'

'And to what purpose did you make these Omnipants?'

'To sell, of course. They were our new line of Manglers or anti-Manglers. He was wiping the floor with us with those new tree-grown underthings of his. You know all this.'

'You didn't manufacture the Omnipants with the intention of overthrowing civilisation?'

'Why would I do that?'

'Power and riches!' hissed Snake.

'I am already the most powerful and richest man in the world,' Hades pointed out. 'What power or wealth could I accrue that I did not already have?'

The door had opened so quietly that Hades had barely registered it. Suddenly a medium sized, immaculately dressed and coiffured figure, as correct and smart as a mathematical equation appeared at the PM's shoulder.

'All the power and wealth that was going to me, Hades. My underpants trees were growing exponentially and pushing you out of the market. The only way you could fight back was to smash everything. Raze and conquer, eh, Sir Hades?'

'Mangler! What are you doing here?'

The prime minister replied while Snake smirked unspeakably. 'Dr Mangler is here to help us restore order and then rebuild from the pants up when we have overcome the current adversity. Meet our new underpants tsar.'

'Underpants tsar? But that's the sort of title that would normally go to me.'

'Honour the man who destroyed civilisation, who robbed billions of people of their dreams and dignity?' asked the prime minister.

'The thing is,' said Mangler, 'we've rumbled your game. We have been investigating the causes of this so-called zombie apocalypse and we've discovered there are no zombies as such. We have established beyond any reasonable doubt that you flooded the market with your Omnipants but you hid in their software a highly destructive programme, one we have termed a berserker programme. On a signal transmitted through the internet the code was activated in all the Omnipants, which then went, well, berserk, with their wearers still inside them.'

The prime minister picked up the story. 'And it was the pants that started the world war, Hades. Same thing: the berserker programme. I was wearing Omnipants that day I flew into Heathrow, Hades. I was wearing Omnipants out of respect and loyalty to you for everything you have done for this country. And my loyalty was repaid by your pants declaring war on the whole ruddy world and humiliating me and this nation — and doing so quite publicly on the international stage, I might add. I won't be able to show my face at the G8 for a decade or two, I imagine.'

'Berserker programme? Is that what this is all about? And what sad little conspiracy blog did you get that off?'

'Forensic analysis of captured Omnipants,' said Mangler. 'We reverse-engineered every bit of machinery, every bit of software, every system in them, and came up with the berserker programme, sitting right in the middle of the operating system and running everything.'

'It's a smoking gun,' said the prime minister.

'Your pants have been made to go quite deliberately mad, which they have done with appalling effectiveness. They have held their wearers captive and forced them to do all sorts of terrible things.'

Hades snorted. 'Preposterous. How could underpants force anyone to do anything?'

'They are not just underpants, Hades.' Mangler was almost whispering with menace. 'They are Omnipants. They are packed with tools, with moving parts — and think where all those tools and moving components are located — adjacent to the most sensitive and vulnerable parts a human has. The corkscrew tool alone would make the strongest person submit to your every twisty whim.'

'Oh, buggery bugger-bags!'

Mangler leaned in close. 'Those pants with all those tools are like iron maidens for your nethers. And what kind of perverted mind thinks up something like that?'

'You tell me, Mangler, because the thought hadn't crossed my mind until you expressed it.' Hades stared back evenly at his accuser, though he didn't feel at all even on the inside.

The PM stepped in with his authority. 'So, Hades, your time has gone. We have announced to the world that Dr Mangler will strip us of the tyranny of Hades' underpants and then lead us into a brighter, future with soft fabrics in a stunning choice of vibrant colours. For you, we have only abject humiliation and ignominy. There was quite some celebration among the survivors of the Omnipants when we made the announcement.'

'In the meantime,' said Mangler, 'the war against the Omnipants continues. But we shall prevail. My entire staff of

124

technicians is tasked with hacking the pants and finding a way to disable them. God help humanity until they do.'

'That berserker programme is nothing to do with me or Hades Undies World. We would not stoop so low as to infect a person's underpants with such a thing,' said Hades, still controlled and meeting the eyes of his accusers. 'A public hearing in a court of law will establish my innocence.'

'Too late.' Mangler smirked triumphantly. 'Using my emergency powers as underpants tsar, I convened a court in secret and had you tried in absentia.'

This was news to the prime minister. 'You did? Emergency powers?'

'Yes, the emergency powers I declared for myself because of the current state of emergency. Following my instructions, the court found Hades guilty.'

'Let me guess,' said Hades. 'The same emergency protocols state there is no appeal.'

'Uncanny guess.'

The tension in the cell threatened to crack even these massive and ancient walls.

26

The bleeping of the prime minister's phone broke the spell. He consulted the screen, took the call, and listened.

Finally, he clicked off and addressed Mangler. 'The zombies are storming the Tower. They are already inside the walls and swarming rapidly and in huge numbers. We are no longer safe here.'

'How did they get in?' asked Snake. 'Did they batter down a gate? Scale the walls? This is the Tower of London, after all.'

'They bought tickets,' said the prime minister. 'In their thousands. This is the Tower of London, after all. But why are they storming this place?' he asked the room generally. 'It's as if they knew that Hades was here.'

'If they are inside the walls,' said Snake figuring things out in his head as he went along, 'it means there is a security problem. We have been —' he enunciated the word with lip-smacking satisfaction — 'compromised. And that also means Her Majesty Herself is in grave danger.'

Hades was so surprised he expostulated. 'You have the Queen here in the Tower of London?'

'Oh, yes,' said Snake. 'We thought, what's the most secure location in Britain, and we thought that's where the Crown Jewels are so no one nicks them, so then we thought if that's the most secure place why don't we stash Her Majesty there with the jewels.'

'Oh, good grief, you incarcerated the head of state in a vault from which there is no escape right in the middle of a zombie apocalypse?'

'But how could they get in?' sneered Snake. 'Have you seen the steel on them doors?'

Hades made a noise like thunder. 'They have tickets, you fool!'

There was a momentary embarrassed silence, which was broken by Mangler.

'Why are you sharing our secrets with our principal enemy, Snake?'

Snake suddenly looked both alarmed and contrite. 'I'm not entirely sure, now you ask.'

Mangler was circling Hades in a predatory manner. 'Yes, very odd, Hades, that your zombies should show up here, just where you are, at this moment in time, when you are manacled in the seat of disgrace. It's as if you were in communication with them. Well, we know there are no messages going through your Omnipants, because they were secured when the police strip-searched you. Do you have a beacon hidden in your beard by any chance?'

'Perhaps I am not the beacon,' said Hades pointedly. 'Perhaps someone else is.' Again, he held his eyes as piercing as a diamond drill on Mangler.

'I doubt it. No one here would want to get into your pants.'

'There's no time for this,' said the prime minister. 'We have to rescue the Queen and find a way out of here.'

'We can exit by Traitor's Gate, straight on to the river,' said Snake impressed with his own idea.

The prime minister was not impressed. 'We're not traitors.'

Snake was not to be deterred; he was going to chase his idea down. 'But Hades is. He can leave by the gate and, er … that thought doesn't seem to be going anywhere. Please ignore it.'

'You're all missing something,' chirped Mangler.

'Brains,' said Hades.

Mangler beamed. 'Ah! A quip! You do like to keep your pecker up in dire straits don't you, Hades. No, brains is not what I was thinking of.' Directing himself at Snake, 'Let's get

Hades unshackled and on his feet. We may need to move very quickly.'

'So what is this we are missing?' the prime minister wanted to know.

'My chaps have been working on this whole Omnipants apocalypse thing, haven't they. As soon as they come up with a solution, which I suspect won't be long, we will be OK. Meanwhile, I have a daring plan to save the Queen.'

'A plan to save the Queen?' the prime minister wanted to know.

'She's clear the other side of the Tower and locked in an underground bunker, and between here and there are thousands of demented Omnipants, and there's just a handful of us, one of whom is in shackles and another of whom is a prime minister, no offence,' Snake pointed out in his reptilian way.

Mangler grinned and tapped the side of his nose. 'It's a Mangler plan and we've all the help we need from my chaps.'

With a flourish, Mangler whipped his phone out of his pocket. 'Get me Dr Merkwürdigliebe. Ah, doctor, if your team is anywhere close to the Tower, now would be a good time for them to swing by. Helicopter gunships, plenty of rappelling ropes and Wagner's Flight of the Valkyries, please. On the roof of the Torture Tower in approximately one minute and twenty seconds …Yes. Yes. I see … See you in a mo. Byeee!'

'So? Is it salvation in the nick of time or are we all going to be eaten in our boots down here in a torture chamber?' asked Hades.

'Salvation is a relative term for you, I'm afraid, Hades. However, Merkwürdigliebe is doing what he can for the rest of us. Meanwhile, he reminds me that this stairwell here is an internal one, and that we should be able to reach the battlements at the top of this turret without interference from those that have been interfered with, as it were. He has arranged for a flight of Mangler Corps choppers and a team of Mangler security chaps to meet us on the roof. They'll pick us up and whisk us over to the Jewel House. While my men keep the zombie hordes at bay, I'll race to the jewel vault and rescue the Queen. How's that?'

'Well, that sounds satisfyingly dramatic,' said the prime minister.

'And how will your men keep thousands of zombies at bay?' asked Hades.

'It's my plan, and it'll go the way I want it to,' said Mangler with some relish and the kind of confidence you want to punch.

The stairwell was, as medieval stairwells are wont to be, unnecessarily narrow and winding and unlit. It involved quite a bit of pushing and shoving and pulling by Snake and the guards to get the portly Hades up. On the battlements, the air was already vibrating and whooshing violently with the proximity of the Mangler Corp helicopters.

'Right. This is going to be pretty tight, so do whatever I say as soon as I say it, OK? Your lives depend on it. Those zombie monsters are probably even now piling themselves against the wall so they came climb over each other to get to us.'

'Whatever you say, Dr Mangler,' said Snake looking as if he were about to unspeakably ruin his own tree-grown pants. 'Just don't let them get me! I have an aspidistra at home that depends on me for everything.'

Mangler threw himself at the battlements, where he looked out over the prospect of the Tower of London and stopped. Surprise prised open his face.

Hades and the prime minister caught up with Mangler. All across the courtyards of the Tower of London, zombies were flat on their backs, wriggling and wailing. The air was full of whirring and clanging noises, which sounded to Hades' expert ears like the death rattle of malfunctioning Omnipants. Sparks and puffs of smoke ejected from the flies and waistbands and hems of thousands of pairs of trousers, dresses and skirts.

Mangler, pulling himself together from a surprise, turned on his beaming smile and announced. 'Well, time to get the Queen out. Not that she's in any danger any longer.

Apparently, my chaps, following my instructions, have hacked the pants and executed an override command that I told them how to make. So there you are. Victory! And just in the nick of time, which is often the best kind of victory. And all down to my chaps and I.'

Mangler turned his back on Hades and hissed into his phone 'Tell me what just happened! I was in the middle of rescuing everyone and becoming a hero when all the bloody zombies went *phut!*'

27

It was no victory for Hades. He was publicly humiliated. *Very* publicly humiliated.

He was forced to parade in chains down the length of Oxford Street — which was pretty much end-to-end branches of Mangler's — in nothing but a very itchy hair shirt and his underpants, a pair of disabled Omnipants, on his head.

Jeering crowds lined the street, jeering in the way of jeering crowds, and throwing rotten tomatoes and the odd pair of mangled Omnipants. The jeering crowds built jeering piles of Hades underpants to which they jeeringly set fire. Pyres of pants blazed at every junction along Oxford Street. Right in front of him, the shattered terrified people of London tore down and stamped on posters of Hades Undies World, the big winking advertisement — that now looked like a wink of provocation to the traumatised citizens of the world — and any Hades shop signs they could pull from the wreckage of their city.

The event was broadcast live on television and streamed online to the world — the whole world.

The government — or Dr Mangler, which was the same thing now — had passed a bill returning Porton Down to government control. The assets of Hades Undies World, Pants Corp, and Hades' own assets were frozen and appropriated. His closest friends and associates went into hiding and grew ridiculous beards to disguise themselves. Even the women grew ridiculous beards to disguise themselves.

The pain of humiliation and dissolution was small compared to a greater pain: the pain of the loss of a daughter.

Hades still had no idea where Victoria was or what had become of her.

At the end of Oxford Street, at Marble Arch, Hades was packed into the back of a flatbed van and driven west, with an escort of police cars and vehicles in Mangler's corporate colours. There was more jeering from the pavements, more things thrown.

Eventually the crowds petered out. The van and its convoy traversed Westway and soon after that, London petered out too. The motorcade powered up the M4 for a while before turning off and delving into the green and leafy countryside. Hades was not interested in where the convoy was going or what it was doing; he was not interested in where he was, nor who he was. He sat on the flatbed like a sack of potatoes well past their sell-by date until the trucks and cars slowed and trundled through some municipal gates into a wasteland of rubbish and smells and squabbling seagulls. Here a pair of police officers climbed up next to Hades, removed his manacles and chains, picked him up and tossed him onto the rubbish pile.

Dusting their hands, the police officers and Mangler's crew got back into their vehicles. One person remained: Dr Mangler said, 'Well, farewell Hades. It was nice knowing you. Toodle-pip!' and he was gone with the loud bang of an expensive and armoured car door. The convoy moved off and Hades remained, half naked, filthy, sitting in the putrescence of the rubbish tip.

Moments later, another car pulled up with a squealing of tyres and shower of gravel. Inspector Snake leapt out and giggling, pulled Hades underpants right down over his eyes before jumping back in his car, which leapt back toward the road amid screams of laughter and tortured tyres and triumphal blares of horns.

Hades pulled the pants off his head with uncertain hands and remained in the muck.

Another car pulled up, a silent black one. Female hands helped him into the back of it and placed a large glass of noggin in one hand and a full bottle in the other.

28

Hades stood by the magnificent lead window of the even more magnificent Tudor manor staring into the new-fallen night. He was cleaned, calmed, fed, and had another glass of noggin in his hand, yet he had not actually spoken since Hilda and Persephone picked him up from the rubbish tip. The two women knew better than to push him. He needed to come back to them from his remote place in his own time.

The horizon was alive with lights, which cast a lurid and hellish glow into the night. The moon was smudged with smoke.

'What is that?' Hades asked at last.

'Pyres,' said Persephone simply.

'Are they burning what I think they are burning?' asked Hades.

'Yes. They are burning your pants. The whole world is. Every pair they can find. It's like some kind of hysterical witch hunt.'

Hades grunted.

'What is this place?' gestured at the magnificent living room that looked like it had hardly changed in the 500 years since it was built.

'A safe house; a bolthole,' Hilda told him.

'Whose is it? They must be running a risk having me here.'

'It's yours,' Persephone told him.

'All my assets — our assets — were seized by Mangler.'

'You don't spend decades as the richest, most powerful man in the world without salting away out of sight of inquiring eyes a few Tudor piles that you can use in an emergency.'

'That was very foresighted of me. Thank you, team Hades.'

Hades went back to scrutinising the bonfires of pants, the pyres of his empire and reputation. 'More important than anything else, any word of Victoria?'

'No,' said Persephone. 'But that might be a good thing.'

'Say what? How can that be a good thing?'

'Because if she had come to harm in London, I'm sure we'd have found her or someone would have told us, which suggests she didn't come to harm,' said Hilda.

'In fact,' continued Persephone, 'I'll wager it means she's up to something. Something that will restore the name of Gousset.'

29

Victoria was lying bound and gagged in an underground cell whose walls, floor, ceiling and spartan fittings were made entirely of rock and ice. It was a cold place. There was no window, no means of exit or entrance but the one door, which appeared to be made of icy granite and hung on hinges of frozen diamond, or something similarly easy to overpower. She assumed that no one knew she was there but her captors, the principals of whom were gathered around her at that moment and plotting her death. She assumed further that her family and friends would be wondering where she was, and that an ice cave in Antarctica was not a place they would consider, her last known whereabouts being dangling on a rope attached to a mortally wounded helicopter over the National Gallery, Trafalgar Square, London, UK.

'Tell me again, Maul, why you brought her here,' said Dr Mangler.

'Because —' Maul spoke as if carefully articulating a very complex idea '— I want to have my disgusting way with her.'

'And do you think that justified you going into my control room and ordering my minions to direct the underpants in London, by remote control, to pick up this woman and deliver to the airship for you?'

'How else was I supposed to get my hands on her?'

'And, tell me again, do you think that was sufficient reason to bring her to the heart of my Antarctic lair, right under my artificially climate-controlled underpants plantation, and thereby expose the fact that you, Flay and I are in cahoots, and few of the calamitous events preceding this point in time were quite what they seemed to be?'

'Fuck, yeah!'

'Tell me again why.'

'Because I get to have my disgusting way with her.'

Flay sighed.

'I suppose,' said Mangler, 'the logic is in it's own terms completely consistent with itself. It's the "own terms" bit that none of us are getting on with.'

Just as her friends and family had no idea where she was, Victoria had no idea what had become of Hilda.

As the helicopter had clawed its way over the rooftops of London, the two women had battled with the zombies that clung to the same ropes. They were flung about in the sky, their fists and feet flailing like the ropes. Zombies tumbled around them, all complaining about being mistreated. With a massive blow Victoria's breath went out of her body, her lights went out, she thought maybe her life was on its way out too. She came to her senses sprawled on the roof of the National Portrait Gallery next to a very large and very solid chimneystack, which, apparently, was the object that had knocked her off the rope. Where had the helicopter gone? What had happened to Hilda? The air was full screaming and crashing and wailing and debris and flying body parts and laughter and Victoria really couldn't get a handle on what was going on.

Then she became aware of the creatures encircling her, all walking with that odd, stilted rocking motion, arms outstretched in attitudes of balance and all moaning bitterly. As they got closer to her, the laughter increased, became more hysterical but rather than tearing her apart and eating her brain, the zombie creatures carried her out to the street, and in procession across Trafalgar Square past the wreckage of the Pants Corp helicopter — which was obscured in another seething crowd of undead — through Admiralty Arch, onto the Mall and to St. James's Park, where the adamantine airship waited, moored to trees, and in which she was spirited at unreasonable speed to Antarctica, the ice cell, and, via a spirited and nearly successful escape and attempt to sabotage Mangler, to the unspeakable desires of Jeremy Maul.

'Well, we can't put her back now, not after what she has seen,' said Flay.

'I'm not keen on keeping her here,' said Mangler. 'She would continue to be a complication, another thing to think about.'

Yes, Victoria had seen rather a lot of Mangler's operation when the adamantine airship had arrived at his Antarctic base before being discovered by Flay.

Back in St James's Park, the zombie horde directed by Maul from Antarctica, deposited Victoria at the top of the gangplank of the airship and tottered off to do whatever damage they could there, such as scare the ducks.

Captain HG Verne and the crew of the airship were expert aeronauts — the best you could find — but they were not kidnappers. The message had come through from Maul that this soot-blackened woman was a prisoner to be delivered to him in Antarctica, but they had no idea and no training in how to deal with captives.

'I've something urgent to do on the bridge,' claimed Captain Verne. 'You deal with it,' he told his second in command, Lieutenant Jules Wells.

'I've something important to listen to in the radio room,' declared Lieutenant Wells. 'You deal with it,' he told the senior hand on the deck, Master Staines.

'I've something crucial to attend to in the bilges,' Master Staines remembered. 'You deal with it,' he told the most junior hands on the watch, airman Bates and airman Mates.

After much thought and brainstorming of films they had seen and books they had read that had hostages in them, they came to some decisions.

'Let's put her in the brig.' The airship didn't have a brig.

'Let's lock her in the cargo hold.' The hold was full.

'Let's throw her in a rope locker.' The rope lockers were full of ropes.

'Let's shut her in a broom cupboard.' That's what they did.

Bates and Mates delivered Victoria's bound, semi-conscious, and exhausted body to the broom cupboard. The crew then got on with the job for which they were actually paid and trained to do and therefrom paid scant attention to the kidnapped woman.

On landing at Mangler's Antarctic base, Maul, hopping with anticipation on the landing pad for hours prior to the arrival of the ship, bounded up the gangplank to claim his prize. Entering the ship he bumped shoulders with the cleaning lady disembarking with arms full of mops and brooms and buckets.

'Ah, Mr Maul, you'll be wanting the captive,' said Captain Verne.

Maul, unaccustomed to be called anything but bugger off, let alone Mr Maul, saluted and followed the pilot to the broom cupboard, which was empty but for Victoria's former bindings looking very limp and silly on the floor.

'That is not according to plan,' said Maul.

Victoria, in her cleaning lady disguise, laden with mops, had made it off the ship without being challenged.

The ship was berthed in a hangar of dizzying proportions. It was not just a hangar; it was a port, a port from which Mangler's product was shipped to the world. Thousands of bales of harvested underpants were stacked throughout the space. Swarms of stevedores were already unloading the adamantine airship's load of essential supplies for Mangler's larders and re-filling the hold with the brightly coloured fruit of the trees.

Victoria paused, disoriented, wondering where to go, where to start, what to start and noticed right away a large and accommodating sign: 'Master Control Room for Everything this way'. She went that way.

Her disguise was well chosen. No one was interested in interrupting a member of the cleaning staff in the execution of her duty in case they themselves were given a mop, and she was able to go into the Master Control Room for Everything without attracting any suspicion or interest of any kind, where she dusted surfaces at random and nudged her brooms around while taking everything in.

The control room was large, airy, comfortable and ordered to the point of insanity. It looked like Nasa's mission control fused with the bridge of a starship.

The place was full of screens. Screens everywhere on every flat surface either horizontal or vertical. Each of the many Mangler minions sat at a workstation with their own screen; there were still more screens stacked on the walls; and the room was dominated by one master screen about the size of a three-bedroom semi-detached house in a nice but unassuming provincial town.

Mangler must have hacked every CCTV network on the planet, every camera phone, every web camera, every tablet camera, every dashboard camera, every camera on a police or army helmet; apparently every Omnipants camera fore and aft; in short, every digital camera on the planet because each of the screens was showing views of the zombie apocalypse from all around the world, and every conceivable angle. At the moment Victoria walked in, the room was full of a very unprofessional and noisy party atmosphere. It was specifically the atmosphere of the kind of party at which a lot of boisterous and adolescent men are watching videos of wipeouts and epic fails on the internet, or watching snuff movies, perhaps. Today, it was the streaming live images of the zombie apocalypse from around the world that inspired the jollity. An old lady carrying shopping bags ran repeatedly into the wall next to the madly slamming doors of the supermarket she was trying to leave, while Mangler's technicians hooted with delight. A young man in a brand hoodie sneaked up behind an academic sort of bloke in tweed and pinned a note on his back reading 'eat my brain' before apparently doing just that. The residents of an old folks home tobogganed down the slope of the roof before hurtling off into space and into the duck pond. Affluent men in business suits crawled on the floor of a boardroom sniffing each other's bottoms. Park wardens danced on the grass next to signs that read 'keep off the grass'. Teachers set fire to the trousers of the school headmaster while he was wearing them, zombies ganged up on and mercilessly tickled non-zombies and then stole their underwear. On the main monitor, the Pope was flashing the devout in St Peter's Square, who were mooning him back.

Victoria was no expert in zombie apocalypses, but this struck her as a remarkably silly one.

As in London, the din of the chaos was mixed with the screech of insane laughter and that vile voice. The voice was the single most unwholesome, perverted thing she had ever heard. If herpes could speak, this is what it would sound like — yet she knew she had heard it somewhere before.

'Oooh! Nice pubes!'

'These pants could do with some more skid marks. Let's drag our anus across the carpet.'

Skid marks! Anus! Suddenly Victoria had the context she needed to recall the voice: It was Maul. Jeremy Maul. Somehow Maul had got into the pants of billions of people around the world — specifically, the Omnipants of millions of people around the world.

More than that, Hades underpants were being hacked and controlled from here: from Mangler's own control centre. The good people of the world had not suddenly turned into zombies, they had been taken over by their own underwear and were being controlled by Mangler from here, Sacred Mountain, his Antarctic base.

Victoria had to get this information back to London. She had to find a way to stop Mangler.

At that moment, the hilarity in the Master Control Room for Everything was interrupted by a tannoy announcement: 'Dr Mangler wants all Omnipants to converge on his location at the Tower of London. He is in the company of the prime minister, has the Queen trapped in the jewel room, and wants to put on a truly terrifying show of zombie power before pretending to rescue everyone.'

The technicians sprang to, and the party atmosphere was replaced with one of intent labour as they tapped and clicked away at the computers in their workstations.

'Doctor Mangler is on the move with the prime minister and his prisoner Hades Gousset, the former underpants magnate.'

Former underpants magnate? Her father a *prisoner*?

They'll be on the roof of the Torture Tower in approximately one minute.

In the middle of the control room, there was single unmanned workstation consisting of a single-legged stand and a large red button labelled 'Omnipants Kill Code: Absolutely Do Not Press'.

No one was looking so Victoria cleaned her way to the button, cleaned around it, and gave it a good whack. Klaxons hooted, lights flashed, the tannoy declared 'Kill code executed' and Victoria was surrounded by technicians who looked both surprised and miffed.

Victoria only became aware that she was holding her mop like a weapon when Flay stepped from the crowd of technicians and took it from her. Flay looked her iciest.

From the control room, it was a short and very direct trip to bonds and shackles and the horribly cold dungeon that was almost as icy as Flay.

'It looks like you'll just have to let me have my disgusting way with her, then,' said Maul, drooling down his front.

'That would be rewarding you for a very stupid and selfish action that could have brought ruin upon our plans and persons.'

Maul inserted a thoughtful finger in his nose. 'OK. Are you going to kill her then? How? I've got an idea. I'll do it.'

Flay ignored him. 'We wouldn't want the body discovered. We can't bury her because out here, that would be like preserving the evidence in a big freezer for perpetuity to discover and laugh at.'

'Well, we won't do that, then,' said Mangler. 'How about taking her for a trip in the adamantine airship to a very remote and wet part of the planet where there are deep oceanic trenches, like the southern Indian ocean, for example, lashing her to something not known for buoyancy, like a piano or anvil, and just drop her off?'

'That would work,' said Flay.

'Darn.' Mangler clicked his fingers. 'I have to use the airship to get back to London and post haste. I have to complete the humiliation of the father of this little captive here and assume my rightful place as head of everything in the world. Domination, you see —' he addressed the trussed Victoria '— is mine for the taking.'

Victoria shouted. 'You'll never get away with it. I'm not done with you yet.' However, due to the gag in her mouth all anyone heard was 'Mwmmh mmmmmmh mwmwm mwm.'

It turned out that Mangler was fluent in Mwm. 'Oh, but we have got away with it. And I can't think what you can do about it, being all tied up and underground far, far away from Ma and Pops.' Something occurred to him. 'Talking of cruel and unusual, why don't we fix up some kind of screen down here so that Daddy's girl can witness the final destruction of Daddy. Just before she dies. Now that would be nice.'

'Go on, Maul,' said Flay, fed up with seeing his finger agitating in his nose. 'What's your idea?'

'First, I kill her. Death of a thousand licks. Very painful, very fatal. They die of revulsion, which is my favourite way of them dying. Then I feed her to pigs because pigs leave no trace. Nothing. Then I eat the pigs so there's no trace of them either.'

'I'm not sure we have pigs here at the snowy bottom of the world,' said Mangler.

'That's OK,' said Maul, looking as if this were actually good news. 'I'll skip the pigs bit and just eat her myself. I don't leave any traces either. Not even plates.'

'I'm afraid that's true,' Flay confirmed to Mangler. 'Won't even leave cutlery. Whatever his faults, he is disturbingly omnivorous and I suspect his digestive system will decompose steel.' She shuddered.

'A bit messy though,' wondered Mangler.

'Not a bit messy, actually. He'll lick the floor clean. He'll make sure every bit of DNA goes inside him. I'm serious, Dr Mangler. Don't even try to imagine it.'

Mangler and Flay turned to scrutinise Maul, regarding him as teachers or parents would a small, enthusiastic, and pizza-addicted child who they were considering entrusting with an important task like putting away safely lots of pizza so that it didn't get rained on but without filching any of it.

'Can we trust him?' asked Mangler.

'Not really. But given his proclivities it's difficult to imagine how he could screw this up.'

'Oh, dear,' said Mangler. 'I fear you're going to get your way after all, young Mr Maul.'

'And I suspect we'd better go and leave you two to it,' said Flay. 'There isn't a sick bucket in the world big enough to contain my reaction to what you are about to do.'

'Goody-goody bum drops!' said Maul clapping his fat and appalling hands together. 'I'd better get on with smacking my chops and salivating in anticipation.'

30

'I should have listened to Victoria,' said Hades still at his
Tudor window watching the gothic spectacle of the pyres.
'And I should have listened to Persephone. I should have
gone with the iPants. Then Victoria would still be here. I
should have gone with the iPants and not the blasted
Omnipants, and then it all would never have happened.'

Hades stopped and turned to face the room. There was
only Persephone and Hilda, both seated in the extravagant
sofas and watching him intently assessing his mental and
physical wellbeing, his capacity for slashing his wrists on his
own noggin glass or for charging through the wall to sprint all
the way to Antarctica to physically tear Mangler apart.

'What did just happen, anyway? I haven't a clue. One
minute we're tootling along as usual, and then up pops
Mangler and suddenly it's the end of the world as we know it,
Victoria's gone, and I'm an outcast, a fugitive. What did go
wrong with the Omnipants? Were they really responsible for
that chaos as the prime minister and Mangler insist? Why did
Pickles include a berserker programme in perfectly peaceful
underpants? We have to get to the bottom of this.'

'But, Hades, we don't think the pants did malfunction,'
said Persephone. Then to Hilda, 'Perhaps you could tell him.
Explain it to Hades like you explained it to me.'

'Of course. Hades, are you ready to hear this?'

'Hear what? I have no idea what you're talking about.'

'Well, as you know, Victoria and I went into London to
collect data to find out what was going on. Despite all the
chaos I managed to upload most of the data we gathered to Dr

Pickles, who has been analysing it. He has also been analysing the servers of the Omnipants network.'

'Jolly good! Lots of uploading, then. Has this got us anywhere?'

'Oh, yes! First, you may remember that people were reporting voices — a hideous laugh, an unwholesome voice. Pickles did a voice print analysis and the voice belongs to Maul.'

'Say what? That Maul with that Flay?'

'The very same.'

'How is that possible? He was blown up and captured by Mangler. We saw it. I denied plausibly that he was anything to do with us.'

'Indeed. One moment Maul was spinning through the air at the bottom of the world, the next he was at the top of the world bringing everyone to their knees. What does it mean?' asked Persephone.

Hilda continued. 'Now, to the berserker programme. When we looked into that we found our servers and firewalls riddled with backdoors and secret tunnels. Not just the net that handles the Omnipants, but everything. Some very clever and very vicious hacker had got in and, well, hacked everything to bits. Whoever it was went through all systems and left this very destructive berserker virus.'

'Mangler? Did Mangler do it?'

'Mangler is the first person to come to mind. But the evidence, such as it is, points away from him.'

'Say what? Does this get more complicated and ridiculous?'

'Indeed it does. Firstly, although the hack was undoubtedly a hack, it was done behind the firewall. It was done from somewhere on company turf.'

Hades absorbed this a moment. 'Mangler has someone inside Hades on his payroll?'

'It's not even that clear. Now listen on. Hackers don't always leave calling cards. But there was one potential giveaway: wherever the hacker went, whatever the hacker touched, there was frost damage to the data and the code. A small amount to be sure, but frost damage nonetheless.'

'Frost damage? In data? Is that usual?'

'Not a bit. Now what do you connect with frost damage?'

'Well, frost, ice, of course.'

'And who do you —'

'Flay! Are you serious? Could Flay have done this? Do we have both Maul and Flay back on the scene?'

'We have no smoking gun evidence. But that's the way it looks. All the signs are there.'

'And what did they have to gain? What's in if for them? And where are they now, anyway?'

'Well,' said Persephone, the technical stuff passed, feeling confident to get back into the story. 'Look who's benefited. The whiff of Maul and Flay is all over the dirty work, but Mangler is now king of the castle.'

'So Maul, Flay and Mangler are in cahoots. But I say again, how did that happen? When can they have arranged all this? I mean, they were in my icebox for months, no contact with the world at all. And how did they get into my systems?'

'We have no idea.'

'So Maul and Flay have concocted an elaborate plot with Mangler, even though they spent months in freezers in my basement with no way to contact the outside world. They have hacked my systems from the inside, even though they weren't on the inside, planted a highly destructive virus that has hijacked all my Omnipants, brought down my empire, ruined me, destroyed the good name of this family, and brought the world to the brink of war.'

'So it would seem.'

'But it's all impossible,' said Hades.

'There's been a lot of that about recently,' said Hilda.

31

Victoria was released from the floor of her cell and bound to a dinner table instead. The dinner table was then neatly set with a place mat, cutlery, napkins, saws, hammers, chisels, knives, cleavers, gouges, an oxyacetylene torch, some romantic candles, and a nice cut-glass vase of flowers.

Once the table was set, a television installation person came in and installed a television — a very large, flat screen jobbie. He installed it on the wall directly in Victoria's line of sight.

'Your daddy's going to be on the television and I am under strict instructions to make sure you see it before I eat you. I suppose it makes more sense than making you watch it after I've eaten you. Perhaps.'

'Mwmmmmwh mwmwmh mhwmhwmhwm!'

'Sticks and stones may break my bones but mwmhs will never hurt me.'

'Mwmh mwmh mwmh mwmh mwmh mwmh mwmh mwmh mwmh! Mwmh mwmh mwmh mwmh mwmh mwmh mwmh mwmh mwmh! Mwmh mwmh mwmh mwmh mwmh mwmh mwmh mwmh mwmh! Mwmh mwmh mwmh mwmh mwmh mwmh mwmh mwmh mwmh!'

'Are you suggesting I spill all our secrets and tell you exactly how we managed to hijack the Omnipants? These are stately secrets, you know, and they're mine, all mine!'

'Mwmh mwmh mwmh mwmh mwmh mwmh mwmh mwmh mwmh!'

'*And*,' said Maul in italics, '*having secrets puts me in a position of power and control over you.*'

'Mwmh mwmh mwmh mwmh mwmh mwmh mwmh mwmh mwmh!'

'Good point. Being that I'm about to eat you, I couldn't be in a bigger position of power and control over you if I had all the secrets of the world stuffed inside one sock and maybe I do, how would you know? Ha!'

'Mwmh mwmh mwmh mwmh mwmh mwmh mwmh mwmh mwmh! Mwmh mwmh mwmh mwmh mwmh mwmh mwmh mwmh mwmh!'

'Fair point. Telling you exactly how we pulled off the impossible would complete your despair and humiliation and since you are about to be eaten, who could you even tell?'

'Mwmh.'

'Not really. It wasn't just cunning and it wasn't just simple. It was more simply cunning with a bit of cunningly simple thrown in.' Maul picked up the biggest, scariest knife and began sharpening it on his fingernails. He began the story. 'Flay was in that ice box for months …'

Flay was in no hurry. She had many other places to be, to be sure, but she wasn't getting to any of them quickly. The locks on the cryopod were heavy and secure. Speculatively, she unpicked the lining of the lid of the pod, using her long, stiletto-sharp nails as tools. This revealed a panel, the other side of which was the control terminal for her pod. She unscrewed that. From there, it was easy to unpick the circuit boards to make a basic interface and hack the system. Once she had done that much she realised that not only was she in the workings of the cryonic storage facility, but had the whole of Pants Corps' intranet to herself.

'Woo hoo!' she might have said, but she was too cool for that and just sort of sneered a bit that Hades could have been so naive as to entomb her in a locked steel box deep in an underground, bomb-proof bunker at the heart of his empire and expect that to contain her. She would just deactivate the lid of the cryopod, jam open the door locks on her escape route while locking down all other parts of the HQ so she could not be pursued, set off the fire alarms, burglar alarms, car alarms, alarm alarms and the sprinkler system to ensure chaos, and just stroll out.

Doddle.

She prepared her escape route meticulously, discovering a hacking genius in her that she had long suspected but never before realised. Eventually, after months of work, she was ready for the final step: she now simply needed to overpower the locks on the lid of her pod and she was away.

The locks wouldn't overpower. They weren't on the grid. A quick check on the outside of the box through the lab's CCTV cameras showed her that they were padlocks. Dumb, iron padlocks from a hardware store.

Bugger! to borrow a term from Hades' vocabulary.

After all that work and genius making Pant Corps' intranet her own, Flay was stymied by two lumps of inert ferrous material. Time to re-think.

'Well,' Maul went on, 'if she wasn't getting out soon, she was going to make damn sure Hades was going to suffer properly. She spent her time from then on constructing a wrecking programme right there inside Hades' own systems, with wormholes in his firewall and everything so that she could access it any time she wanted from the outside world, as well as from her locked inside world, hedging her bets, like. She didn't know what was going to happen, but she figured a vicious little friend on the inside would be handy one day.'

Maul continued to sharpen his carving knife.

'Eventually,' gloated Maul, 'Davinia saw on the news feeds that Mangler had come on the scene, and through the intranet, she saw the chaos his pants were wreaking on Hades' empire, and she thought to herself, that if she got out of there in a timely fashion she might just go pay Dr Mangler a visit and have a chat with him to their mutual advantage.'

'Mwmh mwmh mwmh mwmh mwmh mwmh mwmh mwmh mwmh! Mwmh mwmh mwmh mwmh mwmh mwmh mwmh mwmh mwmh!'

'Ha! Abso-bloody-lutely!' chortled Maul. 'Not only did she get out, but your daft dad delivered us right to Mangler.

At first, the good doctor, on grabbing us in his orchard, was none too pleased.'

'So you were sent here by Hades to spy on my orchard,' said Mangler to Maul and Flay who were shackled to the wall in the interrogation room.

'I expect he has already denied it, and plausibly too,' said Flay very coolly indeed.

'Too plausibly! That's why I didn't believe him for a minute. So what am I going to do with you? I could use you as pawns in a war of accusations over industrial espionage, but that sounds long-winded, tedious, and without clear useful outcome. I could let you go, but that sounds lame and inconclusive. I could, now I think of it, have you taken to a car park in Dagenham and thrashed to within an inch of your worth. Or I could freeze you in blocks of ice and then stitch you together just to see what would happen.'

'Or,' said Flay in that icy way that made people pay instant attention, and clench their sphincters both, 'we could come to a business arrangement. A collaboration, if you will.'

Mangler was very good at being quick-witted, calm, composed and inscrutable and demonstrated these talents now. 'Are you suggesting,' he began after a few beats, 'that you have something to offer that I might be very, very interested in?'

'Mwmh mwmh mwmh mwmh mwmh mwmh mwmh mwmh mwmh! Mwmh mwmh mwmh mwmh mwmh mwmh mwmh mwmh mwmh!'

'At the time I didn't know what Flay was on about,' confessed Maul. 'It was all bollocks to me. But Mangler liked it. I suppose that must be his thing, bollocks. Anyway, no, Mangler hadn't seen that coming but he knew what he liked and he liked what Flay told him. Whatever, it got me on a nice little earner with perks like today's dinner.'

'Mwmh mwmh mwmh mwmh mwmh mwmh mwmh mwmh mwmh! Mwmh mwmh mwmh mwmh mwmh mwmh mwmh mwmh mwmh!'

'If I weren't about to eat you, I'd take offence to that. Now, if you'd like to pay attention to the telly, I'll get my fava beans and Chianti ready.'

Her head being taped to the table, Victoria was unable to look away from the TV. She watched in horror as her father, pants on head, bottom bared to the world, was paraded down Oxford Street to the jeers of the crowd. The BBC commentator went through the catalogue of his sins and crimes, which, summed up, came to attempting to overthrow every government in the world under the guise of a world war he had started himself after sabotaging peace talks and then releasing his berserker application cunningly hidden in the software of millions of pairs of underpants and which caused, well, mass berserking. The BBC didn't stop to wonder why he might have done this. Hades' cunning plan would have worked if it had not been for Dr Mangler, who cleverly figured out what was going on, thwarted the dastardly plan and was appointed world leader as a result.

'Mwmh mwmh mwmh mwmh!' said Victoria.

'Thats easy for you to say,' said Maul, who was fidgeting with impatience and eating flowers from the vase. 'They told me to make you watch this stuff before I ate you. Can't see the point, myself. You won't be remembering any of it once I've eaten your brain.' He tested the oxyacetylene torch on one of the uneaten flower heads, and then popped the blackened, smoking ruin of petals in his mouth.

Victoria struggled in her bonds. Maul laughed. The helicopters of the TV stations followed Hades' motorcade of ignominy over the Westway and to the landfill. When he was dumped in the rubbish, they left him there along with the entourage of ridicule.

Maul danced an obscene little jig, clapped his vile hands and removed Victoria's shoes and socks.

'This little piggy was had for dinner,
'This little piggy was sucked off the bone,
'This little piggy got roasted,
'This little piggy was too,

'And this little piggy cried leave me alone you inhuman bastard, all the way down.'

Maul paused to contemplate his poetry. 'That's what the care worker used to sing to me.'

There was a knock at the door, which opened before Maul could demand 'What the fuck do you want?'

'I want to uninstall your TV.'

'Why?'

'I'm the TV uninstall operative. Before you watch TV the install operative installs it. He already did that. When you have finished watching the TV the uninstall operative uninstalls it. Have you finished watching the TV?'

'Is it normal for TV uninstallation operatives to be blue and to wear absolutely nothing but tiny leopard print trunks and a naff khaki peaked cap?'

'Have you met any TV uninstallation operatives before?'

'No.'

'Then, yes, it's perfectly normal for us to be blue, wear tiny leopard print trunks and naff khaki caps. In fact it's a requirement. Look, the words on the cap say "TV Install Man". If I could have found one that said 'TV Uninstall Man' I would have worn that.'

'Why, if you are a genuine and sanctioned TV uninstall man could not already have a hat that says "TV Uninstall Man"?'

'Because we're very rare, which means that our hats are rare too.'

'Rare?' Maul wasn't following.

'How many people do you know that like to have their TV uninstalled?'

Maul couldn't think of any. 'Is that why you are rare?'

'Yes. And we have to be blue.'

'You look a bit familiar. Have you ever not been blue?'

'What do you mean?'

'You look like someone I once fatally said boo to. But he wasn't blue.'

'That was my twin. People are always mixing us up. In fact the only way to tell us apart is I'm blue and he's not.'

'That makes sense,' said Maul. 'OK, get rid of the goggle box. You'll excuse me if I get back to my foul debauchery.

'The death of a thousand licks,' said Maul turning back to Victoria and tucking an extravagantly large napkin into his neckband. 'There'll soon be nothing left of you but the echo of a scream.'

When the TV crashed on to his head, Maul had no time for a scream himself. He just went face down into the pile of medieval tools on the table and from there to the floor.

Timmy — for it was he — unbound Victoria and tore the gag from her mouth, which he tried to kiss. Victoria dodged. 'Timmy! How did you get here — and why are you completely blue now? You were only a bit blue before.'

'Oh, I followed you in London when they took you to the big airship thing, but I couldn't get aboard, so I stowed away by hanging on to the outside. It was a bit cold, to be honest, travelling at twelve times the speed of sound in the troposphere. This repeated freezing seems to have done something to me.'

'But I saw them boo you — again! And you went right off the roof. How did you survive?'

Timmy shrugged modestly. 'I landed on my steroid-enhanced pectorals. No big deal really.'

'It's so good to see you again. Thank you brave Timmy.' And at last Timmy got his kiss.

'Now we must make good our escape,' said Victoria, and they did. Up to a point.

32

It wasn't so bad up the tree. She could get used to it, Victoria thought in her wildest, most unreasonable moments of optimism — not that there were many of them. However, Timmy was quite enthusiastic about living in a tree since their escape from the ice cell.

'It reminds me, he told her,' reclining on a large and sturdy bough, leaning against the trunk, sun on his face, 'of the time we spent together at Schloss Himmel. Wasn't that perfect?'

After stunning Maul, Victoria and Timmy had trussed him and put him on the dining table in Victoria's place. Being aware of Maul's capacity to eat anything he could physically get in his mouth, they made sure to bind his jaws shut with plenty of gaffer tape looped under his chin and over his head.

Outside the cell, Timmy made for the hangar.

'Where are you going?' asked Victoria?

'We'll have to stow away on the adamantine airship. It's the only way we can get quickly back to London.'

'It's not there. Mangler took it to London. Anyway, we're not ready to go yet. We have to gather some kind of evidence of what Mangler's been up to here to exonerate my father and put Mangler behind bars where he belongs.'

'What kind of evidence?'

'I have no idea. I'll know it when I see it. Let's snoop about a bit.'

The snooping was quickly interrupted by sirens, bells and general alarum. Flay, alerted by the lack of screams in the dungeon, had checked in on Maul.

Which is how Victoria and Timmy found themselves up a tree. Fleeing the hunt for their persons, they escaped Mangler's complex, and once outside the only cover was in the air, wrapped discreetly in Mangler's underthings.

The brief sojourn in Schloss Himmel so fondly remembered by Timmy had not actually been perfect for Victoria. Even putting the best kind of spin on it, the experience hadn't been even mildly pleasant.

Once upon a time, Maul and Flay had kidnapped Victoria twice. Timmy had rescued her from their evil clutches at Paris Disneyland but the rescue had turned out to be his own way of kidnapping her. He held her hostage in the remote alpine castle of Schloss Himmel until she fell in love with him, which would have meant forever if the hostage situation had not been unexpectedly resolved when they were raided by North Korean commandos and propelled into a completely different hostage drama. But that was last year. And Timmy had risked his life to follow her to Antarctica and rescue her again from Maul and Flay. So she decided not to say what an appalling experience life in an abandoned and ice-bound mountain castle had been.

'It's very nice,' she said gently, 'but it doesn't help us help my father.'

'Oh, yes,' said Timmy. 'I'd forgotten about that.'

The low Antarctic sun angled in among the boughs, leaves and underclothes of the tree, striking colours off the fabrics. The professional designer in Victoria couldn't help admiring the vibrancy of the hues. She wondered what kind of dyes Mangler used but corrected herself: this was genetically engineered. The clothes were growing like this.

She looked closer. Vibrant was the exact word: the colour, the fabric seemed to be shimmering. The surface of the fabric was unstill. It had every appearance of being alive.

'That can't be good,' she said aloud.

33

A world away in Hades' Tudor hidey-hole, Dr Pickles was coming to the same conclusion.

'This can't be good at all,' he told his microscope, which said nothing, perhaps contemplating the gravity of what Dr Pickles was implying.

'This most certainly can't be good at all.'

Tudor piles, no matter how well piled, don't normally come with fully equipped laboratories, or even unequipped laboratories, so Pickles was improvising in the barn. A couple of cows and a gaggle of chickens jostled for a look in the microscope to see for themselves what wasn't good at all, while owls and bats peered down from the rafters for a view of the same.

The farm animals also jostled for space with piled non-Tudor computer monitors, centrifuges, quantum looms, pipettes, pirouettes, dinky little hammers, and an espresso machine, all essential tools for the investigation of all matters of matter, and, specifically, undies.

Pickles chewed a temple of his spectacles and wished it were a banana.

Tentatively, he snipped a small square of fabric from the pair of test pants he was investigating — Manglers, bought in a high street shop — and with a pair of complicated scientific tweezers dropped them into a beaker of liquid, which immediately exploded, leaving a small green mushroom cloud roiling in the air. The animal audience retreated a step and looked to Pickles for reassurance. A bat did some very fast laps of the roof space. The remainder of the underpants on the bench seemed to shudder.

'Ooh, said Pickles. That really is not good.'

34

Hilda had ordered an upgrade of the internet connection to the Tudor pile some months ago but since Hades and his crew had taken refuge here, pages had been loading like stroppy kids on their way to school on a wet Monday morning. Ishiguro the butler told her, 'No, Ms Titanium, no gentlemen fitting the description of optical fibre installation personnel have ever visited this house to the best of my knowledge or to the worst of it, come to that.'

Hilda was tempted to ask Ishiguro to call PanOpticon himself but she wasn't that cruel. Calling any service anywhere in the English-speaking world and asking them to actually do what you had already asked them to do, especially if it involved cables that had to be plugged into something as complicated as a socket somewhere, and especially if there was money involved, was not a task she would wish on a sentient being.

Calling any service in order to get service required a week or two on hold listening to Greensleeves as re-interpreted by robots, talking to computer-generated voices that shared none of the intelligence of the computer that generated them, and if you ever got through to a human you would have to face blank denials that you, they, their service, the company, the universe even existed, and if you managed to convince them otherwise, you would have to put up with glib and empty promises that something would be done in the full knowledge that it wouldn't.

No, Hilda didn't have the heart to inflict that on dear old Ishiguro. She would have to try it herself.

'Hello,' said a very pleasant if dreamy voice. 'PanOpticon. My name's Lisa. What's yours? How may I help you?'

Hilda was suspicious. First, she had got through right away. Second, the customer support lady had not greeted her with immediate defence, denials, hostility or a combat stance. 'Several weeks ago, I requested that this address be fitted with an optical internet connection with enough bandwidth to carry all the world's oil tankers, fully laden to the moon and back in the merest twinkle of an eye, but it seems that the necessary work has not been undertaken. In terms of connectivity we have all the speed of an old lady on a 19th century shopping bike on a very muddy farm track going in the wrong direction.'

'Oops!' said the customer support lady. 'That doesn't sound too good. If you'll bear with me —' clickety-clackety on a keyboard — 'yes, you're in the system but it seems no one has bothered to do the job yet. Shall I flag you for priority attention since you've been waiting six weeks already?'

'Oh. Yes. That would be very nice. Are you sure … ?' What Hilda wanted to say was "Are you sure you're not taking the piss?" but her better instincts forbade her.

'All good. No probs. There should be someone with you in —' There was a ding at the front door and Ishiguro strode smartly off to answer it. '— a sec. Or now. Is that all right?'

'Apparently, yes. Thank you very much.' Moments later, Ishiguro put his head around the door to say that there were some very pleasant gentlemen from PanOpticom here to upgrade the internet connection.

'Are you sure they aren't apparitions or pranksters?'

'I did ask them, Ms Titanium, and they assured me they were not.'

'Better let them in then.'

'Heigh-ho,' said the men from PanOpticon together.

'Like, so good of you to call us out to work on your broadband connection. Very cool, indeed,' explained one.

'Super cool and awesome, both,' the other elaborated.

'Like, show us the way and we'll have it done in a jiffy.'

'Are you OK? Are you stoned or something?' Hilda wanted to know.

The men from PanOpticon beamed at her. 'High on life, ma'am!' said one.

'Wow!' said the other.

Hilda knew then without a glimmer of doubt that something else was very wrong in the world.

35

The airliner hurtled across Scotland, then England, passed London and zoomed on over France.

Captain Star came out of a reverie to find himself at the controls of that plane. Next to him was the co-pilot Captain Twinkle, staring ahead through the windshield with a beatific smile on his face and just a bit of drool creeping down his chin.

Star wondered where they were. He checked landmarks: sky, clouds, earth. Well, that narrowed it down a bit. He was between the sky and the floor and adjacent to clouds. Cool!

Speed: very fast. That was very cool too, but he had no idea why. Altitude: yup, they had altitude, so that was good too because it meant they weren't flying on the ground or under it, which would be, well, you know, uncool, if not outright silly. But that was OK.

'Hey!' Star roused Twinkle. 'Hey.' He didn't feel the need for an exclamation mark on the second hey. It was, like, you know, a bit incongruous with the general groove of coolness here in the cockpit. He just let the second hey wander around a bit and find its own conclusion in its, like, own, you know, time.

'I feel great,' said Twinkle.

'You know, I was thinking. And you know what I reckon? I reckon we're somewhere. That's what I reckon.'

'That's so cool.'

'I was thinking about it — quite a lot. And you know another thing I reckon? I reckon I'm pretty sure there's a way of figuring out where this somewhere is.'

'Why would you want to do that?'

'You know. Whatever.'

'That's so cool. So you could try the GPS. That's usually pretty good at knowing where we are.'

'GPS. Right. I knew I was forgetting something.'

'Hey. You know where the GPS says we are? We're over France.'

'I like France.'

'Me too.'

'Kind of near Orléans. That's right in the middle. But if I think about it, I don't think we're supposed to be in France.'

'Wow. We should have stopped way before here.'

'Yeah. We should have stopped at London.'

'Wow. That's cool.'

They sang a few bars of the Marseillaise and when they realised they didn't know more than the few bars they broke off into some *hon hon hon* noises and Gallic shrugs.

'I totally didn't notice we'd gone past London.'

'Me neither. I was feeling great.'

'Do you suppose the passengers noticed?'

Both the pilots swivelled in their seats to look at the undisturbed cockpit door. The flight engineer was sitting at his station sucking his thumb.

'Nobody said anything.'

'I guess they're OK, then.'

'Shall we head back to London?'

'That would mean turning the plane around, wouldn't it.'

'Probably.'

'Heigh-ho.'

36

It was coronation day for Dr Mangler. As saviour of the world he was assuming his newly and justly appointed role as World Leader (Not Pretend). When civilisation was on the brink of collapse through zombie apocalypse, and the underpants of the formerly trusted father-figure Hades Gousset had run berserk, Mangler was the one who had shown the leadership, the composure and the almost preternatural knowledge to stem the hordes and restore TV and proper shopping.

He was robing in the luxurious robing room of his new suite at the United Nations in New York. He would soon address the world from the assembly room of the same esteemed institution.

The ermine robes draped on him by his flunkies purred and embraced him. They were grown on one of his especially special trees. He stroked them as a reward for their affection. While the flunkies busied themselves preparing Mangler for his appearance before the world, the great man himself conferred with marketing people, speechwriters, event planners and the Secretary General of the United Nations who was on the floor polishing Mangler's shoes.

Everything must be perfect because on this day the world would change forever.

Mangler was looking at a photo slide show on a tablet. He was looking at a photo gallery of hundreds, perhaps thousands of users of Manglers pants. Some of the subjects were on the street, disrobed to their undies or wearing their treasured Manglers on the outside of their day clothes as was the fashion of the moment. Others were apparently photographed in the privacy of their own home through windows or the lenses of web cams. Other photos were clearly intercepted chats, selfies. The subjects were all three genders, all races, shapes, sizes and ages.

You see, said Mangler, this one does not look so good in the pants. He has too much bulk. And this one, what does she eat all day? Pure fat and sugar? I'm amazed she can stand. She shouldn't be wearing such beautiful pants. What is she doing? Now this one. The pants are just hanging off him. No shape at all. And this? My God, she's just lopsided. Does she have no shame? This one? Old? She should be buried already. Him, his pants do not match his complexion. The clashing colours are making me feel seasick.'

'Well, that's humanity,' said the Secretary General still at Manglers feet. 'We are a frail and faulty and diverse species, we humans.'

'Oh, I'm sorry, Secretary General. Did I just kick you in the face? It's this involuntary spasm I have. It goes off when I hear sobbing-heart liberal shit. Oh, I'm sure with the best minds in the world at your disposal you can get the bleeding staunched and the shirt cleaned up before the ceremony.

'Now look at this one? Racially impure. And this one, should sue his ancestors for crimes against DNA.

'And this one is a degenerate, you can see it in the way he stands, hand on hip, twinkle in his eye, for God's sake.'

'But it can't be helped. This is just the way people are.'

'Oh, sorry, did I just kick you again? It's that spasm. Now I'm World Leader (Not Pretend) I should get it attended to. On the other hand, now I'm World Leader (Not Pretend) I have no need to get it attended to. The world that I lead can just get used to it.'

At a signal, a member of Mangler's black-suited entourage presented the prone secretary general a box topped with a big gold bow.

'Mangler Premiums from the new underpants range. The fibres contain platinum drawn and refined from the foundations of the earth through the roots of my trees. Wear them now. Wear them at all times. You'll find it will soothe my unfortunate spasm.

'Now kowtow, everybody. I want to check my neck tie in the reflection of my glory.'

Mangler strode to the great hall of the of the United Nations General Assembly. This was a place where historic things had happened. Here president Kruschev of the Soviet Union had banged his own shoe on the table, Colonel Muammar Gaddafi spoke for six hours without teleprompter or notes about his pet gerbils, General Colin Powell tried to convince the world that a pizza delivery truck in Iraq was a threat to world security, Abba had performed live and caused a riot, and on and on.

Triumphal music and pomp led Mangler to the lectern. Here before the world: the Pope, the heads of state of the most powerful countries, kings and queens. The Secretary General was already at his big desk, wodges of blood-stained tissue paper stuffed in his nose.

Archbishops intoned like a chorus in a Greek drama while Mangler was seated in his marble throne and crowned and blessed. Choirs of what appeared to be actual angels floated in the air and sang Mangler's name as he was confirmed as World Leader (Not Pretend).

Finally, still draped in a very proud and alert looking ermine, with the crown on his head, Mangler rose to address the world.

He stood at the lectern and his image gazed down on the packed hall from the two vast screens flanking like wings the gold-coloured wall. Elaborate pennants made of hundreds of Mangler pants hung from the lighting dome and cascaded down the walls. Directly above Mangler's head the emblem of the United Nations had been replaced by the Mangler tree of life logo — orthogonal, regular, evoking — to pick another symbol completely at random — a swastika, perhaps.

Mangler had moved into the UN and the world looked on beatifically, at peace, and with only a little visible drool on its chin.

Mangler dropped, a pin to test the silence. He gestured for more quiet, dropped the pin again, cupping one ear with a hand. Satisfied, he began.

'I congratulate the people of the world for recognising my contribution to defeating the zombie menace caused by Hades' berserker virus. A truly hellish trick. How much lower can you go than infiltrating the underpants of the population of the world?

'It was not just luck, but, I feel, most humbly, destiny that I was on hand and ready to save the world. So, yes, you're welcome. And this coronation today is most just and appropriate.

'There will be some changes around here. All for the greater good, of course; all for the benefit of your DNA. The world will be run to the highest principles of natural order, such as that to be found in the tree of life —' he gestured at the emblem above him. 'Scientific principles discovered over generations in the search for genetic perfection are made manifest in this symbol, and I have reached into nature's genetic heart and tweaked it to perfection.

'The future is clean. Purity of purpose and form and composition is ours.

'Fundamental to the principles of this natural order is the fruit of nature, the fruit of my magical trees; the fruit of this perfected DNA: my pants. My Überunderpants.

'Oh, by the way, that's the new name for my line in inner wear: Überunderpants. Expressive, huh? So, to lay the proper foundations of our orderly New World, we must have the appropriate foundation wear. And so that this New Order can be shared equally by the people of this planet, pants must be equally available to all. There must be no inequality between undergarments. I am therefore announcing an underpants free-for-all.

'Yes, from now on, all Mangler's Überunderpants will be free to you, whoever you are, wherever you are.

'As of' — he looked at his watch — 'now, all Mangler pants will be absolutely free! And you and you and you and all the people sitting or standing near you and everyone near them and everybody! Everybody, I tell you! And not just one pair of pants but unlimited pants! Everyone shall have as many underpants as they want in as many colours they want, any shapes because all the available shapes have been properly authorised.

'And all this courtesy of me: Dr Hieronymus Mangler.

'In the future no one will covet their neighbour's underpants. There will be no more fights over underpants. There will be no more wars about pants.

'However, ultimate freedom and perfection does not come without its responsibilities.'

Mangler paused. He looked out at the world, his eyes full of sorrow.

'I regret that some people on this planet, on account of degenerate genes are not physically, spiritually or intellectually compatible with Mangler pants.'

The giant screens above him filled with the images of the unfortunates who didn't look gorgeous in Mangler's product, the images Mangler had been judging before taking the lectern.

'It is imperative that the planet be cleansed of this imperfection in order for the Mangler Überunderpants to flourish in the best possible environment, bringing humanity to its peak, fully realising the potential of this race.

To this end, we are opening resorts around the world for physical and moral reconstruction. Individuals who do not fit the mould as defined by the Überunderpants will be invited to these resorts — absolutely free and at no expense to themselves — where they will remain until they look fantastic and think like beautiful people. Though some may be asked to, you know, step inside showers or ovens from time to time to just take a look.

'And in addition to all this, in addition to the pants free-for-all, and the free corrective resorts, I will ensure all trains will run on time from now on.

'You may cheer ecstatically.'

Which the world did, from New York to Sydney, from Buenos Ares to Tokyo, from Longyearbyen to Dr Mangler's orchard in Antarctica, the world whistled and cheered. Those who had hats tossed them in the air. Others tossed cookies. Some people cheered a bit quietly, taking a thumb from their mouth in order to do so, and immediately putting it back. The more demonstrative of the world's population hugged their family, their pets, their neighbours or themselves. The more expressive danced a jig or a fling, a flamenco or even a kazachok or two.

To a casual observer some of the cheering may have seemed a tad languid, but this was not a lack of enthusiasm, this was because some people were just *sooooooooo* happy.

Dr Hieronymus Mangler had arrived and the world was about to get shaped in his image.

37

'Is it normal pig behaviour,' Persephone asked, 'to be flat on the back with trotters in the air, drooling and grinning inanely?'

Hades, Persephone, Hilda, Pickles and the barnyard animals were clustered around a pair of delirious, supine porkers.

'Not really,' said Pickles. 'What's more, I've been telling them about sausages and all they do is giggle. The fact is, I've been experimenting on them. Didn't have any guinea pigs so had to use the full-size ones.'

'And what sort of experiment involving giggling pigs would be relevant to our predicament?' Hilda wanted to know.

'Ah! I'm glad you asked. I think you'll find this interesting. I've been feeding them Mangler's underpants and this is what happened to them — they came over all zonked.'

'Say what, Mr Man?' Hades was not impressed. 'You've been feeding undies to piggies? What on earth is the point of that? Have you run out of useful things to be doing?'

Hilda fixed Hades with one of the hard stares he could feel even from under her burqa.

'OK,' said Persephone. 'You may need to walk us through this because the relevance of daft pigs to a worldwide coup d'état by a dangerously crazed über-loon is eluding us.'

'It's all very simple and very evil,' said Pickles, 'except for the actual science, which is all very fiendish and extraordinarily evil. I was investigating the properties of these

Manglers, getting to know the enemy, hoping to back-engineer them and I discovered some interesting things.'

'Go on,' said Hades watching as one of the pigs appeared to rapture and ascend to another plane of being.

'First, the pants seem to be alive.'

'That can't be good,' said Persephone.

'That's exactly what I said, funnily enough,' said Pickles. 'On the other hand, being organic and being grown on trees, this is not mind-blowingly surprising. The next thing I discovered is the sinister bit. The pants produce and secrete an organic tranquilliser that is absorbed by the skin of the wearer. This produces a mild feeling of wellbeing and contentment.'

'Mild?' Hilda gestured at the pigs. The porker that hadn't yet raptured was staring in fascination at something that didn't actually exist — not is this dimension, anyway.

'Well, eating the pants delivers a stronger dose than wearing them.'

Persephone was impressed. 'Lucky pigs.'

Hades always spent a while a step or two behind the conversation before getting ahead of it. 'If you fancy a quick trip to Never Never Land, you just eat your pants. You'd think Mangler would mention that in the marketing. Is it even legal?'

'Legal is beside the point now. Mangler is the law.' If Hades wasn't up to speed yet, Hilda was.

She went on. 'Haven't you noticed anything strange lately?' she asked.

'Well, just a zombie apocalypse,' said Persephone.

'My public humiliation and destruction,' added Hades.

'The installation of a worldwide dictator who happens to be providing free to the everyone in the world organic underpants that secrete a pacifying psychotropic,' suggested Pickles. 'That's something that doesn't happen everyday.'

'Yes,' said Hilda. 'And despite the horror and the mayhem and the extreme dubiousness of the manner of Mangler's takeover, no one is complaining. Not only is everyone OK with everything but everyone seems happy and distracted. No complaining or surly shop staff. No irascible drivers on the road. No grumps or gripes about the weather or your soul-destroying job. Certainly no objections to Mangler's power grab.'

Hades caught up. 'And they're not complaining because they are stoned on Mangler's pants.'

Persephone mapped it out. 'Mangler produces these mind-altering underthings, disposes of his chief rival, and while everyone is blissed out on his tranquillisers, seizes power and begins to shape the world in his twisted image — an image that's twistier than a coil of eugenically-buggered DNA.'

Hades continued. 'What doesn't make sense, though, is the berserker programme. That's what brought me a cropper. It has Flay's ice-prints on it, but she was in suspended animation at the time the programme got into our systems, locked in a box in the basement of Porton Down. Immediately before that she was busy trying to kidnap Victoria and steal the secrets of our military underpants applications. When did she collude with Mangler?'

'Locked in a box in the basement of Porton Down. Why am I getting alarm bells?' asked Hilda.

'Alarm bells aside,' said Pickles, 'there's more.'

'I'm not sure I have room for more,' said Persephone.

'Well,' said Pickles, 'I don't know whether Mangler is aware of this or whether he cares, but like all genetically modified organisms, his underpants are dangerously unstable.'

The bats in the rafters took flight and embarked on mad circuits of the roof space.

'What do you mean dangerously unstable?'

'The first clue is that they are secreting varying amounts of the tranquilliser. There is no consistency from one pair to the next and even individual pairs seem to vary their amounts from hour to hour. Next, I have been looking very carefully at the fibres and they aren't happy. Some are degenerating. Others are writhing. Others are pumping themselves up as if on steroids. Some are just exploding or mutating. Under the microscope it's a bit of a monster's ball in your underthings.'

'Is it a monsters' balls up?' wondered Persephone.

'What does this mean? What's going to happen?' asked Hades.

'I don't know yet. They could just sort of disintegrate. Or the opposite, whatever the opposite is. Meanwhile, people are getting massive doses of these tranquillisers. It's not a recipe for a happy-ever-after sort of ending.'

'So what should we do?' Persephone wanted to know.

'Crikey! I don't know. You might run for the hills. Or you might dig a hole to hide in. Put a blanket over your head? Why does everyone ask me? Ask Hilda, she's the ideas person. Ask Hades, he's the great leader.'

'We need to get everyone in the world out of their pants,' said Hades. 'And we need to do it now.'

38

Muriel Thingerbottom looked at the razor wire with a mixture of peace, contentment and puzzlement. Peace and contentment because, you know, she felt great, and really, if you thought about it, or perhaps if you didn't think about it, everything was, you know, *great*. Puzzlement because Mangler's Sunny Happy Days holiday resort was located in a vast plain of devastation that might once have been a verdant rain forest. The land was soot black and overlaid with the ash and spikes of charred wood and the cremated bones of animals that had once lived there. In places, the ground still smoked despite the miserable drizzle that drenched everything. Water dripped off the steel-link fencing, the barbed wire, the machine gun towers, the men holding the machine guns, the search lights, and the expressively rude wooden sheds that seemed to be the accommodation for the Sunny Happy Days campers.

It might not have been drizzling. She wasn't sure. The airborne wet might have been the humidity, which was at drowning levels. The heat boiled away at her contentment, threatening to evaporate it completely.

A centipede, livid red and poisonous orange and the size of an alligator scurried over her Crocs making her jump. She was sure she heard it growl as it passed.

Camp Sunny Happy Days did not look the way she expected when she was asked to move here — told to move here. Told nicely to move here. The name Camp Sunny

Happy Days, and its location in exotic South America conjured images of palm trees, golden beaches, fluorescent cocktails and intimate adventures with wax. This place wasn't exactly sunny or happy. It certainly looked like a camp but the jury was out on sunny and happy.

Her path to Camp Sunny Happy Days began a few days previously at Gloucester bus station where she liked to hang about, despite the permanent cold and gritty wind. She was standing outside the newsagents eating a Twonky bar or three, and a bag of hedgehog and vinegar flavour crisps — just one family-sized one — and maybe a tub of durian and mangosteen ice cream. It was just a thing she did, this eating. Everyone has a thing. Eating had always made her feel good. It made her feel good after getting depressed as she usually did after looking in the mirror and seeing what the eating was doing to her. And she generally did the eating thing outside Gloucester bus station because it was the first eating stop after the bus stop at which she arrived, and which precluded any further waiting around for food after sitting on the bus for howeverlong wishing she hadn't eaten the munchies she brought along for the bus journey quite so fast, like before the bus even arrived and that. Anyway, she was doing her eating thing on the street outside Gloucester bus station when two men approached her.

It was not unknown for her to be approached by men, especially in Gloucester bus station, but they were usually not the wholesome kind and were invariably covered with stuff that would probably never wash off even if exposed to the most biologically active or caustic detergents and generally proposed things to be done in bushes or toilets that would produce more stuff that would never wash off. These men today were a different kind of men. You could tell right away because you couldn't hear them breathe. These gentlemen wore impeccable black leather trench coats and impeccable black fedoras and impeccable sunglasses and had impeccable blond hair and impeccably handsome jaws. They remarked upon her snack and all the many other similar snacks she had apparently enjoyed before and showed her gleaming gold badges, like police ID, but these had the Mangler tree of life logo and the title 'Bottom Inspectors'.

The Bottom Inspectors measured her with a measure they just happened to have on their person and weighed her with some scales they also happened to have on their person. They then checked her teeth and studied her from various angles and invited her to Camp Sunny Happy Days.

She said she ought to tell her mum.

'Does your mum like snacks as much as you do?'

'Oh, yeah! She's brill!'

'Well, perhaps you'll see her there.'

A black van pulled up. It was emblazoned with the Mangler tree of life logo, which was very swish, and she felt quite someone as she climbed in the back. She smiled happily at the nice ladies and gentlemen, lads and lassies that were already in there.

'Hi!' she said happily.

'Hi!' said the others dreamily.

'I feel great to be going to Camp Sunny Happy Days. Are you going there too?'

'Yes, we are,' said a nice old lady who looked like a turkey that had only half escaped Christmas. 'Are you?'

'Oh, yes!'

'What a coincidence,' said the young man with the red face and the torso that appeared to be back to front. 'So are we.'

'Woot!' said Muriel.

'Just get in and sit down,' said the men in the black coats.

The gates of Camp Sunny Happy Days expressed some audible pain as they opened to admit Muriel and her fellow happy campers. A vulture lifted itself off the gatepost and flapped belligerently away.

Just as Camp Sunny Happy Days didn't look like a resort, it didn't behave like one.

Where, Muriel wondered, was the big swimming pool that looked like an advert for rum, around which were congregated men who looked like the men who congregated in adverts for rum? There were a few waterlogged craters but no pool. Where, Muriel wondered, was the beach? In place of cocktails there were battered and rusting tin cans filled with a greasy, grey water that contained globs of something like tapioca and which was apparently alive. As for the lavish buffets and piles of lobster you were supposed to get at resorts? Well there was plenty of food if you considered charcoal to be food.

'Lots of energy and totally yummy,' the camp leader, whom everyone addressed as comandante, would say before stressing, 'Have you ever had a barbecue without charcoal? Point made.'

Another feature of resorts, Muriel thought, was an abundance of doing nothing, a huge amount of lazing about, an absence of anything compelling to keep her from her sun bed or night bed or bed of roses. At Camp Sunny Happy Days, however, there was always something to do. She and all the other resort guests were up at dawn and trudging out to the vast orchards of Mangler pants that were, even as she laboured, being planted where the forest used to be. All the hours of daylight Muriel was up and down ladders carefully but quickly detaching the Mangler-wear from the trees and piling it in baskets and she spent most of the dark hours baling up the clothes and stacking them for shipping.

However, there was a plentiful supply of clean undies, which was nice. And the camp staff were very keen to see that you had all the pants that you needed. There was something specially comforting and reassuring to slip into clean things after a day up the trees and a night in the shipping sheds.

Some of her new pals even took to keeping a spare pair at all times in their mouths, slowly sucking and chewing throughout the day. They looked very peaceful and dreamy indeed, so much so that they would occasionally forget they were on ladders and stroll off into space and down to earth very abruptly or end up absentmindedly in the baling machines, which they would gum up with their insides and jam with their bones.

So, no, it wasn't what Muriel expected and she missed her mum in a distant sort of way, and despite all the comforts of Camp Sunny Happy Days, she missed the odd home treat like the Twonky bar and the ice cream and the daily kilogramme of sugar. But she was happy. Wasn't she?

39

Hilda and Hades watched the protest march from the sidelines, anonymous if not inconspicuous inside their burqas.

The placards of the protestors read 'Free your mind, burn your pants!'

'Pants are slavery!'

'Liberate your bottom!'

'No to pants! Yes to life!'

They were chanting: 'What do we want?'

'A pants-less world!'

'When do we want it?'

'Now!'

'Our kind of people,' observed Hades. 'We must make contact with them.'

Opposition to Mangler was growing. Some naturists and other free thinkers accustomed to doing without undies had remained free of the tranquilliser and they were mounting a fightback, this demo being one battle.

Making contact was not a simple matter of saying a cheery hello. The protest was well attended by police, thousands of whom lined Charing Cross Road and funnelled the marchers to Trafalgar Square for a spot of kettling.

The police were restless and twitchy, in complete contrast to the dozy and docile grins of the few onlookers. A side effect of Manglers tranquillisers was a complete loss of curiosity. It didn't really matter to the citizens that someone had found cause for discontent in this chemical utopia, they had pants to admire and collect, and what a cornucopia of under-drawers Mangler had contrived! The big bookshops of the West End had been emptied of reading matter and filled with displays of the most desirable underthings yet seen on this planet or any other,

Hades grimaced inside his burqa. 'The cops don't look too docile. Did they forget to put their underwear on this morning do you suppose?'

'We've heard that Mangler is giving the police and the military pants that secrete a different kind of chemical. Apparently it's like a cocktail of amphetamines and cheap coffee. Turns the wearer into an irritable twitching mess. Pickles is trying to get a sample to analyse.'

They drifted in the same direction as the protest, pretending to be as nonchalant as possible, though whether it is possible to be nonchalant inside a burqa is a matter still subject to heated debate in several international forums.

Nonchalance notwithstanding, they were being shadowed by a couple of Mangler's black-coated, Bottom Inspectors, his notorious and privatised semi-secret police and enforcers.

'Don't look now, but we're being followed.' The message flashed up in the lens of the iGlasses Hades was wearing.

'Don't look again: our followers are being followed,' Hades flashed back.

'So they are,' signalled Hilda.

The two sinister shadows watching Hades and Hilda had their own sinister shadows: two men strolling seemingly as oblivious as any of the shoppers or tourists on Charing Cross Road, wearing the same dreamy-far away expression as everyone else. It was their eyes that gave them away. Their eyes had life and purpose. No amount of acting could hide that.

'Well, this is an interesting turn up,' said Hades. 'What do you suppose it means?'

'If they are tailing the agents that are on to us, it means that they must be on to us too.'

'Are we that bloody obvious?'

'Well, you are six foot one and a hundred kilos in weight. Even in a burqa, that's a bit standy-outy. I also suspect that your big bushy eyebrows are escaping through the vent for the eyes in the front of the burqa hood.'

'Oh bugger! Well, I suppose we could just call it a day here and double back to the Angel on St Giles High Street for a pint. Damn fine pub.'

'Go for a pint while dressed in a burqa?'

'We could be apostates,' said Hades reasonably.

'It's a bugger to drink in this hood. You need a straw about two feet long. I've tried.'

'Well, in that case we shall just go with the flow and see this mission through.'

The flow took them down to Trafalgar Square where suddenly there were police on every side. There were police on foot with riot shields and helmets and batons, even though there was no riot going on. There were police on horseback, police with water cannon, police in armoured vans, police with dogs, police with cats, giraffes, elephants, pigs and hamsters. The thick blue line had closed behind the demonstration, blocking Charing Cross Road and any way back. The cordon of authority tightened, baton arms were raised, bludgeoning objects became airborne, and assertive hands grasped Hilda and Hades and pushed, pulled, and hurled them through the melee and suddenly they were in the clear and legging it down Duncannon Street toward The Strand, as fast as a hitched up burqas would allow. Whoever it was that pulled them from Trafalgar Square was running with them and when the time came, hurled them onto another course, away from any thoroughfare of size or significance and into the convolution of narrow streets that is central London, and in which both Hilda and Hades completely lost track of where they were, which was probably the point.

'In here,' they were told and they were through a graffiti covered door and clattering down some rickety wooden stairs into a basement that was full of dark and the unknown. It crossed the minds of both Hades and Hilda that descending into the bowels of a building of uncertain location with persons unknown, having just fled a pitched battle might not be a good idea, but this was where the flow and the momentum of the events of the day were taking them, so this was where they went.

40

It was dark, very dark indeed in the basement, as befits underground basements that have no windows or other apertures to the outside world. Hilda switched her glasses to night sight, which didn't help a lot because instead of a lot of dark filled with mysterious masked figures she was looking at a lot of green filled with mysterious masked figures.

Lights came on, which had the effect through Hilda's night vision of nearly blowing out her optic nerves. She switched her iGlasses to tropical beach mode. Now, rather than a lot of dark or a lot of green filled with mysterious masked figures, there was a lot of light filled with mysterious masked figures. About a dozen in all, dressed entirely in black, military-style fatigues with balaclavas that completely hid their faces.

'Sit down.' The mysterious hooded figure had a woman's voice and a woman's body to go with it, which was convenient. She was standing arms crossed in a no-nonsense stance that suggested very much that she was in control around here, and generally not one to accommodate nonsense. The two crowbars strapped cross-wise on her back, hooks protruding over each shoulder, said the same.

Hilda and Hades sat at the rough chairs they were offered, which were at a tasteful restaurant table. Indeed, the basement had much the feel of a restaurant or cafe, one that had once been haunted by London's beautiful people, especially those that had beautiful bank balances. Its understated colours and elegant lines bore the imprint of the kind of interior designer whose name you could drop any time you wanted a free dinner anywhere. However, it also bore the more recent imprint of having been long forgotten about and entirely left to things not remotely beautiful nor possessing anything like a bank account.

Hilda and Hades could feel that this was a hideaway for these mysterious hooded figures. From the place to be seen the basement restaurant had gone to a place to go not to be seen.

With a sinister squeal, the doors to the kitchen swung open. The individual that came through them was hunched, wizened, hooped, hobbled, wrinkled, runkled, and comprehensively unkempt of dress and skin. The individual that came through the doors was of uncertain gender, indeterminate species and unguessable age; not particularly animal, mineral or vegetable and not clearly alive; and evidently bore the mixed DNA of gnome, walnut, lump, and troglodyte. It wore a chef's hat, chef's apron and carried a big cleaver. Stopping in the door, it surveyed the masked figures in the restaurant in the way that suggested it was sizing up something that was crawling on the counter tops in his kitchen that shouldn't be crawling on the counter tops in the kitchen and which he was about to kill with a blow from a frying pan. The masked figures regarded the wrinkled one with some awe and trepidation and stood back a little.

'Jellied eel all round, is it then?' asked the creature in the chef's garb.

'Yes, please, Tarquin,' said the one with the woman's voice.

'Right you are then,' said the individual that had come through the doors, and turned and went back through the doors.

The woman stood over the seated Hades and Hilda.

'Why would the ex-underpants magnate Sir Hades Gousset and his personal assistant Hilda Titanium be hanging around an anti-underwear protest?'

Hades was appalled. 'How did you know it was us?'

'Ms Titanium's burqa. A dead giveaway. And you, Sir Hades, your eyebrows are escaping from the eye vents of

183

your hood. Only one person on this planet has eyebrows that fecund.'

'Were we that obvious?'

'Well, Mangler's men had no more problem spotting you than we did. You may have noticed that.'

'Oh, buggery bugger-bags!' Hades pulled his hood off and breathed a sigh of relief at having his head back in the world. 'I fondly imagined they only wanted to share some interpretations of scriptural verses.'

There was a loud and persistent thudding and thwacking in the kitchen that made the pictures jump on the walls.

'Thank you for spiriting us away from that mass beating — but may I ask, who do we have the pleasure of thanking?' asked Hilda.

'It is safer for everyone if you don't know our names or see our faces. All I can tell you is that we are the Commandos.'

'Commandos?' wondered Hades. 'It's very brave of you to take on Mangler's thugs, but the name is a bit dramatic, don't you think?'

Even behind the dark glasses and masks he could feel hard stares, and there was another coming from Hilda's burqa.

'We're anti-underpants. We are therefore the Commandos.'

'Oh, I get it.' Hades felt a bit silly for being slow.

'So, I say again,' the leader said again, while the other Commandos closed in, making a circle of mysterious black around Hades and Hilda, 'What is an ex-underpants magnate and his PA doing out and about when we're tearing down the underpants of oppression?'

'A bit less of the ex-magnate there, old girl.'

'Well how else would you describe yourself?'

'More sort of between empires, really, I suppose.'

'We wanted to make contact,' said Hilda. 'Discreetly. Hades is somewhat inconvenienced with regard to his popularity and approval at the moment and with the general public all over the world wanting to lynch him, etcetera, etcetera.'

'And why would you want to make contact, discreetly or otherwise? What could we possibly have to talk about?'

'We have a common enemy,' Hades told him. 'Mangler.'

'We do not have a common enemy.' Hades was taken by surprise.

'But Mangler —'

'Our enemy is underpants.'

'Underpants? Your enemy? But that's preposterous! Underpants are innocent bystanders. Underpants are our friends. They are just there to catch drips.'

'Underpants are repression. They have always been there, just out of sight, constraining us, insulating us from our true natural state. For generations, for millennia, there are those of us who quietly abhorred underpants and worked for the day we might rid ourselves of this bondage. It was Robbie Burns who wrote, "Where'er ye be, let your tackle go free, in church or chapel let it dangle".'

'Burns wrote that?'

'Oh, yes, he did. People only remember the cleaned up, bastardised and safe version of it these days. Now events have vindicated us. The true, insidious nature of underpants is out in the open.'

The door to the kitchen squealed open again — this time with perhaps a little more pain. The wrinkled thing named Tarquin emerged laden with bowls — more bowls than a person ought to be able to carry. He appeared as a perambulating, teetering pyramid of bowls.

'Jellied eels,' the chef announced.

'I really don't think —' started Hades.

'You'll enjoy the jellied eels!' said the masked woman in tones of cold steel that suggested 'enjoy' was a command not a prediction.

'I say,' said Hades examining his bowl, 'this jelly does rather seem to be strawberry jelly, rather than the eel jelly one associates with jellied eels, and the eel head embedded in it does seem rather — what's the technical word? — uncooked. As in raw. As in still twitching.'

'It's Tarquin's special recipe,' one of the other Commandos assured them.

'Well, that's good, then,' said Hilda, jabbing Hades in the ribs.

'That's *jolly* good then,' expanded Hades.

'You're very welcome,' said Tarquin, who had emerged from under his pyramid of bowls.

'So, jellied bangers, is it? Righty-ho. Won't be a jiffy.' The wizened chef retreated back into the kitchen.

'This place,' said the woman gesturing at the walls of the restaurant, 'is called Les Deux Fesses. It has been for many generations — no one knows how many — the hub of London's secret community of the pants-less ones. Our people are spread all over the world. We are an international people, and an ancient one. We are at once everywhere and nowhere. We are among you but not of you. You may at any time be sitting next to, doing business with, be friends with someone who has eschewed underpants for a simpler more honest way of life, and you wouldn't know it.

'Through the millennia, we have been reviled and misunderstood and persecuted but we have persisted. Governments and religions have tried to eradicate us, but we disappear before their eyes and emerge again on our own terms. Places such as this around the world have provided hubs for the diaspora. A place to meet people like ourselves, to be ourselves without the pressure to artificially swaddle our loins for some facile moralistic prejudice.'

'You mean, you come here to eat without pants on,' clarified Hades.

'You may have noticed the lockers at the foot of the stairs. That's where customers can stash their articles of oppression when they come in.'

'OK,' said Hades. 'You are a secret society of people who go without pants. And …' He gestured at the kitchen door.

'Tarquin is the last in the long family line of owner-chefs at Les Deux Fesses. Aside from being a shelter to us, the restaurant has been famous for its excellent cuisine. Was famous for its excellent cuisine. Is … has been famous for its excellent cuisine. Whatever. Tarquin has continued that fine tradition and in recent years he has added to it by getting aboard the new wave of British gastronomy. These days he offers his re-interpretations of classic British dishes.'

'So,' said Hades, 'we couldn't be in a better place to strike back at Mangler. We have secrecy, history, and a network on our side, and grub to hand.'

'Really! Mangler's the enemy.' said Hilda driving home the point. 'He's deceived us all and forced the world into his Überunderpants.'

'Mangler's the enemy and you're not?' asked the Commando woman in a tone that was both scathing and incredulous. 'All we know is one minute we're minding our own business when there's this terrific zombie apocalypse and everyone's pants go nuts. Turns out it's a berserker virus hidden in your most intimate regions. Next thing is, another underpants magnate — Hieronymus Mangler — has taken over the world. Everyone has to wear his pants because there's no choice and people who don't look good in them are being disappeared. Now, what do Hieronymus Mangler and Hades Gousset have in common? Yes, they're both underpants magnates! And what do our two recent catastrophes have in common? Yes, underwear made by Hieronymus Mangler and Hades Gousset! I think it's pretty bloody clear who our enemies are.'

Hades could not contain himself. 'But this is what we are talking about. It was Mangler who corrupted our Omnipants with a berserker virus to bring me down.'

Hilda continued. 'Mangler's organic Überunderpants are secreting a kind of sedative that's pacifying everyone while Mangler gets on with taking over the world.'

'Everyone's so stoned on his things they probably haven't even noticed or don't care,' added Hades.

'You've been saved because you habitually go commando.'

The Commando leader was silent for a moment.

The kitchen door butted into the pause. 'Jellied bangers,' announced Tarquin proudly, distributing bowls among the Commandos.

'The jelly's green this time,' observed Hades.

'Gooseberry,' said the Commandos in unison.

'And the sausage …'

'Not cooked. It's Tarquin's own recipe.'

'Don't tell me you're one of these people that cooks his sausages!' said Tarquin and shuddered visibly. 'So passé! Have you not heard of Heston Blumenthal?' He went back to the kitchen.

'You expect us to believe this about Mangler?' asked the Commando woman.

'It would be very helpful,' said Hilda.

'You can prove what you say?' the leader wanted to know.

'We can prove the Überunderpants are secreting tranquillisers. We have the analysis.' Hilda showed them on her tablet.

'That doesn't mean much to me. I'm a plumber. Jim, here, though, met a scientist once in a pub in Camberwell, didn't you, Jim. Let him have a look.'

Jim had a look.

'Wot? Eukaryotic cells, is it? Crikey! That's going back a bit. Let's have a shufti.' Jim shuffled over and lifted his sunglasses a tad to get a better look. 'Hmm. Ribosomes, yup. Endoplasmic reticulum … I'm sure the bloke in the pub mentioned that. Translocation to the ER lumen, glycosylated proteins, molecular chaperones — tick, tick, tick. There's your Golgi apparatus … vesicle fusion, and your porosomes; exocytosis … Looks, kosher to me. Mind you, it was Camberwell, so you never know.'

'Here's the jellied mushy peas,' said Tarquin busily serving. 'You'll note the quiet irony in this dish: the mushy peas are cooked but the jelly isn't set.'

The woman sniffed thoughtfully. 'Makes sense,' she conceded. 'It would explain why everyone has gone so dappy. And what about that virus he planted in your Omnipants, the berserker programme? I don't suppose you have evidence for that do you?'

Hilda and Hades explained as best they could about the hacking trail, and the planted code, but Hades had to admit, 'No, we don't have that smoking gun. If we did, we could go public with it and save everyone a lot of time and trauma.'

'Here are the jellied pork scratchings in case anyone still wants a nibble,' said Tarquin.

'Well,' Hilda wanted to clarify, 'even if we did have that evidence no one would care until we had a means to get through that tranquilliser. The way things are at the moment we could beam real-time images of Mangler eating live kittens and everyone would just go "that's soooooooo awesomely cute!" and that would be that.'

The woman exchanged consulting glances with her colleagues and pulled off her balaclava. 'My name's Alice.' Alice had gorgeously dark, tousled, collar-length hair, icy grey eyes that could cut diamonds and a complete set of luscious features. She was of such striking appearance she should have been a film star. 'All right. You have our attention. But if you're having us on, we'll shop you to Mangler's Bottom Inspectors so fast your elastic will go ping.'

The rest of the gang pulled off their own hoods to reveal a variety of ages and shapes and genders, which all shared the same mien of dramatic determination. Jim put an old tobacco pipe in his mouth and applied a match.

'And to finish off, here's the jellied jelly. I know this one's a favourite,' said Tarquin.

'So, how do we work this?' Jim wanted to know.

'Communication,' said Hilda emphatically. 'Communication is crucial.'

'And cracking heads,' Hades added with passion. 'I always find that cracking heads works wonders, don't you?'

'Cracking heads?' asked Alice. 'More like cracking bottoms. Let's make a plan!'

41

Originally it was a famous bookstore in London's West End and then it was converted into a massive store dedicated to Mangler's pants. After that, it became a blazing fireball.

As the effects of Mangler's tranquillisers took hold on the population, the corporate apparatus decreed that there was no need for anything like thought, and all its accessories such as books were removed, like Hades, to the nearest landfill. The empty stores were filled with Mangler's product and instantly became a 24-hour It's-a-Small-Minded-World fantasy attractions for the dazed population — attractions where you could take the fantasy home with you and wear it. Formerly responsible and productive citizens abandoned family and workstation just to inhabit full time these cathedrals to nether wear.

Flame poured through the show windows in an angry torrent and up into the sky, sweeping with it the ash and dust remains of Mangler's manna to the masses.

The people stood in the street, despite being well past the witching hour, in large gawping crowds. Some were impassive. Some were were strangely, confusingly torn between a deep inner happiness and a powerful sadness and fear. Others walked, arms outstretched in grief or slow-motion rescue — there was no way to tell which — into the flames.

Bottom Inspectors tapped their feet impatiently waiting for a very chilled fire service to arrive and confront the conflagration.

By the time the fire brigade did show up, in dribs and drabs and in a sort of ad hoc fashion, a large part of a large and venerable city block was ablaze.

42

There was not much traffic on the motorway, most people being, you know, too happy to bother driving; everyone had whatever they wanted wherever they were sitting or standing or lying. With the road to itself, the convoy of articulated lorries proceeded at a sensible pace, just fast enough or just slow enough to accommodate the unpredictable attention spans of the drivers, who were fitted with special pants that delivered a reduced dose of happiness and distraction. However, the dose was still high enough that when the drivers saw the first diversion sign they followed it without a second thought.

'Hello, big convoy: Diversion this way', said the sign, which included a helpful arrow pointing the way to London's M25 orbital. The convoy didn't actually want to go anywhere near London. They were travelling from Southampton toward the heart of the country, but, you know, the sign said go this way, and the drivers were feeling happy and content, so whatever and they followed obediently the 'Hello, big convoy: Diversion this way' signs and arrows onto the M25 and then around and around that because the signs had been placed in such a way that any obedient driver would simply rotate around the capital until running out of petrol.

Within a couple of days, the M25 and the roads feeding it became jammed and clogged with stalled vehicles. Nothing moved in the south east of England. Since the lorries were carrying cargoes of Mangler's Überunderpants imported from his overseas plantations, this meant that much of his distribution network was immovably snarled and tangled in just one corner of the country.

The population of the United Kingdom were suddenly in danger of running out of underpants.

43

Meanwhile, in the secret Les Deux Fesses basement restaurant and bunker off Wardour Street …

'We can't do any more fire attacks,' said Hades emphatically.

'I thought they were a roaring success,' Alice differed.

'We didn't factor in a comatose fire brigade,' Hilda told Alice. 'Yes, we removed some distribution nodes around the country —'

'We lit a fire under their bums, all right.' Jim chuckled at the thought.

'The great fire of London was very cleansing,' thought Alice. 'It got rid of the plague.'

'It also got rid of most of London,' Hades pointed out.

'The way we disrupted distribution was effective,' said Hilda in her best assessing the situation tone of voice. 'And it has bought us a window of opportunity. Supplies of pants are running low. Those pants in circulation have a limited life of secreting that stuff. One more push and we might be able to get through to people.'

'But not long,' warned Alice. 'Mangler is flying in supplies now and there are too many ports and motorways in this country for us to cover properly with our numbers.'

'Oh, yes,' added Jim, 'the Bottom Inspectors are moving fast on our diversion signs. We don't have long to press this advantage.'

'Well, I do have a suggestion,' put in Dr Pickles, pinging a ball pen off his copious scientific teeth.

'I do like it when you have a suggestion,' said Hades encouragingly. 'It means I don't have to come up with a suggestion myself.'

'Simple. We tackle the general population in much the same way that we tackled the convoys of lorries.'

Alice was alarmed. 'Divert them into the traffic jam on the M25? How will we do that?'

'We'll need some more signs,' said Pickles, looking indecently relaxed and confident.

44

The burning of the pants shops had been dramatic but in the bigger scheme of things was not going to stop Mangler. Looked at from a certain perspective, urban Britain was one giant shopping centre. The logjam on the M25 was far more trouble than the fires, but in the major cities it was still business as usual while stocks lasted.

Queues of underpants seekers and admirers lined up wherever there was a pair to be had.

But just to be safe, Mangler ordered the conversion of all department stores to just one department — guess which department.

The morning after Hades' last meeting with the Commandos, when the staff at Selfridge's eventually remembered what they were supposed to be doing they opened to the doors to the thousands of happy shoppers outside who didn't move. If the store staff felt any curiosity or concern at the lack of interest in the doors to this cornucopia of underthings, it was overwhelmed by their sense of tranquility, so for quite a long time nothing happened and nobody did anything about anything.

In time, Hermione Harrods, the floor manager, drifted from the shop to maybe, you know, take a look at something, or whatever. It turned out that all the shoppers were staring at a big sign on the pavement outside the store. In jolly letters, the sign read, 'Just look at this sign!' and that's what everyone was doing.

So engrossed in the sign, the crowd failed to register the arrival of a troupe of motley-clad individuals until they whipped away the hypnotising message.

'Now look at us!'

The crowd beamed in approval. The motley was derived from Mangler's own pants, stitched together in a fantastic multi-coloured dream coat. The individuals twirled to give the audience the full affect.

'Oooh,' said the audience.

'I'm the Pied Piper of, er, Tower Hamlets,' said Alice, for it was she.

'You have too many colours on you to be pied,' said Dr Pickles who was along as scientific advisor and who occasionally missed the spirit of things. 'Pied means having two colours. You have about 80 percent of the visible spectrum on you.'

'Do you think these people give two hoots about whether I'm pied or not?' Alice hissed at Pickles.

'Not really, but it's the principle of the thing,' insisted the scientist. 'You are misrepresenting yourself to people who are in no mental condition to evaluate what you say.'

Alice was too busy and too tense about possible intervention from Bottom Inspectors or police to spare any number of her own hoots about Pickles' objections. 'Ladies and gentlemen! We have a wonderful underpants-themed show for you and a real treat it is. And it's absolutely free. All you have to do is follow the music and dance this way!' She struck a jolly chord on her ukulele.

'That's not a pipe,' said Pickles. 'You said you were the Pied Piper of Tower Hamlets, whoever that is, the Pied Piper everyone knows was from Hamelin and that's in Germany, and anyway he was called the Pied Piper because he played a pipe. And wore clothes of two colours. You're wearing lots of colours and that's a ukulele, not a pipe.'

'Look, I can't play the pipes, so a ukulele will have to do.'

'But you're a plumber. What kind of plumber can't play pipes?'

'I'm a bloody good plumber. I can fix pipes, I just don't play them.'

'This whole thing is feeling a mite inauthentic, now, Alice. I just want to mention that.'

'How about, I am a figurative Pied Piper playing figurative pipes.'

'How does Tower Hamlets fit into this? Is that a figurative Tower Hamlets or the real Tower Hamlets?'

Luckily for Alice's mental wellbeing and Pickles' physical integrity, Hades was also there. 'Dr. Pickles, would you like to go off with a small team of bodyguards and assistants to do some scientific research or other? I'll assist the multi-coloured ukulele player of Tower Hamlets —'

'Dalston, actually. Dalston has no h in it, so —' said Alice not at all helpfully.

'So I'll assist Alice in her mission,' finished Hades. 'Let's go.'

Alice's first chords of John Philip Sousa's The Liberty Bell may or may not have been directed straight at Dr Pickles' head, but the merry band of brightly coloured Commandos set off with a hoppety-skippety dance while the very large crowd of Mangler's shoppers happily followed and even made a few amiable stabs at the dance steps themselves.

Removing evidence and providing extra incentive to follow along, a couple of spare Commandos picked up and brought along the captivating sign.

The procession set off across Oxford Street. Somewhere on Duke Street, Alice modulated into It's a Long Way to Tipperary, but despite that they all soon arrived where they were going: a narrow street formed hundreds of years ago of a gap left absent-mindedly between important-looking buildings that for all the centuries had housed important men in wigs, whether wigs were necessary to their function or not or even in fashion. It was the kind of alley that, when it formed all those generations ago, was probably full of foul refuse dumped from upper windows and full of foul people with warts and bad teeth and worse accents who would lie in wait, their hat brims collecting the excrescence dropped from above, for any passersby who were even a little bit less foul than themselves, who they would cudgel and rob. In these non-cudgelling days the alley would be deemed officially picturesque and contain nothing more sinister than quaint cafes designed to trap tourists. Normally.

Today, as the crowd of shoppers were led in, had anyone been alert enough to know or care where they were, they would see a return of the furtive presences in the shadows, readying themselves to pounce. The desire of these lurkers was not the wallet, the purses, the watches, the lives, or the teeth of passersby, but their underwear.

Muggers had never had more compliant victims, but relieving the stoned of their undergarments is not something many of us learn at school, so despite the lavish preparation for this operation there was still some debate about the best modus operandi.

Does the victim remain standing? Should they be laid on the ground? What if they protest or struggle? Could you be contaminated by the very pants you were swiping?

Alice stood akimbo in the little street and whipped the two crowbars out of her back holster, spinning them on her fingers like a gunslinger spoiling for a fight. 'This how I do my debagging!' she declaimed.

'Oh,' said Jim, 'I don't suppose you have dozens more of those do you?'

Luckily, there was one Commando who had learned the art of removing undies from the stoned at school. He had attended a private school of considerable repute, where, he insisted, it had been an essential skill. Teams of three were the thing: two to tip the victim upside down and one to do the necessary swiping. Following this method the Commandos got through the workload in no time.

Hades, as the hands-on leader type, threw himself into the task with everyone else. One, two, three, head down, bottom up, off with the Überunderpants, on with the Hades, all stop!

Jim removed the briar from his mouth in a manner that meant trouble. 'What are you doing?'

'I'm re-potting the poor soul in some sensible underpants,' said Hades, wishing he too had a briar he could whisk from his mouth in a manner that could only mean corresponding trouble for anyone who removed their briar at him.

'And why would you be doing that?'

'Giving the chap some security. After the ordeal he's been through he'll need some nice snug, woolly undies. Calm the frayed nerves, you know. Make you feel the comfort of home even if home is a million miles away.'

'And who are you working with?' asked Jim.

The other Commandos stopped what they were doing. Alice stopped playing her ukulele. Everyone was looking at Hades.

'We've spent millennia — millennia! — fighting for the liberty of humanity. We've had to live incognito for fear of persecution. Do you know what has happened throughout history to brothers and sisters who have been caught with their pants off just living the way nature made us? Torquemada had an especially sadistic version of the iron maiden just for us. And now, and now that our moment has come, right in our faces, you try to put new underpants on a person we have just liberated? You may be an ally, but you are still a man who made a fortune out of underpants.'

'I see you have a point there,' announced Hades.

'Well spotted,' said Jim.

'I'll just toss these underpants nonchalantly over my shoulder as if I didn't even have them in my hand in the first place, shall I?'

'What underpants?'

'Right,' said Alice, 'let's get back to it, and launched into an especially strident version of Beethoven's Ode to Joy.

Sudden deprivation of your addiction, not to mention your unmentionables, can cause trauma and all kinds of panic. Hades and the Commandos had requisitioned a number of the endearingly corporate cafes and restaurants on the little street and were seating the bewildered citizens with a biscuit and a nice cup of tea, as you would a blood donor, which is where they had got the idea.

Specially trained Commandos gave gentle counselling to the newly liberated citizens about what had happened to them and the world, and were told emphatically that if they wanted to stay clean they needed to stay away from Mangler's peddlers.

They were also invited nicely to join the Commandos, and assured that there were biscuits and plenty more tea for all members, not to mention a table at Les Deux Fesses.

'How many have we done today, do you reckon?' Alice asked Jim.

'Oooh, hundreds, I expect.'

Alice rubbed her hands. 'Another sixty-odd million to go and we're there.'

45

'Oi, it's the Bottom Inspectors. They're coming down Oxford Street mob-handed with the rozzers,' hissed their lookout in a stage whisper a second before the police sirens told Hades and the Commandos the same thing.

The signs disappeared releasing the un-liberated Mangler wearers from their trances and back into bewilderment and befuddlement.

The men and women of the resistance disappeared into the shadows taking with them the liberated citizens.

'Look at them,' mused Hades aloud. 'One minute, secure in enslavement and oblivion, the next alert, free, but running with fear and uncertainty. What kind of addled world is this?'

'We'll have to split up,' said Alice. We'll be in touch in the usual way, whatever that is. And can I suggest making it sharpish?' and she was gone too, leaving her motley fluttering to the ground behind her.

Hades and his party made off into central London, taking the narrowest, most obtuse and pointless little streets they could in order to keep out of sight, regardless of where they actually went. The sirens came and went, and eventually went without any more coming, by which time their evasive walking had taken them right back to the West End.

There were scarcely any fewer people here than in normal times, all attracted, as in those normal times by the bright, hypnotising lights, the crowds, but unlike in normal times, by the plethora of shops dispensing brightly-coloured undies at no cost.

With the day falling into night, Hades and Hilda wandered into Piccadilly Circus, and here they found Dr Mangler — dozens of Dr Mangler, scores of Dr Mangler.

There is nothing more powerful to the unwary mind than a person on the telly, so to the tranquilised people around Piccadilly junction, Mangler must have appeared like God. He gazed down from giant TV screens mounted on the walls among the famous lights, on rooftops, around Eros's base, in all the shop windows, and three flat screens were cleverly rigged up as a sandwich board on a sandwich board man.

In order to make sure every citizen everywhere was within easy intimidation distance, The World Leader (Not Pretend) had rigged up huge video screens in every public space. This much propaganda power pointed right in the faces of the populace would make despots past and present glow green with envy.

Mangler was making a speech. His voice boomed and echoed around the world like the end of days itself.

'I am honoured, privileged and humbled by the task bestowed on me by the people of the world to provide underwear to each and every citizen. I do not shirk this task. I do not waver. I will live this commitment for as long as necessary.

'Regrettably, even though underpants grow on trees, the task of farming and bringing these essentials to you is not without its burden and price. I shall not trouble you with the dull economics of this.

'I have promised the pants will be free and always will be. It would be a betrayal of your trust if it were any other way.

'And yet, for the sake of hardworking people everywhere, we have to make hard decisions, and it is irresponsible to future generations if we do not live within our means now, and if we wish to avoid a hard landing for the world's economy we must swallow the hard bitter pill of realism now. Belts will be tightened, for the better, but Mangler's wares come in all sizes.

'I have therefore decided that it is in everyone's best interests that I levy a flat-rate levy on all citizens. This way, we will ensure the permanent supply of Mangler's super duper Überunderpants.

'The levy will constitute just eighty per cent of individual income and national GDP. And this world leadership promises not to hike the levy until we do. No, don't thank me, it's what I'm here for.

'I want to thank everyone for their hard work. If we all pull together as a team, we can make Mangler's Überunderpants even more fantastic than they already are.

'This is Hieronymus Mangler, World Leader (Not Pretend), touching you in the places other world leaders cannot reach, and signing off.'

The image crossfaded to another of a beaming Mangler with a 'Cheer Now!' caption. The aimless crowds in Piccadilly Circus and across the nation cheered, though it wasn't clear to either Hades of Hilda that they knew why, and at the end of Shaftesbury Avenue, an awkward-looking, pear-shaped man was bundled roughly into a black van by Bottom Inspectors.

Hades and Hilda put their heads down and kept walking.

46

The director signalled the end of the broadcast, the feed was cut, the cameras backed away from World Leader (Not Pretend) Hieronymus Mangler, and the crew began clearing up.

'Here are the production figures for today, Dr Mangler,' said the president of the United States, shuffling forward on his knees.

'Everything is going according to plan,' cooed the president of Russia.

'What do you mean everything is going according to plan?'

'The world is as acquiescent as a light and fluffy soufflé,' said the chairman of China, sounding more dove-like than the president of Russia.

'When was a soufflé ever acquiescent? And how can you say things are going according to plan when they plainly aren't?'

The former leaders of the world, who were gathered round Mangler's throne in what was formerly Westminster Abbey, frozen in diverse postures of supplication, self abasement, and grovelling, hid this troubling news in the fog of chemicals in their brains and waited for elucidation, enlightenment, amnesia or, if it was their lucky day, a deliciously hefty kick.

'Germany!' barked Mangler, and whistled as you might a dog. The chancellor of Germany skittered forth on all fours.

'Drop!' said Mangler. 'No, not your trousers. You can put them back on. The thing in your mouth. Drop that.'

The chancellor wasn't aware that he was carrying anything in his mouth. He removed the obstructing tablet computer from his oral cavity, depositing it in Mangler's hand before embarking on a ten-fingered search of the same place looking for whatever might be in there that his master wanted.

Mangler consulted the tablet. 'In the last week alone, around the world, there have been 227 assaults on convoys of Mangler Überunderpants, 463 outlets or warehouses have been burned down, a further 700 have been sabotaged with 'Look at this' signs, and thousands of people have been forcibly debagged. There is a well-organised resistance out there and it's getting stronger.'

Mangler paused to scrutinise the reactions of the former world leaders, which ran the full gamut of 'Fab!' to 'Groovy!', which was entirely the wrong gamut to run.

Sigh.

'Lucky I came along and saved the world. Left to you lot, it would have gone to hell in the paper bag you couldn't fight your way out of and because you were unable to find the hand basket things usually go to hell in.

'Let's see if you can get it right this time. One more chance, OK?' Mangler barked again, this time to clear his throat. 'Now, the science reports. Oh, yes, the science reports. Scientists! Where are you? Yes, come forward. Sit in a circle around the throne. That's good. Thumbs in mouths please. Mouth, Werner, mouth, I said, not your — Your *own* mouth, Richard. Thank you.

'As of yesterday, nearly thirty per cent of the world's population was standing in front of open fridges wondering what they were looking for. Most of these people have been standing in front of the open fridge for a week or more, and the number is increasing every day. Another ten per cent are staring at a wall. A further five per cent are staring at a wall and singing to it. Another seven per cent of the world's population has decided it is a teapot and is perched on the kitchen counter next to the kettle. On top of this, fifteen per cent are spinning slowly in the street staring up at the sky for no particular reason. Productivity is falling. Nothing is getting done.

'No, it's not a good thing. I told you only one more chance — now pay attention. Without productivity no one will be able to pay their levy and I won't be stacking the loot in my own vault.

'What's worse, with all this dribble everywhere how can we have purity? When did you ever hear of purity out of dribble?

'The pants, dear scientists, are unstable. The DNA is wonky. What does this mean?'

'It means that today is Tuesday,' said NASA's chief rocket scientist.

'No. Somebody try again. Why is the DNA wonky?'

A Nobel-winning geneticist suffered a moment of lucidity, as a real thought slipped out of the deeper brain and emerged unscathed from the chemical chaos of the Überunderpants. 'It means that the tampered DNA is inherently unstable, a problem common to all modified organisms, great or small.'

'Guards! Have this man sent to Camp Sunny Happy Days, and make sure you bang his head accidentally on a few walls on the way!

'No, gentlemen, it does not mean the DNA is unstable. It means you have not done your jobs properly. You have not adequately implemented the very simple instructions I gave you. I provided you with the blueprints of the perfect DNA. All you had to do was make sure it was put into practice perfectly. Now go back and fix things so that they are the way I want them! And you need to do it now. No, not now; now's already too late. Do it yesterday — before breakfast yesterday, if not earlier. Have a very, very early start yesterday, oh yes. And while you are about it, increase the secretion rate of the compliance juice in all standard pants so we can get those imbeciles out of their refrigerators and working for me.'

'You ought to be able to get something for the teapots on eBay,' said the secretary general of the UN, to a general murmur of assent.

Mangler sighed homicidally.

47

Dr Edwin Pickles was back in his barn, eyes fixed on his microscope. In truth, it was difficult to concentrate with the pigs barging his legs and tugging at his trouser seat with their teeth. The effects of the Manglers had worn off, but the greedy porkers wanted more; it seemed to Pickles that they were addicted to the underwear.

Despite the pigs, the afternoon of researching while Hades had been debagging had been very fruitful indeed.

'Wriggling,' Pickles told the pigs. 'Definite wriggling. Haven't seen that before. You see,' he explained to the cows, 'I noticed while walking around London today, that people were wiggling their bottoms in a most peculiar way. The Manglers are supposed to cause pacification, not wiggles. Wiggles and pacification are two different things, take it from an old boffin. Most odd. Let's get a closer look, shall we?

'Oh, yes,' Pickles told the chickens on the worktop. 'Very odd things going on under the lens here. Let me snip a larger sample — ouch!' The chickens and the cows and even the pigs looked concerned.

Pickles was concerned too. 'You know. Odd as this sounds, I do believe these bloody underpants just bit me.'

48

Hades and Hilda laid low at the Tudor pile for a couple of days, letting the heat in the city cool off a bit.

'Pickles, is eccentricity a prerequisite for a career in science, are you trained in the trait at university, or is there some esoteric occupational hazard invisible to lay-people like me that turns you all a bit odd?'

'Depends which kind of eccentricity you mean,' said Pickles poking a pair of Mangler Überunderpants through the bars of a cage with a lecturer's telescoping pointer.

'The kind of eccentricity I mean is the kind that compels a rational mind such as your own to lock underpants individually in a variety of rabbit hutches, gerbil cages, aquaria and specimen jars, and then poke them with a pointy thing.'

Pickles sidled over to Hades, and waving the pointy thing in his face, said in his best stern voice, 'The buggers bit me.'

He showed his boss the tip of one finger, which Hades had to privately concede was looking a bit red and swollen if you were looking for redness and swelling.

'And you haven't personally been ingesting any of these pants,' Hades confirmed.

'That,' snapped Pickles, waving his pointer perilously close to Hades' proboscis, 'would just be silly. One needs a clear and functioning mind at this time of crisis. Scientific research doesn't mix with psychotropics.'

'You weren't experimenting on yourself, then.'

'Of course not. If I want to experiment, I have pigs.'

As intelligent as pigs are, they are not known for their linguistic skills. Nevertheless, the two attending at Pickles' ankles both looked up and apparently uttered an enthusiastic 'Yes, please!'

'Moreover, I've been observing samples of these buggers very closely. Something very odd is going on.'

'Yes, good doctor, we've noticed. Mangler has tranquillised the entire population of the world and completely taken over the place.'

'I mean even odder than that.'

'I like to think I have an open mind, and one that has been forcibly broadened by peculiar experiences up to and including meeting aliens, but I am having a hard time conceiving of anything odder than this, Dr Pickles,' said Hilda.

'Can you be more specific?' Persephone wanted to know.

'No,' said Pickles, 'Except to say the buggers tried to bite me.'

'Were you by any chance prodding them with your pointer in an effort to make them bite again?' Hilda's mind was made of more analytical stuff than her colleagues.

'I was. And what's more, apart from biting, they've been doing other weird stuff.'

'Other weird stuff? Like reading books or building matchstick models of the Taj Mahal?' Hades wanted to know.

'Like wiggling. Visibly wiggling. Especially under the microscope.'

Hilda and Persephone took Hades urgently by the arms.

'If there are any developments, send us a message. We all have our iGlasses on,' said Persephone.

'We're going back to London to hook up with the Commandos. We have to plan our next moves.'

'Right-ho,' said Pickles, turning back to the caged pants and brandishing his pointer in a threatening manner. 'Mind how you go. I fear things are about to take a turn for the worse. Back! Back, yer buggers!'

49

They approached Les Deux Fesses, the secret headquarters of the Commandos, just off Wardour Street in a roundabout, spiralling sort of way, circling their destination at a distance and getting closer and closer. It was a precaution, a chance to reconnoitre the streets for any excess of activity from the Bottom Inspectors or police, of which there was none.

The giant flat-screen televisions peered down at them from rooftops and out of shop fronts. They observed a new forest of CCTV cameras sprouting from just about every upright — lamppost, street sign — in the area. They kept their heads down and drifted toward the restaurant.

'Keep walking!' flashed Hilda through her glasses just as they were about to make the final turn into the alley off Wardour Street where Les Deux Fesses lurked below the streets.

'Say what?' Hades flashed back.

'The Commandos: Mangler's got them. The hideout's blown. Keep walking, slow and dopey. Let's hope the Bottom Inspectors haven't spotted us.'

'What do you suggest?' Persephone wanted to know.

'Let's get out of town as fast as we can without drawing attention to ourselves.'

'Bollocks to that,' Hades signalled. 'Let's see if the Coach and Horses is open. If this doesn't demand a pint, I don't know what does.'

50

The staff nor the customers at the Coach and Horses showed any reaction to Hilda propping up the bar with a pint while wearing a burqa. This was one advantage of an entirely zonked citizenry.

'But Hilda,' said Hades, sucking foam from his extravagant moustache, 'What do you mean Mangler's got the Commandos? There were no Bottom Inspectors or coppers to be seen.'

'The rough patch of wall in bad need of pointing, on the building on the corner where we normally make the turn off Wardour Street?'

Hades shrugged. 'A rough patch of wall in need of some work? That would be a first in London.'

'Would Jim ever be separated from his briar?'

'Not on your Nellie or anyone else's,' said Persephone with passion. 'He was born with that puffing thing in his gob.'

'Well,' said Hilda, 'it was wedged by its stem in a crack between bricks. Just sticking out as if the wall itself were having a smoke.'

'Oh,' said Persephone and Hades together and took deep draughts of their drinks.

'Jim must have wedged it there as a warning, perhaps while escaping or while being captured. We don't know.'

'Mangler's boys could well have been waiting for us at the Les Deux Fesses. We might have walked into a trap,' said Hades.

'I don't doubt it for a second,' said Persephone, already halfway through her pint of pink gin.

'Well spotted, Hilda. I think you just saved our bottoms.'

'Yes. Thank you.'

'We must assume,' Hilda continued, 'that the entire resistance network has been compromised. We can't risk trying to make contact again.'

'If they've busted the restaurant, do you think they've hit Pile House?'

'Well, none of the Commandos knew about it, so they couldn't be coerced into telling the Bottom Inspectors where it is. Nor have we had any alarm messages from Pickles or anyone at the house. You would think someone would have got a bleep out if they had been raided.'

'So. No more resistance. Where does that leave us?' asked Persephone, waving her empty glass at the bar staff.

'It leaves us in a pub with several hours before closing time,' said Hades.

51

Outside the Coach and Horses, the West End continued much as it ever did, oblivious to the drama and power struggles being worked out in the pub on the corner and, indeed, all around. Visitors and locals, business people, and seekers of the good time alike plied the streets wide-eyed at the lights, the spectacle, the huge TV screens beaming Mangler's face. Some were out looking for a good time, many were finding it in their underclothes. Couples walked hand in hand, not always out of romance but in case they absentmindedly drifted off in different directions.

One such happy couple strolled down Old Compton Street together.

'Gosh, Fiona, I feel great.'

'Double gosh, Sebastian, I feel great too.'

'I feel great because I'm with you, Fiona.'

'And I feel great because I'm with you, Sebastian.'

'And I feel great because my underpants are wriggling in a most unusual manner while I'm with you, Fiona.'

'And I feel great because you feel great because your underpants are wriggling in a most unusual manner while you're with me, Sebastian.'

'Aren't your underpants wriggling too — just a bit — Fiona?'

'Yes, Sebastian, they are wriggling, as a matter of fact, and more than a little bit.'

'Oh, Fiona!'

'Oh, Sebastian!'

There was a squishy, crunchy, splatty sound and Sebastian said 'Oh!' again before falling to the pavement in two distinct pieces and a fountain of blood.

'Oh!' said Fiona, maintaining the theme of the conversation.

With more wriggling, gnashing and splatting, most of the two distinct bits of Sebastian disappeared and became very indistinct bits.

'Oh!' exclaimed Fiona a little more shrilly and joined Sebastian on the ground in her own two distinct bits.

'Oh,' said Hilda at the window of the Coach and Horses. 'That's not good.' She zoomed her iGlasses on the puddles of blood and pink foam that had been Fiona and Sebastian, making sure she had a recording.

'What's that?' Hades and Persephone wanted to know.

'That's our cue to get moving back to Pile House, and there's no need to finish our drinks. I think I've just seen what Dr Pickles had almost figured out when we left.'

'Are you sure about the bit about not finishing our drinks? I was just getting on so well with this one.'

'Yes, Persephone, I'm afraid it's that serious.'

52

It was dark by the time Hades, Persephone and Hilda got back to Pile House.

It was a long and frustrating journey.

Hilda had taken the precaution weeks before of hiding a number of fast getaway vehicles around London for just such an eventuality. Fast, as it turned out, was an irrelevance. In order not to attract attention to themselves, they had to drive very slowly and with the opposite appearance of competence in order not to draw attention to themselves. Hilda had to wander, wobble, slow down, stop thoughtfully whenever she changed gear, stall, start again, take wrong turnings, vacillate indecisively at every junction, circle every roundabout 27 times, move on, come back, circle the same roundabout another 38 times, and all the while edging toward one of the very few locations where she could drive over or under the jammed M25 and escape into Berkshire.

Once out of the city limits she gambled on fewer CCTV cameras and drove like a normal person — though still avoiding motorways and A-roads as much as possible. Once in the vicinity of the hall, they took the same precautions they had in London when approaching the Les Deux Fesses, circling in the lanes and looking out for signs that the house might have been raided.

Nothing.

There was no moon and the countryside was lost in mystery. For anyone afraid of the dark, Oxfordshire was a grim place to be tonight.

Finally, they crunched up the long drive to the house itself.

Ishiguro stepped out to greet them, and Hades, Persephone and Hilda leapt from the car radiating instructions about needing to see Dr Pickles and how Hades and Persephone needed topping up, and it was this moment that Mangler's gun-toting, black-clad team of crack Bottom Inspectors had been waiting for. They dropped out of the night sky from silenced helicopters, emerged from the bushes and trees, screeched up the drive in a convoy, and splashed out of the ornamental carp pond in scuba gear.

The Goussets and associates were herded at gunpoint into their own living room and commanded to sit. Pickles was also fetched from the barn and prodded in on the end of a carbine. Once they were all sitting helplessly, Dr Hieronymus Mangler himself, immaculate in his black suit and immaculately black hair with its immaculate side parting and his immaculate insanity, strolled in.

'Well, well, well. Here you are at last.'

He smiled. Even his minions cringed.

'It seems that just a few of us can't get with the plan. No matter. We've got your ukulele-playing chums under lock and key and in Mangler's super duper correctional Überunderpants.'

Persephone was appalled. 'You put Alice and Jim, and the Commandos in underpants? Überunderpants?'

'After a lifetime of avoiding underthings of any kind?' thundered Hades.

One of Mangler's minions stepped forward with a tablet and showed a live stream of a cell at an unspecified location. Alice and Jim were sitting on the bare concrete floor, each with a pair of Überunderpants stuffed in their mouth. They were cross-eyed and drooling, and they wobbled and swayed even though they were sitting.

'You inhuman swine!' Persephone told Mangler.

'Please! I am a superhuman swine. Oh, yes! In only a few days, I'll have you out of my hair, we'll have the M25 cleared. There's nothing you can do now to stop me.'

'Oh, buggery bugger-bags!' said Hades.

53

Victoria was reclining on her branch of the underpants tree, back propped against the trunk, considering her options and a plan of action to take down Hieronymus Mangler. This is what she was always doing when she wasn't snooping around Mangler's Sacred Mountain facilities looking for something to sabotage, or scavenging for food.

She still had no cunning plan to thwart him, but where there was a will to mischief, there was a way.

Something stirred in the branches near her, and she became very alert and wary. Whatever had stirred in the branches it wasn't the breeze.

There was more movement.

'Victoria!' called Timmy. Victoria didn't answer because she had her eyes very much on the underclothes hanging in the tree.

'Victoria!'

Victoria kept very still indeed and let only her eyes do any work.

'Victoria! Erm, Victoria! Erm!'

Something lashed at her and snarled and barked at the same time. Victoria leapt to the ground in one movement, went low and stayed low. There was a loud thud as Timmy did the same.

'Victoria, something very erm just happened.'

'I know Timmy. It happened to me too.'

'I think the underpants just tried to bite my face off.'

'I do believe that's exactly just what happened to me.'

'Underpants shouldn't do that, should they.'

'They most certainly shouldn't, Timmy.'

'Something is very wrong, isn't it, Victoria.'

'Lots of things were already very wrong,' said Victoria. 'Now they are extremely, bafflingly, scarily wrong.'

'Why,' Timmy wanted to know,' would a pair of underpants want to bite my face off, and yours too?'

The tree shook and dozens of plain y-fronts and pretty pink panties lunged and snarled at the two of them, held to the thrashing tree and restrained by their stalks.

Victoria and Timmy rolled a bit further from the insane pants and collected their wits, which was a much quicker and easier task for Timmy, having fewer of them.

'Right, Timmy. I suspect this makes things rather urgent. Imagine if all the Mangler pants are behaving like this all over the world.'

'Why are they doing this?'

'I don't know. But it's another thing on my list of jobs to do, along with overthrowing the maniac who created these beasts.'

'What do we do?'

'Get back into the Sacred Mountain facilities and this time we stay there until we've done the job we came here to do. Luckily, we are both dressed for the task.'

Victoria happened to be dressed in her stolen uniform, the uniform that disguised her as one of Mangler's many minions: military style grey overalls, a naff peaked cap and big clumpy boots that might have been worn by Action Man in the 1970s.

Timmy was also wearing his stolen uniform.

'It hasn't yet grown to your size, then,' Victoria observed.

'No, Victoria. Seems not. Was it supposed to?'

'Not really. I was just hoping.'

They hadn't been able to steal a uniform Timmy's size. Mangler's men were simply not built like Greek gods. His overalls stretched to breaking in the pecs and biceps, sagged sack-like in the middle, and rode high above his wrists and ankles. Nor did they make him appear any less blue. In certain hipster neighbourhoods of east London, like Dalston or Shoreditch, his appearance might earn him a lot of very cool friends and invitations to the most exclusive parties. Anywhere else in the world he looked like a prat who didn't fit into his clothes.

'Sorry, you're too conspicuous. I'll try to steal something more your dimensions, Timmy. Meanwhile, you stay here and guard the insane pants. I'll come back for you if I can, but otherwise, I might just have to abandon you here.'

Timmy's face fell to the ground in a puddle of despair.

'I don't mean a word of it, Tims. I'm just teasing. We are a team, and if we need to suddenly leg it, we need to be together.'

Timmy's face leapt back onto the front of his head.

'But do try to stay in the shadows, eh?' Victoria winked and they were off into Mangler's Antarctic lair to continue their search for a means to defeat the mad dictator and restore honour to her family and free the rest of the world.

'Oh, wait a minute,' said Timmy, who leapt into the lower branches of the tree they had just escaped. Something like a dogfight broke out immediately, but Timmy dropped back to the ground and bounded back over to Victoria.

He held up two very drab, utilitarian, corporate, very buckety buckets.

'Always carry a bucket,' recited Timmy. 'When you have a bucket no one asks what you are doing. A wise man once said that.'

54

Mangler's secret base was expansive and sprawling and quite
Byzantine in its structure. Vast hangars and warehouses
stuffed with Mangler product were connected to underground
bunkers and all were connected by tunnels and walkways and
utility rooms and tea rooms on different levels so that the
complex burrowed into the ground like a vast ant nest.

The place was full of secrets and must one day yield them.
Each occasion Victoria set out, she had no idea what she was
searching for, but she was convinced she would know it when
she saw it. When she failed to find secrets, which happened
every day so far, she would forage. She collected food,
clothes, useful things and emergency backup buckets.

How many days had she lived like this? She had lost count
but surely something must break soon.

Information was not hard to find in the lair, just not the
information she could use. Every room, chamber, hallway,
closet was fitted with computer terminals and TVs, all on, all
tuned to and beaming Mangler's propaganda machines: Fox,
Sky, CNN, BBC … Manglers face and tree of life motif, and
a constant commentary on underpants production targets and
ideal lifestyle slots were the permanent backdrop to Victoria's
explorations. Each show was designed to convince the
population of the planet that they wanted nothing more or less
than a lifestyle that revolved around Mangler's underpants,
that everyone in the world was happy and blessed because of
the hard work of Dr Hieronymus Mangler himself, and so
every trip into Mangler's lair impressed on her the growing

urgency of the situation, as Mangler fastened his grip on the world.

As they did every day, Timmy and Victoria strolled unchallenged with their buckets into Mangler's Master Control Room for Everything. Dusting around the desks and monitors, Victoria tried to scrutinise the data and images on the screens. Timmy seemed to be polishing the air as such, waving his cloth around in wild gestures of conspicuous effort. Apparently nobody minded or cared. The alternative to not minding or caring would be to engage with seriously odd behaviour, and anyway, the tranks were keeping things nice and even for everyone. Why, you know, sweat it?

Victoria's own dusting became a mite aggressive. She thwacked and whipped the dust and generally beat it up, perhaps belying a little of her frustration at not being able to find any data she could use in her fight against Mangler. The pants must have a flaw, a weakness, a way to be disabled, an allergy, an antidote, and that information must be here somewhere.

'Is everything all right?' Victoria's thrashings had penetrated even the blissed-out consciousness of one of the guards.

'Oh, yes,' said Victoria rapidly composing herself to the look of the mildly zonked. 'I have a bucket.' She held up her bucket for the guard to examine.

'Your bucket seems to be in order,' said the guard, but a mote of thought ploughed a little furrow on the man's forehead. 'Are you —' he began, and was cut off by music, a jolly, upbeat-ish sort of music with an electric guitar refrain that could only be produced by a doddery old grandad who thought he was being wild and with it, and an electronic bass line that sounded like a quaint and old-fashioned coffee grinder.

It was Bottom Gear, the favourite TV show of all Mangler's minions.

'Yay!' cheered the minions and abandoned their posts to cluster at the TVs.

'Oh, crap,' said Victoria as the presenters came on to their stage, which was cleverly contrived at a height that they appeared to be walking on the heads of the studio audience.

Victoria rallied herself again to seize this moment of distraction to have a more careful search for whatever it was that would prove their salvation, but the televisual antics claimed her appalled attention.

55

'Brum-brum! Brum-brum! Hello. That's me pretending to drive a car,' says Jeremy Clarkbloke, very importantly and making car driving gestures.

'Vroom-vroom! That's me pretending to drive a car too,' says Richard Hamster like a squirt of fresh diarrhoea.

'Neeeeeeeeeeeeeeeeowwwwwwwwwwwwwww! And that's me pretending to drive a car faster than Hamster.'

'Gosh that was fast, Jeremy. I wish I could be like you.'

'Yes, it's jolly exciting being me. Being me is almost as exciting as pretending to drive a car.'

'I must say, it's pretty exciting wanting to be like you!'

'Shut up, Hamster. So, welcome to another fast-moving edition of Bottom Gear. Our special guest presenter this week to help present this fast-moving edition of Bottom Gear is the extremely funny comedian, Jimmy Voiture!'

'Yay!' say the audience.

'Hello,' says Jimmy Voiture from inside a suit that looks like it is made of carbon fibres and costs enough money to cause a normal person to vomit.

'Yay!' say the audience.

'He's so funny, isn't he!' squeaks Hamster.

'Shut up, Hamster!' say Jeremy and Jimmy together.

'Jimmy and I are very excited about chumming up and presenting this edition of Bottom Gear because Jimmy and I are complete twats, aren't we Jimmy.'

'Absolute twats, Jeremy. Absolute chummy twats.'

'Am I a twat too?' asks Richard.

'No! Fuck off, Hamster!'

'Oh, please can I be a twat?'

'No,' says Jimmy. 'You're a clinker. A specky little clinker.'

'Yeah, a specky little, clingy-onny clinker,' confirms Jeremy.

'And your mother is too. I saw her once, so I know.'

'Yay!' say the audience.

'What a cracker of a show we have for you,' says Jeremy. 'Not for you, Mr Clinker-Hamster. For the audience.'

'Yeah,' says Jimmy, 'for the audience, not for you.'

'Yay!' say the audience.

'Yes, here we are in Bottom Gear, the show about stuff for bottoms: underpants, underthings, foundation wear, undies, kecks, bloomers, knickers, skimpies, panties, pants …'

'Shorts, Y-fronts, thongs, French knickers …'

'And we're going to have lots of gratuitous jokes about foreigners, poor people, welfare scroungers, women, Mexicans, Asian people, black people —'

'Poor foreigners —'

'— anyone less English, white or middle class, privileged, affluent or self-important than us, in fact.'

'Hey, that reminds me, Jeremy,' says Jimmy. 'Why did the disabled person cross the road?'

'I don't know, Jimmy, why did the disabled person cross the road?'

'To get away from me. I was driving very fast on the pavement.'

'Yay!' say the audience.

'And when he was crossing the road, I runned him over anyway,' says Richard hopping from one foot to the other.

'No, you didn't,' says Jimmy. 'I was there driving on the pavement, so I knows. So there.'

'Yeah, shut up, Hamster,' says Jeremy.

'Yay!' say the audience.

'So, tonight, we've got some fantastic underpants for you.'

'Yes,' says Richard. 'We'll be nicking pennies from beggars, and finding out whose underpants will help run away the fastest.'

'Which underpants will add heft to your kick when you're putting the boot into the homeless? We'll be road testing on the some of the poorest streets in the poorest parts of the country.'

'When you're driving your brand new, top of the line Jaguar, which pants will help you feel most smug?'

'But when it comes to underpants, there really is only one pair. Isn't that right, Jimmy? Isn't that right, Hamster?'

'That's right, Jeremy,' says Richard.

'That's right, Jeremy,' says Jimmy. 'And the only pair to have, let's face it, are Mangler's super duper Überunderpants.'

'That's right, Jimmy. They really seem to do everything,' Richard agrees.

'And they really have everything, don't they.'

'Oh, yes, indeed. They have colour, and they have glamour —'

'But it's not just about good looks.'

'No, not at all, because these babes actually have holes in you can put your legs through.'

'And the male version has the extra hole for putting the extra thing through.'

'A bit redundant in your case, though Richard,' japes Jeremy.

'Yay!' says the audience.

'And that's not all. In addition to having holes that will accommodate your limbs and extremities, they have elastic!'

'Elastic?'

'Yes! At the waste and at the legs!'

'Yay!' say the audience.

'They are made of the latest living Mangler fibres that are actually — wait for it — grown on trees! That surprised you didn't it!'

'But we don't like trees, do we? They're mostly lesbians and scroungers and they get in the way of our cars when we drive very fast.'

'Shut up, Hamster! We're getting paid to like trees today.'

'Yes, indeed, these Mangler pants can go from nought to 120 in six days or less, with only the help of a very fast car. Isn't that right, Jimmy.'

'That's right, Jeremy, and unlike other brands, such as Hades Omnipants, to pick a name at random —'

'Yay!' say the audience.

'They are completely safe!'

'That's — oh!' said Richard.

'Don't say "oh!" Hamster! Only pinko lesbian black people say "oh!" — Oh!'

With a crunchy, squelchy, splatty sound, Richard fell to the stage in two pieces.

'Yay!' say the audience.

'Pull yourself together, man!' says Jeremy a nanosecond before he too drops in pieces to the stage, blood fountaining all over the front row of the audience, which say 'Yay!'

'Oh,' says the director in the director's booth. 'And this is going out live all over the world.'

'Oooh, what a c —' And down goes Jimmy. Seconds later, the three chummy presenters are a big, unstill puddle of blood and lumps of chewed offal.

'Yay!' say the audience.

56

Victoria dragged Timmy out of the command centre, and when eventually she had stopped laughing, she exclaimed, 'This is serious, Timmy! The Überunderpants are turning on their wearers. We've got to do something and do it now, or as close to now as we can possibly manage. Poor Jeremy!' and she dissolved in laughter again.

'But what are we going to do?' asked Timmy, quite reasonably, there still, after all these days, being no obvious course of action.

'I'm fed up with this.' Victoria took a firm hold of her bucket and led Timmy by the arm to the towering glass atrium which was hub and centre of Mangler's HQ. Pointing in a direction at random, she announced, 'I am going to march purposefully down this corridor, and open a door at random, and inside that room I'm going to find the solution to our problems.'

'Goodness gracious, Victoria! That does sound like a plan. Do you think it'll work?'

'Of course it won't. I'm clutching at straws here. But clutching is all I have,' and Victoria set off with martial purpose, the ever-perplexed but forever trusting, Timmy following.

The corridor, like every other here was long and corporately bland, decorated in off-white, off-grey, off-brown. The corporately regular doors were marked with cryptic names or cryptic numbers. Nothing suggested a clue, an idea or even hope.

The hallway was curved following the elegant sweep of the outer wall. They could, reasoned Victoria, end up where they started, or this could just drive her round the bend.

'Are we there yet?' asked Timmy.

Victoria sighed. 'No,' she said without breaking her stride. 'Ask me again in a second.'

Timmy looked at his watch. On they went.

They were now running out of corridor. The hall terminated ahead in big fire doors and huge floor to ceiling windows let in the insipid Antarctic light and views of the icy wastes outside.

'Are we there yet?' asked Timmy. 'You said to ask you again in a second.'

'In that case, we're there,' decided Victoria. She stopped.

They were standing outside a door. It looked the same as all the other doors, had an unhelpful label in code, and was guarded by a fearsome security panel on the wall beside it. The security panel had a keypad for code numbers, a card swipe for swipe cards, a retina scan for retinas, a finger print checker for fingerprints and bells for alarums. This suggested to Victoria that her chosen door was locked, which it turned out to be. So near and yet so far, she thought.

She rapped on a card scanner on the security panel. 'Oi!' she declared and held up her bucket to it.

The door opened.

'There you go,' she told Timmy and in they went.

'Oh, my gosh gracious!' said Timmy. 'I think you may have found the bingo.'

The room was a laboratory and there was no one in it. You could tell the room was a laboratory by all the gadgets, pipes, tubes, pipettes, bubbling things, and the whathaveyous all over the place. You could tell it was an important laboratory because it was big, and assertive in three dimensions. At the far end was some kind of observation area, separated from the laboratory proper by a big window that was apparently made of bulletproof glass or something similarly not to be argued with. Inside the observation area, were some vicious looking plants. Plants are not normally vicious in appearance, but these left the observer in no doubt that if they weren't contained by that glass they'd be out and growling and eating things that didn't want to be eaten, like tables, chairs, innocent bystanders, you. Their big leaves hung in a thick tousled coat, the shadows behind the leaves seemed to snarl at you. Victoria was sure one was standing akimbo. They rustled and shifted and craned their stalks as Victoria and Timmy crept into the room and when the two humans put their noses close to the window for a better look, the plants lashed out, thudding on the glass.

'Gulp,' said Timmy.

'I'll go along with that,' said Victoria.

'So what are these things?'

'See the colours and the patterns in the leaves, Timmy? This one is a sort of malevolent polka dot pattern. This one, dangerous-looking hoops.'

'This one seems to have a quaint floral print, which ought to be OK for a plant but seems odd for some reason.'

'And this one's a demented kind of paisley.'

'And this one might have pink frills, though they might be fangless gums.'

'No, Tims, those are pretty frills, all right.'

'The one at the back has Hello Kitty designs all over it. What is this?'

'The terrifying truth is, Timmy, that these are underpants.'

'Underpants?'

'Yes, mutated underpants. Underpants mutated beyond recognition. I'll bet they are Mangler Überunderpants that have reached the far end of their metamorphic process. What you are looking at, Timmy, is the future of humanity's underwear if we don't do something quick.'

One of the plants with odd black-tipped foliage swept diagonally across it and covered in Mangler Tree of Life logos, gave a stiff, open-leaved salute.

'The answer to our problems is in this room somewhere. But what does it look like?'

Timmy held up a pair of secateurs. The plants thrashed at the window.

After a couple of thoughtful circuits of the lab, Victoria settled on what appeared to be the main computer terminal and clicked through folders and directories at random.

'Bugger. It would help if I knew what any of this meant,' she muttered.

'You don't know what this means?' asked Timmy sounding a little awestruck.

'Funnily enough, no I don't, Timmy. I think I must have skipped class the day we did advanced genetic engineering at fashion design school.'

'Oh. That's not very convenient.'

'Ah ha!'

'What? Have you found something?'

'I most certainly have. A whole stash of downloaded funny cat videos.'

'Oh. That's good. But why's that good?'

'Because if it turns out that we've imagined this whole catastrophe because of ingesting, say, a bit of gone-off pork pie with hallucinogenic properties, and that there is no crisis threatening the existence of humanity after all, we'll have something with which to while away our suddenly empty hours.'

'Oh.'

57

'Can I help you with something?'

Victoria screamed. 'Oh, Jesus Christ Almighty! You can help put me back in my skin because I just jumped out of it.'

The ugly man in the green-stained white lab, the one in the wheelchair, the one with the mad upright hair and the insane sticking-out eyes shrugged. 'OK. Head first or the right way up?'

The odd man, the beautiful woman and the other odd man, the blue one, regarded each other.

Victoria held up her bucket. 'Cleaner.'

'Cleaner than what?' asked the man with the hair.

'Cleaner than mine,' shouted Timmy in a panicky sort of way and holding up his own bucket.

'Nice try, Timmy,' said Victoria out the corner of her mouth.

The man twizzled the lever on his wheelchair and whirred round the workstations to get closer to Victoria and Timmy.

'I assume you've sneaked in here to try to find a way of stopping the Mangler Überunderpants before they take over the world and eat everyone in it. Are the buckets part of your plan to save the world? I must say, I hadn't thought of buckets. I'd thought of most other things. I'd thought of salt water, secateurs, plagues of aphids, urinating dogs, scythes, lawnmowers, thermobaric bombs and thermonuclear devices, but buckets hadn't occurred to me. I wonder if they should have. Do they help?'

'We're not sure yet. We're carrying them as a sort of matter of principle.'

'Principles! Ha! I remember those. Possibly.' He frowned and shook his head in the way of someone reminded of the folly of youth. He wore black leather gloves and the left hand crept about his chest and midriff as if it had a mind of its own, and looking like an especially large and scary spider. 'Rum do, these Überunderpants. I told Doctor Mangler, not yet, they're not ready, but he wouldn't listen. No, not at all. Now look at the mess. They're all over the place, eating the very people the good doctor is supposed to be subjugating, but he won't accept it, you know. No, not a bit. Won't accept it at all.'

Victoria had believed, as far as she had permitted herself to think about it, that discovery would have meant alarms, klaxons, sirens, bells, dozens of heavily armed thugs, a brutal seizing and probably a lot of pain and inconvenience. She didn't expect a benign chat with an ugly old dwarf who had a wandering hand. 'May I ask who we have the honour of speaking to?'

'What?' said the man. 'I thought there was only us three here. Has someone else come in?'

'No, there is just the three of us. I am asking about you.'

'Oh, I see. You said "honour" and confused me. People don't normally consider it an honour to talk to me. But I suppose you were being ironic.' The left hand leapt into the air at Victoria and Timmy and the man caught it with his right, over which he seemed to have more control. 'Anyway, you are in my laboratory, shouldn't I be interrogating you?

'That's a good point,' said Timmy. 'I hadn't thought of that. Go ahead, please.'

Victoria no longer had a clear idea of what was going on here. She decided to take a risk.

'I'm Victoria Gousset, daughter of Sir Hades Gousset, and this is my personal assistant, Timothy Adonis. You've already met our buckets.'

The left hand twitched horribly. The right hand held it down on the arm of the wheelchair. 'Ah. Of course. I recognise you from the fashion shows in Paris and Milan, and from the fashion magazines and the wanted posters. Yes, my original surmise was correct. You are indeed here to save the world. No doubt you were rummaging in here in the hope of finding a fatal flaw in the Überunderpants.'

'Well,' said Victoria. 'I've explained who I am.'

'Oh, yes, I'm Merkwürdigliebe. Doctor Merkwürdigliebe.' The hand shot up in the air in a straight-armed salute. Again he had to tame it back to his side while speaking. 'You can call me Merkwürdigliebe. Or Doctor. Or Doctor Merkwürdigliebe. Don't call me Al.'

'Why not?'

'It's not my name. Anyway, I am Doctor Mangler's chief technician.' He announced this as if it cleared up a lot of things, which it didn't at all. The left hand scuttled playfully to his right shoulder and sat there. 'I've been helping Doctor Mangler with the quite amazing science of his underpants trees. The big breakthroughs were all his. The insights, the genius connections, the inspired innovations. But I've been with him all the way, helping to make his fantastic idea a reality.' Yet again the arm leapt into a salute and was wrestled back down.

'Fantastic idea? With respect Doctor, I wonder whether homicidal, people-eating underpants, er, under*plants*, is a fantastic idea.'

'Oh, no, that wasn't the idea at all, Ms Gousset. Of course not. Where's the profit if your product eats all the customers?'

'Down the pan, presumably.'

'Quite so. No, the original plan was the nice pants. The pants that made you feel good. The perfect pants that would help create a perfect world full of perfect people. Pants that would bring stability and unity through order and uniformity. Order is a beautiful thing.' He sighed. 'One world, one pair of pants, one leader. Elegant! Sublime!' The left hand thought so too and struggled to get airborne.

Victoria couldn't ask what went wrong because there wasn't anything right with the original vision. 'So, how about the, er … ?' Victoria gestured over her shoulder at the plants.

One of whom, apparently bothered by the absence of meat was nibbling speculatively on a neighbour.

'Too soon. Too soon, you see, Ms Gousset. All genetically modified organisms are by their nature unstable. I tried to tell Doctor Mangler, but he was convinced the technology was ready. He wouldn't wait. What could go wrong, he wanted to know. It's just trees and underpants. The technology was a perfection of scruffy nature. He was convinced of that. So we didn't stop to find about the long-term affects of these organisms in the environment. Now we are finding out.'

'But Doctor Mangler has all the resources of the world at his disposal. Surely he could control these things. Stop shipping them out. Set the forces of law and order on them. Tell people not to wear them, get rid of them. I dunno, spray weed killer on them or something.'

'Oh, he could. But he won't.' The hand had crawled into an armpit where it was apparently washing itself.

'Why ever not?'

'Because this is his life's work, for one thing. More than his life's work, this is his brainchild. This is an extension of him.' Boing into the air went the hand. 'How can he admit his extensions have mutated hideously and started eating people? No, he is in deep denial. He is in a profound state of delusion. This isn't happening. If he even acknowledges that his creation is destroying the world, he will claim it is sabotage. Or that the plants were created by someone else to discredit him, that his plants are a, are a … plant. No, he can only see what he imagines to be perfection. If we try to do anything, he may even try to defend his little monsters. There would be a bloodbath.'

'Doctor, you mentioned a fatal flaw. You said when you found us you thought we were looking for a fatal flaw. Do they have a fatal flaw?'

Merkwürdigliebe shrieked and his rogue hand flung itself at the window containing the plants. 'Fatal flaw? You're bloody looking at it! They've mutated into flesh-eating monsters. How can that not be a definition of fatal flaw?'

Merkwürdigliebe wheeled over to a cabinet and clattered inside. He held up for their inspection: 'A perfectly normal can of cat food. The can is sealed. OK?'

'OK,' said Victoria.

When Merkwürdigliebe tossed the unopened can, through an access hatch and into the observation space, the plants moved with a frightening speed for vegetables — it would have been a frightening speed for a velociraptor but these things were the same phylum as cabbages. They were an insane pack all throwing themselves on the tin and snarling horribly. Shredded leaves made a blizzard, severed branches span through the air. A spray of vile green splattered the inside of the window and then with a dull clang, a ripped and mutilated ex-can of cat food hit the window and dropped back into the seething mass of foliage.'

Merkwürdigliebe stood with his arms outstretched in triumph. 'There. I give you one fatal flaw: extreme and violent mutation.'

Timmy clapped.

'I meant the other kind of fatal flaw, the kind that is a weakness that we can exploit to put an end to these horrors,' said Victoria.

'Oh, that kind of fatal flaw. I feel a bit silly about the theatrics now. In truth, Dr Mangler's strategy is to stabilise the things not defeat them. I'm attempting to correct them so they do what they are supposed to do. We are so close to success with this one, that it really sticks in my bum that it hasn't worked properly.'

'Isn't there time for correcting the DNA later and trying again? Don't we need to stop these creatures from eating people now, clean up the bad ones to make way for the good ones?'

'I suppose,' said Merkwürdigliebe in the tone of voice you would use when someone suggested you put a gazebo in the garden but you weren't too enthusiastic yourself, not really seeing the point of it.

'Weed killer,' asked Victoria. 'Can we spray the buggers with something to make them go away?'

'Tried it. They like it. They get high on it and then get belligerently drunk. Meanwhile, attempting to spray them we'd probably kill every green thing on this planet except them. There would be no salad for generations.'

'Predators, parasites. How about slugs?'

'You know what I'm going to say, don't you.'

'The plants ate the slugs.'

'Yes. And the rhinoceros.'

'The rhinoceros?'

'Yes, a rhino will eat anything vegetable. Anything. Shrubs, small trees, branches, leaves, bark, tubers, bulbs — anything. They also weigh over a ton, have their own armour plating, horns that could eviscerate a tank, and they are extremely aggressive. Can you think of a better herbivore to match with these insane plant things? Well, they ate the rhino. Every bit of it. Took about a minute. Horrible. Truly horrible.'

'Music,' said Timmy. 'My mother always sings to her flowers. She says it calms them down.'

'Pacification,' suggested Victoria. 'It might make them less aggressive.'

'Ah! Music! We did try a bit of musical experimentation.'

'And?'

'And this.' At the first notes of the sublime Bach cantata Merkwürdigliebe streamed into the observation room the plants struck up a cacophony of raspberries, farts, catcalls, and there was much gesturing at the speakers with what appeared to be the vegetable equivalent of a two-fingered salute.

'Not much pacification there,' Victoria conceded.

'So, out of curiosity we tried this.' The Sex Pistols' Anarchy in the UK was much more to the taste of the plant things, who immediately began pogoing and slamming and spitting at the speakers.

'A little more,' said the doctor. 'Something happy.' Pharrell provoked a shower of what appeared to be plant excrement.

'So much for music then.'

'Could we forget to water them?' offered Timmy. 'You know, neglect them? We could go for a couple of weeks in Ibiza. That usually does for my plants.'

Victoria approached Merkwürdigliebe. 'Is there really nothing else?' She leaned in close in to the scientist — at great risk to herself because she had no idea what the hand might be up to or whether the cratering on his skin was contagious, and if it was, at what range.

Merkwürdigliebe tapped and clicked at his computer terminal without enthusiasm.

'Well. There is this one thing. But it's only the germ of an idea. I don't see how it could really work.' On the monitor, a 3D molecular diagram rotated. It was a very spiky collection of molecules, very barbed and vicious.

'Itching powder,' said Victoria. 'Could it really … Haven't I said all along that we have to get people out of their pants? Then without the tranquilliser addling them, they can at least look after themselves.'

Merkwürdigliebe was sceptical. 'But you've seen what these plants can do. It's out of the frying pan and into the kettle.'

'It's better than what we have now. And think, doctor, think! This was one of the basic concepts we learned at fashion design school. One of the most absolute antitheses on this planet is …'

'Underpants and itching powder,' finished the doctor. He waggled his head, shrugged his shoulders and waved his arms about. 'Like fire and ice, like chalk and cheese, like matter and antimatter. Ach! I am not convinced. Would it do any good? How would we apply it? Are you going to sneak up to each and every person in the world and slip this in their underwear? What then?'

'Trust me, doctor. I have a feeling about this.'

'And if it works, everyone in the world is going to have a feeling in their bottom about this.'

'Can you manufacture this stuff here at Mangler's base? Lots of it?'

'Can I? I already have. Just as a precaution, but in the end I couldn't see the point. I'm a scientist not a prankster.' The hand hopped around in its own private ecstasy.

'That is fantastic! Doctor, are the computers in this room linked to Mangler's intranet?'

'Of course.'

'So we could hack the manifest of the airship and change the cargo.'

Merkwürdigliebe shrugged. 'But now, you have awakened a conflict within me, Ms Gousset,' he said as the hand leapt to his throat as if to strangle him. 'You are asking me to act against the man who provides my research funds. No greater loyalty is there in the universe than a scientist has for his source of funding.' The hand jumped into what appeared to be a kung fu fighting pose. 'None. Mothers and children? A mother will renounce her children many times over before a scientist does anything against the writer of his cheques. So, it has been an academically interesting conversation but I must now press this little red alarm button and summon a commotion of thugs. And then I must destroy our vast stocks of itching powder before you find another way to exploit them. Ein Volk, ein Reich, ein Funder!' Another stiff-armed salute.

'No!' shouted Victoria. 'If there is no world there will be nothing to fund! You are throwing away your future!'

'If there's no future, then it's not my problem!' Mangler stabbed the alarm button. Sirens screamed and whooped, red lights flashed and whirled, the door banged open, a large number of armed men in black uniforms stormed in, and Victoria and Timmy dived under the nearest desks.

Merkwürdigliebe was suddenly in front of the big window of the observation room in which the Überunderpants plants were taking a renewed interest in the outside world.

The scientist waved his arms and bounced up and down in his wheelchair. 'Don't whatever you do shoot the glass! Don't shoot the glass!'

'Yoo hoo!' called Timmy bouncing up and down right next to Merkwürdigliebe and waving his arms, very much in front of the glass. 'Shoot the glass! Shoot the glass!'

The body language of the big plants seemed to be saying,'Hello? This looks interesting'.

'Don't fire!' yelled Merkwürdigliebe.

'Do fire!' yelled Timmy.

Like dogs with a steak they've been told to absolutely leave on the table and not touch, the base nature of the men with the guns overcame what they knew they shouldn't do and they fired. The glass of the observation room exploded inward. Merkwürdigliebe's screams were swallowed in the tsunami of green that engulfed him, and a bloody and chewed wheelchair span emptily in the air.

The gunmen were confused. One moment they were fighting intruders, then the doctor was being eaten by pot plants and … yes! The intruders! Where were they?

The pants plants were already on the move rushing the security team who opened fire without great effect on the targets but with dramatic and spectacular destruction in the office and as lab equipment and computer bits and files exploded willy-nilly.

The top of the desk under which Victoria was sheltering ripped off in a hail of splinters. On one side the Überunderpants, on the other, the mad dogs of base security and in between a storm of bullets. Two strong arms surrounded her and then, as if everything weren't sufficiently disorienting already, she was on the ceiling, along which Timmy, keeping a secure and reassuring hold on her, scampered over the heads of the security team who were at that moment all dying in a futile struggle with the veg.

And then they were out of the lab, the door slamming behind them and Timmy was placing Victoria upright and safe on the floor.

'How did you do that Timmy?'

'Funny thing, when we were searching the lab, I opened this big plastic box that was like a fish tank with no water and got bitten by a spider. I've been feeling even more fantastic than usual since and I have this great urge to go climbing walls and chase flies. Fab really. I wonder what it can mean.'

'Don't question it, Timmy. Go with the flow. Talking of which —' The sirens and alarms were still in full cry. There was a mighty thudding on the lab door, under which a rich mix of dark red and dark green liquids oozed. 'We need to make some distance between ourselves and this spot and we need to tweak our plan a little. Do you still have your bucket? So do I. Let's go.'

'We have a plan?'

'We most certainly did until that fool Merkwürdigliebe went all corporate on us, but not all is lost.'

The corridors were full of people running in all directions and getting muddled up with more teams of armed security trying to go to the aid of their late colleagues in Merkwürdigliebe's lab.

'If those plants get out of that lab, as I suspect they will, this whole place is for the mulcher.'

58

The chaos put Victoria's plan back on track for her. As workers fled in panic they left office and lab doors open wherever they went. Victoria found the privacy she wanted in an empty office, and at the computer terminal calmly located the manifest for the airship and the base's inventories, did some switching about.

'Timmy. You've ridden on the outside of an airship. Have you ever fancied a ride on the inside? May as well. Complete the set.'

Timmy didn't know what to say. He fancied Victoria, not the airship.

Victoria stopped in the hallway so abruptly Timmy collided with her.

'Oh, yes. There's something I've been wanting to do for days, and now is the perfect time.'

The corporately anonymous door she stood in front of was marked simply 'Thermostat Room. Absolutely no admittance whatsoever at all, even a little bit, under any circumstances of any kind.'

'That's us,' declared Victoria and marched in. So emphatic was the notice on the door, security had seen no need for a lock.

The thermostat control centre was white and empty but for one pedestal right in the middle, on which was mounted a dial thermostat. Victoria wound it back to 'Off', beat it with her bucket until the dial and stand were a pile of splinters and broken wires, and legged it giggling.

Outside, the idyllic blue skies over Mangler's pants orchard dwindled to steely grey and the first ice crystals began forming on the trees.

59

The adamantine airship was moored where it was supposed to be, and with impeccable timing one of the rampaging plants broke into the cargo processing area of the hangar, scattering stevedores and crew in all directions and allowing Victoria and Timmy to sprint across the tarmac and get aboard.

'This is good, Victoria. Where shall we stow away?'

'Stow away? Whatever for? We're going to hijack this thing.'

'Oh. That took me by surprise a bit, Victoria, but whatever you say. How do people go about hijacking airships?'

'Dunno. I haven't tried before. Let's find out.'

When they tried it, it turned out that hijacking an airship involved running insanely through the salons and crew areas yelling 'They're coming! They're coming! Run for your lives!' which the already spooked crew were only too glad to do. On the bridge, Timmy and Victoria found the captain was made of sterner stuff.

'A captain goes down with his ship,' he told Victoria and Timmy stoically.

'But the ship is down. You're berthed in the hangar.'

'Jolly good! Tick "going down with the ship" off the list of things to do.' The captain scarpered.

'Jolly good!' echoed Victoria. 'Now all I have to do is manoeuvre us out of the hangar and fly around the world at great speed. How's that?'

'Easy peasy pudding and pie,' said Timmy, not really sure what he was agreeing to. 'You really are awfully clever to be able to fly one of these things. I can barely fly a bicycle.'

'Well, to be honest, I haven't ever flown one of these things.'

'I see,' said Timmy.

'But I was once in an alien spaceship and I did see aliens flying that. How different can it be?'

'Ah. Aliens taught you how to fly.'

'No. Not quite. I just saw them doing it. They pushed levers, except when they pulled them. I notice they did quite a lot of tapping things on touch sensitive screens and occasionally they put their hands inside holograms and wibbled them about a bit.'

'Hollow whats?'

'I don't actually see any holograms on this ship. I may have to improvise. Infer. Guess.'

'I was never very good at guessing. I could never understand what the correct answer was supposed to be.'

'No. Well. I need you to try to find the controls that will close all the doors, seal and pressurise the cabin areas, and then the controls that will cast off the mooring lines. Can you do that?'

'Yes, of course. Except I have no idea what you are talking about.'

'Excellent. We are all on the same page, then. You know, Timmy, I have an even better idea. Why don't you stand guard and stop anyone who tries to stop us.'

Timmy's face lit up like an especially cheerful dawn on a particularly glorious day in paradise. 'I can do that.' He adopted a guarding posture by the door.

Most of the controls were labelled, which Victoria thought was useful, but knowing what they were called didn't necessarily help her understand the names or tell her what to do with them.

When the mooring ropes disconnected themselves and the doors sealed, the crew on the ground realised that something very unauthorised was going on and ran around trying to catch the loose tethers as if they could pull the giant craft back to the ground themselves.

An enterprising bod in a control tower somewhere also realised the airship was doing something it didn't ought to be doing and hit the button to close the vast hangar doors. At about the same moment, Victoria found the throttle on the aircraft and leaned on it. The enterprise of the bod who was closing the doors stopped short of actually considering what might happen if this giant vessel that was full of very volatile hydrogen crashed into the doors. Nor did his enterprise stop to acknowledge that the adamantine airship was made of, well, adamantine, the most unreasonably tough substance known to humanity, and as a consequence had not considered what would happen if ship and doors met at speed. Embarrassing clang? A massive hydrogen explosion that would demolish the whole hangar and bestow fiery death on everyone therein? Or what?

Each of the hangar doors was about half the size of a football pitch, but the airship took them with it. The doors flapped inanely like broken insect wings on the ship's back before crashing to earth.

Victoria powered the airship up and away from Mangler's secret base. Behind them, the continent of Antarctica dwindled to a map of itself.

'We'll be back soon, Timmy,' said Victoria as she twirled the ship's wheel, setting a course for Britain. 'We'll come back to dismantle Mangler's idiotic base and restore Antarctica to its pristine beauty.'

'Okey-dokey,' said Timmy, still in a guarding posture at the door to the bridge.

'But first,' Victoria told him, 'we're just going to nip around a bit, rescue everyone in the world from certain death, defeat Hieronymus Mangler, restore the good name of my father and my family, and put to right everything that's been put wrong.'

'Righty ho,' said Timmy.

60

'I don't know how you managed to infest the world with these foul perversions of nature but you're going to pay for it.'

Mangler was apparently of the opinion that generously feeding his enemies their own fine food and fine wine while threatening them with pain and death and gloating about his victory was very sophisticated because this was what he was doing, and he was looking very smug and self-satisfied, and was affecting an air of urbanity.

Hilda made faces at him from inside her burqa.

Mangler was sat at the head of Hades' big dining room table, on which he had commanded the lavish spread, and twirled a glass of a famously expensive and celebrated single malt in his fingers. He didn't drink anything other than single malt. He was into purity.

Hades, Persephone, Hilda, Pickles and their retinue were also sat at the table, each with an armed guard watching over them. They were served by Ishiguro and his staff, whose actions were also directed and overseen by guns.

'Get something inside you. Keep your strength up. I suggest we're all going to need it,' Hades told his wife and colleagues, heaping more cold meat on his plate. None of them lifted a fork and remained in obstinate silence. Despite the eating, Hades watched Mangler intently, scrutinising him; apparently attempting to dismantle him with his eyes. An individual less insane than Mangler would have felt very uncomfortable or intimidated.

'Your attempts to undermine me are quite pathetic, Sir Hades, I assure you, and quite futile.'

Hades stuffed most of a whole gherkin into his mouth and munched thoughtfully.

Mangler took another swig of Hades' fine scotch. 'The people are not stupid, Sir Hades. They can see through you and your attempts to discredit me, to deny them the utopia that is rightfully theirs.'

'The people are not stupid, they are stupefied,' said Persephone. 'They don't know what's going on. They don't know what day of the week it is. Those that are still alive.'

'There you are wrong. The people are serene.'

Hades crunched loudly on a radish but didn't speak.

'The deaths are all your responsibility. I can clearly see you have been tampering and plotting. There's no point in denying it. You have a whole laboratory set up in the barn. I have seen Dr Pickles' equipment myself. You have been trying to destabilise the fabrics and then make it look like the Überunderpants are malfunctioning.'

'Pah!' said Persephone. 'You're living in cuckoo land.'

Mangler held out his glass for a refill from Ishiguro.

'I am living in Buckingham Palace since the Queen abdicated in my favour. You don't get Queens throwing their thrones at you if you are hanging about with cuckoos.'

Now Hilda spoke up. 'Dr Mangler, we have seen it with our own eyes. The Überunderpants are mutating dangerously. They are eating their wearers. You have to take action now. Millions of lives are at risk.'

'You see,' added Pickles, 'we have no idea yet whether all the pants are going to complete this mutation into the dangerous state, or just some of them. We have no idea what the mutated pants will do, whether they will mutate further, whether they will become stable — or the opposite, become yet more unstable. We just don't know. We are only sure that there is considerable danger and it's happening now.'

'My underpants,' exclaimed Mangler 'are beautiful. No one accuses my underpants of being dangerous. My underpants are simply conducting their task — ordained by destiny of cleansing the planet of the impure and spreading peace and harmony.'

'Cleansing the planet of the impure? These are just ordinary people suffering like this. There's nothing impure about them!'

'Impure, impure, impure! There is a reaction between certain unworthy individuals and the Überunderpants. The impure may be physically or mentally unsuited to the Überunderpants. For these individuals, proximity to the Überunderpants can be —' he paused to find the right word '— transformative in a number of ways. This process is entirely right and completely separate from your various acts of terrorism.'

'And what kind of peace and harmony is it that is enforced by chemicals in your underpants?'

'A very manageable peace and harmony, Lady Persephone. No different from what the world has done for along time with schools and TVs and religion and TV and shopping centres. A manageable peace and harmony that keeps everyone in the orchards and the shops creating and consuming my underpants. Don't —' he shouted '— tell me you would do otherwise if you had the means. The difference between you and I is that through my purity I have the clarity of vision to conceive and implement this plan.'

Hades waggled his eyebrows at his wife and colleagues in a way that said, don't pursue it, the man is bonkers, and we'll deal with him rather than reason with him.

'What do you intend to do with us?' Hades waggled his eyebrows at Hilda in a new gesture of approval of the question.

'Oh, simple. I can't have you meddling with my plans again. First, I will force from you the methods you have used to subvert my underpants. If you have nothing interesting to divulge, I will have the compensation that force was used to establish that there was nothing to divulge. Then, when I have purged the planet of your toxic influence, there will be a rather grand show trial and you will all be publicly beheaded on Tower Hill. My new world order will last for another 1,000 years at the very least.'

'Only a thousand years?' asked Hades. He shrugged and stripped a chicken bone with his teeth. 'Hardly seems worth the bother.'

'I think it is you who is away with the cuckoos,' suggested Mangler. 'Here I am outlining your fate and you mock.'

'Bologna, anybody?' asked Hades offering round a plate of sliced sausage and stuffing a few pieces in his own mouth.

'Where are you going to take us?' Pickles wanted to know.

'For now, you are under house arrest until I have arranged a suitably vile dungeon in my Sacred Mountain headquarters. The adamantine airship arrives tomorrow and I will ship you back on that. You will then be truly out of harm's way as far as the innocent population of the world is concerned — and very much in harm's way from your own point of view.'

'Jolly good,' said Persephone. 'We'll look forward to that then.'

Mangler was gone, but his armed goons very much were not. Hades stared after Mangler in his inscrutable way and piled much, much more food on his plate.

61

Hades insisted they gather in the drawing room for brandy and cigars after his sumptuous dinner. No one was really in the mood for fun, but assuming something was going on in Hades' busy brain, they went along with his suggestion.

'Ishiguro, good chap. Please bring along the oldest, finest, most self-indulgent brandy we have in the cellar. Thank you very much.'

The former King of the Undies World, the most self-made man in the world, lit a big, fat Cuban cigar. 'Jolly fine grub. Cook has pulled off another blinder. Good on cook, that's what I say. Nice night too. There's a moon, a cloud and even a star or two. The temperature's about right, I would say. Not too warm, not too cool. Quite possibly optimum, I should think. Saw some ducks on the pond the other day. Seemed to be quite enjoying the water.' While he was talking complete and utter rubbish, the semaphore signals he sent with his eyebrows read: 'Can't talk here. Too many hostile ears. Any suggestions?'

'Oh, is that semaphore? I only do morse,' flashed Pickles with his eyes. 'Can you do morse? Hilda? Persephone?'

Persephone waggled 'Hilda's wearing a burqa. She's going to be a mite left out of any conversation that relies on eyebrows.'

The eyebrows of the sergeant of the guard butted into the conversation. 'All the guards are marine commandos. We all read semaphore. And morse. Duh!'

62

It was a long, difficult night. Hilda wandered the corridors of the Tudor pile looking for inspiration, Hades and Persephone looked for the same thing in bottles. Pickles sensibly went to bed at a sensible time where he swatted up on semaphore before turning out the light.

Wherever Hilda went she was followed guards. There seemed to be no privacy and no escape.

Under cover of the burqa, Hilda could use her mobile phone and tablet without being seen. But with her device in her hand she could think of no one to contact. Alice and Jim and the rest of the Commandos were captive. The rest of the world was under Mangler's chemical spell.

Hilda fired off some speculative texts and mails at Victoria updating her on the situation. She assumed Mangler's spooks at GCHQ would read those.

Eventually even the shadows seemed to sag in the halls and nooks of the Tudor pile and looked knackered. Hilda went to help Hades and Persephone with the bottles.

63

Dawn broke ominously. Hilda had never known the dawn to break ominously before, and thinking about it, she wasn't sure what she meant by the feeling that dawn was ominous and wasn't sure why she felt that way at all.

The time of day, consulting her various devices under the burqa for verification, didn't really have much to do with dawn. It was, by the clock, embarrassingly late to be waking up.

Perhaps it was her location, on the floor of the drawing room, wrapped affectionately around the legs of the drinks cabinet. She wasn't convinced it was her posture, though it was not helping to dispel the ominous feeling. There was, she was sure, an ominous air in the ... in the ... well, in the air. Getting a bit more specific, there was a vague but dense noise of sort of foreboding everywhere.

She unfurled herself from the legs of the cabinet and straightened the hood of her burqa so that she could see out.

Persephone was sprawled full length and face down on the table. Hades was on the chaise longue, on his back with his legs propped vertically against the wall. Empty bottles lined, lay, fell, rolled, or staggered on every flat surface in the room. But still that wasn't the source of the foreboding.

Hilda noted that there were no armed guards in the room. That was odd, though not on its own menacing.

Hades abruptly leapt to his feet: 'God's bollocks, I feel good! What a splendid dousing of the whistle. Much needed. I feel utterly repaired for it. What's for breckers, Ishiguro?'

'Vast amounts, Sir Hades, vast amounts.' With precision butler timing, Ishiguro had entered the room a precise nano-second before his name was used. He was carrying an over-laden tray and was followed by several other over-laden trays, beneath which laboured several members of the household staff. 'On observing sir's Olympic-Sized bladdering last night, I took the liberty of preparing an equivalently sized breakfast containing everything that's bad for you. Bloody Marys and dog-hair juice are available on request.'

'Oh, dear. I fear we need some table space or some such in order to put out this spread,' said Hades, looking around the drawing room for a spot to land the trays. Persephone rolled off the big table and onto the floor taking most of the empties with her.

'Ah, you can put the nosh on the table if you would be so good. Thank you very much.'

'Um, Hades,' Hilda reported, 'There don't seem to be any armed guards with us this morning.'

'Nipped out for a ciggie, I dare say,' said Hades mauling a full English.

'If I may interject,' Ishiguro offered, 'I believe they nipped out to fight an army of Überunderpants that surrounded the house during the night. They don't appear to have returned. Any of them.'

'An army of Überunderpants, you say? Where is this army now?'

'Surrounding the house with apparent intent to eat anything that it can get its fronds on.'

At which Persephone got to her feet, drained whatever was left in the bottle she was holding on to and swooshed open the curtains.

'I wouldn't —' attempted Hilda and Ishiguro together.

The big, expansive windows of the drawing room offered a view through a diamond lattice of the beautifully kempt lawns of the Tudor pile. Or normally they did. Now they looked out on an army of unkempt Überunderpants, some members of which were festooned with tatters of uniform and webbing of Mangler's guards — one wore a peaked cap belonging to the same. The plants, spotting breakfast — not Hades' full English — rushed the window as one and bounded inside in a spray of shattered glass. Persephone taking long fast swings with her bottle, batted a great many back outside but it was not a fight she was going to win. Hades grabbed her by the waist, and with his free hand a tray of sausages, and flew to the door, which Ishiguro smartly held open for him.

Hilda forged herself a path to the door with deft and violent use of a chair and both she and Ishiguro ducked through together. On the other side, they both clung to the door knob.

'How are they with mechanical things? Door handles? Have they figured them out?' Persephone wanted to know.

The plants had their own workaround to contraptions like door handles, which was to batter the obstruction down. The door thumped and jumped in its frame in a way that suggested the wall might come down with it.

'Right,' said Hades, 'Bright ideas, anyone?'

The drawing room door splintered and Hades and his crew fled into the hallway and up the stairs, on the way appropriating from the displays of medieval armour various pikes, halberds, maces and axes. As the plants swarmed into the downstairs hall, the humans withdrew to the upstairs and, momentarily, out of sight of the homicidal veg.

'This is not a bad defensive position,' observed Hades.

'They don't seem to realise we are here,' Hilda pointed out. If we are quiet, we may be able to keep eluding them.'

'Morning all. Off to war, is it? A mass insurrection against Mangler perchance?' It was Pickles in his pyjamas and clutching his teddy bear.

'Shhhhh!' he was told, and then he was told why.

'Cripes,' said Pickles. 'I wish I hadn't bothered getting up now.'

'Bugger!' said Hades peering cautiously over the balustrade. 'They heard you, Pickles. They're investigating the stairs. We don't have more than a fleeting moment to concoct a plan that will save our lives.'

Hilda's tactical brain was working ahead. 'Ishiguro. You know this house better than anyone. Are there any safe ways out?'

'Yes, indeed,' put in Pickles, 'these places were made with priest holes and boltholes and hidden rooms and all sorts of things.'

'Would a secret underground tunnel running from this house and under the adjacent fields for about half a mile to the pub in the next village be of any use?'

'A secret tunnel leading to a pub? Do lead the charge, Ishiguro, old chap!' said Hades.

'There's a secret stairwell through the core of the house from the roof to the tunnel entrance beneath the basement. There's access to it on every floor, but if the plants haven't found it, and there's no reason they should, it should be serviceable.'

'Here they come,' said Hades, 'they've sniffed us out.'

They ran, pausing to haul heavy lumps of furniture in their wake to slow down the plants. Their flight paused briefly at a blank, oak-panelled wall while Ishiguro briefly manipulated a candleholder and tweaked the nose of a brass gargoyle thing. A panel slid open and they were inside with the panel closing out the charging plants behind them.

'In the older, more turbulent days in which you could be persecuted and executed for dancing to the wrong madrigal, this was a practical means of escape,' explained Ishiguro quite unnecessarily while they all clattered toward the basement. 'In more recent times, the owners of the house used it for discreet trips to the inn, for party pranks, and the like. The servants used this stairwell as a means of getting to and from chores without disturbing their masters and mistresses. I fear a few of the staff have lately been using the stairs as a place to shoot up, judging by the number of discarded needles and blackened spoons I have been finding.'

The stairs were lit by feeble little bulbs dangling on exposed wiring that would set a fire safety inspector's passions ablaze, so Hades, on point with a halberd, had a fleeting view of foliage as it tried to ambush him. He stood his ground even in the narrow stairwell and whooshed his weapon to great effect.

'There are too many of them! The whole basement is stuffed full of the bastards! Back up! Back up! Some idiot must have left the bottom door open while being eaten!'

Hades, Persephone, Hilda, Pickles, and Ishiguro ran back up the cramped and narrow stairwell. All around them the walls seemed to be alive with a rhythmic thudding as the plants outside tried to batter their way inside.

Eventually the humans burst, screaming with muscle pain onto the roof, where Persephone tackled a potted shrub before realising it was not a manic pair of Überunderpants trying to devour her.

Ishiguro, Pickles, and Hades braced the roof door closed with their halberds and a couple of stone plant pots that idled nearby.

'Are there any other ways on to the roof, Ishiguro?' asked Hilda.

'Oh, absolutely. We'll need to barricade each before the pants reach them.'

Something across the roof and just out of sight broke with a momentous crashing, like the impact of a glass tsunami.

'That'll be the rooftop conservatory,' said Ishiguro calmly. It would seem they've found a way onto the roof by destroying the place we keep the plants. Very apt, if I may remark on the irony.'

'Oh, yes. Please do remark on the irony,' said Hades in grim mien and testing the weight of a very spiky mace in his hands. 'I like a bit of irony when the chips are down.'

Pickles was still on the escape plans.' I wonder whether we could shimmy down a drainpipe.'

The sun went out. The sky blackened and a heavy shadow smothered the roof and all hope thereon. Above them, the adamantine airship, newly hove in out of the blue, hovered just metres above the Tudor pile.

'Now what?' asked Hades, quite reasonably.

64

Victoria was pleased to find that without any training whatsoever, and quite unreasonably, she was in fact a dab hand at flying the adamantine airship. She powered up to scramjet flight and hurtled through the stratosphere quite enjoying the spectacle of continents and oceans flashing by beneath. The proximity to space made her spine tingle.

From the ground the airship appeared like a large orange meteor speeding across the heavens. Heat flashed on the adamantine shell and she reflected that one small crack, one hairline fissure in that shell at this velocity would result in the entire ship being incinerated in a second. This thought added yet more tingles to her spine.

Pleased at her ability to power up to mach 24 for the flight, she was even more pleased to find that she could power down to make a stop right over the Tudor pile where she believed her parents to be, assuming Hilda's last messages were no fake.

As the airship dropped gracefully back into the troposphere, somewhere over the Mediterranean, something odd and disturbing started to happen. The controls began to freeze. It wasn't that they froze in the conventional sense of becoming rigid or immoveable, though that was definitely part of the problem. Ice was forming on the control surfaces, in creeping white fractal patterns.

Momentarily, Victoria wondered whether there was something wrong with the environmental systems but the truth hit her as cold as the ship's wheel: Flay. Flay was hacking the flight systems.

'Timmy, we have an issue.'

'I don't have any issues. The box makes a strange lump in my leopard print trunks, so I don't normally bother with it.'

'No, not tissues, Timmy. Issues. We have issues.'

'That's nice, Victoria.'

'Timmy, issues are bad things, not good things.'

'I see,' said Timmy in a voice that suggested he was going to be massively patient until he had got to the bottom of this issues thing.

'Flay is hacking the flight systems. She's hijacking the airship.'

'But I thought we had already hijacked the airship.'

'We have.'

'This is all very complicated, Victoria. Can't we do away with the difficult bits?'

'Yes, it would be very nice to do away with the difficult bits. I think that's the beginning of a plan right there.'

'But we're nearly back home. Why did Flay wait until now to hijack the ship?'

'My guess is that she's actually hiding on board and wants to get to the UK. Regardless, hacking the airship in scramjet flight would have been incredibly dangerous. If the hack had accidentally cut the engine power, the effect of air resistance at that speed would cause a sudden deceleration that would be like running into a brick wall. Who knows whether even the adamantine would survive such an impact, and even if it did, anyone inside the ship would have been mushed into jam by the jolt. No, she's waited until now to land us where she wants and deliver us right to Mangler.'

'As I said, can we do away with the difficult bits?'

'But you know what this means, Timmy? Where there's Flay, there's Maul.'

'Hello, everyone,' said Maul. He was standing in the middle of the flight deck with the barrel of a gun up his nose. He had slipped in while Timmy and Victoria were plumbing the concept of issues.

Maul removed the end of the gun from his nose and gestured at both Timmy and Victoria with the green-clogged end. 'If either of you moves, the other gets it.'

'Darn and pish,' said Timmy.

'Me and Davinia are taking control of this big balloon thing. Gousset-girl, move away from the ship's wheel. I said, move away —'

'You won't get away with this you know, you horrible little man,' Timmy told Maul, who rolled his eyes.

'Shut up, you big meat-wank. We *have* got away with it. Me and Flay is taking this ship back to Mangler who will reward us big time. Unless we decide to keep it.'

'I think you should put your gun down now before you get hurt,' Timmy insisted.

'Oh, yeah? Oh yeah? Like I even need a gun to deal with you, you big blue, er, thing, you. All I need to do to do away with you is say boo. I done it before. Dead cool it was. Do you remember, Mr Arnie-head?'

Timmy stood his ground. Timmy seemed to grow in his ground and beamed defiance and disgust from his face right at Maul's.

'Leave Timmy alone, Maul. It's me flying this ship. Your argument is with me, not Timmy.'

'Absolutely not the point,' said Maul. 'My argument is with anything that I can bully. All right there, Timbo, me ol' mate? Ready for what's coming?'

'Maul! I said leave him!'

'Shut it! I've got a gun aimed at you and a little word beginning with boo aimed at Mr Corny Beef here.'

'It's OK, Victoria. I can deal with Mr Squirt. My only worry is that after I've dealt with him my own head will fall off with laughing.'

'Timmy! You know what happened last time — and the time before that, and the time before that. We'll just give the little creep what he wants for the time being. He's not worth you dying.'

'Dying? I'm dying to see this blob of grease cry like a baby.'

'All right Spam-man. You asked for it. Boo!'

Victoria screamed. Timmy didn't flinch. He remained akimbo and kept his stare on Maul.

'Hello? I just said boo? So boo again to you-hoo! Boo!'

Timmy stared down at Maul and Victoria realised that he knew something neither Maul nor she did.

'Oi! Boo! Fucking boo boo boo, OK? Ha ha ha ha ha! That got yer didn't it!'

Timmy looked over at Victoria and smiled reassuringly.

'I said boo. Boo boo boo boo boo boo boo boo boo boo boo boo boo boo boo boo boo boo boo boo boo boo boo boo boo boo boo boo boo boo boo! Boo boo boo boo boo boo boo boo boo boo boo boo boo boo boo boo boo boo boo boo boo boo boo boo boo boo boo boo boo boo boo boo boo boo! Eh? Ha!'

Timmy glanced at the clock on the wall and yawned.

'Boo-wop showaddywaddy, boo-wop she-boo boo! Boozy boozy bums and boozy! Boo boo be doop boo! Booble booble boo boo booble boo! Boo boo black sheep have you any boo-boo? Boo for fuck's sake! Fucking boo, innit!' Maul was now red in the face and bouncing up and down. 'Are you so fucking stupid you've forgotten what boo does to you? Collapse and die, you bastard!'

'I was bitten by a spider. I have super powers now,' said Timmy simply and whacked Maul over the head with his bucket. Maul went down straight as a pole.

'Well, er, that was exceedingly cool,' said Victoria.

'Was it? Oh, thank you.'

'We're just coming up on Pile House and Flay is somewhere on this ship hacking the control system. I can fight her from the flight terminal here and try to delay her. Can you find her actual person and disengage her from whatever it is she's doing?'

'Happy to oblige,' said Timmy, tucking the inert Maul under his arm. He sprang to the ceiling and scuttled off the bridge at great speed.

The controls were now under a mantle of hoar frost. Victoria scraped at the hard, white shell. Beneath the bridge window was Pile House and on the roof she could see Hades, Persephone, Hilda, Pickles and Ishiguro — and she could also see a horde, an army, a swarm, of Überunderpants closing in on her family and friends. Whatever she was going to do, she had to do it fast. At that very moment Flay accessed the core of the flight systems and Victoria became aware of the light foliate rustle of a mad Überunderpants plant sneaking up on her from behind.

Victoria sighed and summoned all her multi-tasking abilities to deal with the situation.

65

Hades took in the charging horde of green and the hovering airship.

'Right! Jolly good,' he said. 'A tight spot. Haven't been in on of those for a second or two,' and the airship leapt backward at great and sudden speed, nearly all the way to the horizon.

The Überunderpants stopped their charge and craned their stalks in the direction of the giant ship. What was it doing?

The ship was spinning laterally, like rotor blades. It dodged sideways a few times in a variety of different sideways and did a loop-the-loop.

On the Tudor rooftop all combat remained suspended as the airship twirled vertically like a Catherine wheel and lapped Oxfordshire like an excited dog in a park. There was another loop that took it to the edge of space, from where it returned spinning on its axis like a torpedo. Hades winced mightily against the presumed impact with the Tudor pile.

The airship didn't crash. Yet again it juddered to a halt over the old house. This time it stayed put. A cargo hatch opened and ejected, as if they were being spat out, a man, a woman, and an insane plant, who landed on the roof between Hades' group and the still-transfixed Überunderpants.

'Maul and Flay,' said Hades, Persephone, Hilda, Pickles, and Ishiguro all together.

'Yum!' the Überunderpants all seemed to say together, and 'Charge!'

'Bugger off, we're on your side, you stupid vegetables!' said Maul as he disappeared beneath the avalanche of green.

'Look out below. Anti-pants procedures commencing,' said a booming voice from the airship, a voice that sounded, adjusting for boom, a lot like Victoria.

'Victoria!' exclaimed Hades, Persephone, Hilda, Pickles and Ishiguro.

'You may want to get your pants off folks. They are just about to become pretty obnoxious,' boomed Victoria.

Vents opened on the underside of the ship and clouds of yellow dust billowed at the roof.

'What is that?' asked Persephone. Moments later when her bottom caught fire, she knew.

'Itching powder, everybody! Aaaaaaaagh!' The Goussets and friends legged it behind different chimney stacks — of which there were plenty — to escape their underthings and the torment they were bringing.

For the Überunderpants, there was no escape, being genetically 100 per cent underwear they could hardly slip out of themselves. They shook, they juddered, they writhed, they twitched.

Hades might have felt sorry for them and had to remind himself that these were utterly callous flesh-eating mutants who themselves knew no pity or remorse.

The pants convulsed and as they did so, they began to fall apart. Leaves took to the agitated air. Stalks span off in all directions. The plants came apart in a thick, twitching carpet of foliage — a thick, harmless, twitching carpet of foliage.

'Hey, Dr Pickles! I can see your bare bottom,' laughed Victoria. 'OK, all. Not a moment to lose. I have to save the world. A few circuits of the globe dumping this stuff into the major air streams ought to do the trick. Back by teatime, I reckon.'

The adamantine airship powered away with a triumphant wiggle of its tail.

'That's our daughter, you know,' said Hades to Persephone.

'Erm,' said Pickles. 'Mangler owns every major airforce in the world. Mind you don't get shot down, or anything.'

There was movement in the middle of the pile of shredded Überunderpants.

'Don't tell me the buggers are still alive after that itching!' bellowed Hades and charged —his kingly robes preserving his modesty — halberd and mace aloft in his hands.

'Ow!'

'Ouch!'

'Bugger off!'

'The Geneva convention gives us the right to surrender — does it give you the right to cosh defeated people?' Maul and Flay, covered in green stains and bite marks, raised their hands in both surrender and an effort to ward off Hades' blows.

66

Mangler paced manically in the glass expanse of the top floor of the Shard.

'Shoot it down! Shoot it down!' He was referring to the adamantine airship. Mangler had understood from Flay's last broken messages from on board that Victoria had some kind of plan, some kind of secret weapon and that she was fighting back.

Westminster Abbey was Mangler's ceremonial and symbolic home, the Shard was his nerve centre: the hubris of adopting the tallest building in western Europe excited him, and besides, it was difficult to find anywhere in the city big enough to accommodate his ego and madness. To Mangler, the vast glass tower was like a panopticon built inside out. From here he could spy on every corner of London at once, turning the city into a vast prison.

'Have you shot it down yet? What's keeping you?'

His minions were, you know, OK about this shooting down the airship thing.

'Move! Move! Move! Move! Move! Move! Move!'

They were totally chilled about, like, you know, calling Strategic Air Command or whatever and scrambling the fighters, but first, like, you know, they had to space out a minute. But, you know, that's cool.

'Get on with it! Get on to the NSA, tell them to remotely hack the flight systems. They're doing it to airliners all the time.'

'Er, hi, yeah, Dr Mangler? Mein furrier? Yeah, Strategic Air Command say the adamantine airship is like flying too high and too fast to shoot it down? They guess it was, like, designed like that?'

'Imbeciles!' Mangler screamed. 'That Gousset woman is going to ruin everything.'

Mangler's minions liked the way everything was sort of rippling around them, and the ripples if you didn't look at them too directly, yeah? made all these colours kind of float into the air so it's like snowing light? Far out!

'OK. This is what we do. Tell security to go find Hades and his vile brood and kill them. Just kill them! No mucking about! Now get on the radio and tell that hideous bint in my ship that unless she comes down right now we are going to stuff her parents inside the biggest big guns we can find and shoot them at her! Do it now! Why are you doing nothing? Get on with it!'

'Could you, like, explain that bit again?'

'What bit?'

'The bit where you told us what you wanted us to do? Wow!'

Mangler followed the minion's rapt gaze into the sky and to the orange fireball hurtling across London.

67

Muriel Thingerbottom woke, or half woke, or became dimly aware that somewhere in the ocean of her contentment she was in great pain. It was a burning, insistent pain with a large note of hilarity in it.

The first thing Muriel did was fall off her ladder. Lying on her back on the scorched earth, she located the pain in her clothes, in her underpants to be exact, so she wriggled out of those. The relief was instant. She remained lying on the ground and light began to trickle back into her synapses.

It was drizzling. She hadn't noticed that before. The Mangler pants dangled like wet rags in the trees. The sky was horrible. It was grey and suicidal. The ground was horrible too. It was black and had apparently already committed suicide or had been murdered. All through the orchard, workers and guards writhed on the ground or staggered groggily, waste-down naked.

The commandante, naked as everyone else, stared at his clipboard as if he had never seen it before.

Camp Sunny Happy Days, thought Muriel. That was the name of where she was. Camp Sunny Happy Days. Some part of her mind that had been bound and gagged for many weeks was suddenly able to speak: this place was never happy or sunny. She had been kidnapped and forced into slave labour. How had she not seen that before? The pants! She had been drugged with underpants. But now she was free.

The pants in the trees, they were no longer just dangling. The trees: they and their fruit were shaking, thrashing and flailing; they were shedding the pants, shedding their leaves, shedding their own branches. They were falling apart.

Something quite bonkers was happening.

Muriel found her trousers and put them back on and headed for the camp gate. She missed her mum. She missed her Twonky bars and sugary, salty things. She even missed Gloucester bus station. She was going home, and she didn't care what the commandante or the Bottom Inspectors or Dr Mangler thought.

68

'That woman is rampant! What does she think she is doing? How dare she defy me like this?' Mangler stepped on to his command podium in the middle of the office from where he liked to shout his most extravagant demands.

'Do something!' he ordered.

His minions turned bright red, screamed, convulsed and threw themselves on the floor where they tore at their clothes.

Mangler could feel the pain too but declined to give in to it. He was made of insaner stuff than his staff.

'The bitch! The monstrous bitch! She is spraying the world with itching powder! She is destroying everything!'

69

When Hades burst into his office, he found the prime minister of the United Kingdom bare-bottomed, on his knees, and beating his underpants with a heavily framed portrait of the Queen.

'You! You! You bastard! Look what you've done to the country! Look what you've done to the world!' The prime minister stopped beating his pants, leaped to his feet and attempted to beat Hades instead.

Persephone threw herself in the way and tried to grapple the picture from the PM who didn't want to let go.

'Bernard! Please listen!' said Hades in his best imploring voice.

'I'm George! Bernard was four governments back!'

'George! That's what I said! Listen to me! We've got Mangler on the run. You have to help us bang him up once and for all.'

'You can't even get my name right you blithering nincompoop! Why should I ever listen to you again? Why should I ever listen to another underpants magnate again? First you try to destroy the world with those bloody Omnipants, then you try to destroy the world all over again with your bloody war against Mangler! Get out! Get out before I kill you!'

Persephone didn't like it when people spoke to her husband like that. She somersaulted the prime minister across his own desk and into his chair where he landed bottom first, with his feet on the table and without any dignity at all. She turned her back 'And put some bloody trousers on!' She screamed the word trousers in such a way that even the portraits on the wall seemed to wince and all the molecules in the glass of the windows considered running for their lives.

The prime minister, on the other hand didn't feel his was a life worth preserving. 'No, Hades. No way. Absolutely out of the question.'

'I haven't told you anything yet.'

'No need! Whatever you say, it will be dangerous nonsense and I'm not listening. The landfill was too good for you. I'm going to create for you your own special prison fashioned from a cesspit.'

'I'm telling you, Prime Minister, this mess is all Mangler's doing. He sabotaged my Omnipants to discredit me and then he unleashed his genetically modified Überunderpants on the world.

'Well, you would say that wouldn't you.'

'Edward —'

'George!'

'George! Have you put your trousers back on yet? I'm asking because I don't want to have to tie a half-naked man into a knot for not listening to my husband.'

'Then you'll just have to not tie me in a knot because I'm not going to dress for your torturing convenience.'

'I may not want to, Hilary, but I will if I have to.'

'Damn you!'

'Stand by for an important announcement from Dr Mangler!' said a screen on the prime minister's desk.

'You have a dedicated link to Mangler?' asked Persephone in incredulity and contempt.

'Mangler put that there to tell you what to do, didn't he,' remarked Hades intercepting the escaping eyes of the prime minister. 'The first executive office of the United Kingdom has a direct line to Mangler on his desk by Mangler's orders. I see.'

Liberated of his über-obedience-pants, the prime minister now thought this pretty odd too, but he wasn't going to say so in front of Hades.

'Prime Minister! Howard, or whatever your name is. That madman Gousset is attempting a coup d'état. He mustn't get away with it. Get onto his people right now and close them down. Shoot everyone. Immediately! I'm going globally live in thirty minutes to put things back to rights.' Mangler paused a beat. 'You're not wearing any pants, are you. Damn you!'

Mangler was replaced on the screen by a broadcast countdown.

'Well, that's you told, isn't it,' said Hades with another one of his penetrating looks.

'Get out,' said the prime minister quietly.

70

The Goussets headed up Whitehall and into the West End. The rooftop screens, the massive screen set up in Trafalgar Square, all announced the imminence of Mangler's broadcast.

'This should be interesting,' Hades pointed out.

The streets were littered with discarded, twitching, dying Überunderpants. The occasional pile of brown leaves marked the demise of a fully mutated pair.

'Yes. Mangler's captive audience is suddenly not so captive.'

Thousands of people milled about on the streets, looking tired, confused and not a little angry. The Goussets continued on to Leicester Square.

Hades heard the clack of the bolt of the gun pointed at the back of his head.

'We have orders to shoot the both of you on sight.'

Hades and Persephone put their hands up and turned round to confront the pair of leather-coated Bottom Inspectors and the posse of Mangler's black-clad enforcers.

'Ah!' said Hades. 'I had failed to anticipate that. Silly me.'

'Bollocks to orders,' said the Bottom Inspector and lowered his gun. 'There's something very weird been going on and we're going to find out what, and then we decide for ourselves who to shoot.'

'Spoken like a very wise man, if I may say so. Thank you very much.'

Before Hades could move on, 'But you two are staying with us. We haven't ruled you out as someone to shoot.'

'Oh dear,' said Persephone. 'I do hope something happens in the nick of time.'

'That would have to be about now, I think,' said Hades, as the broadcast on the rooftops began.

'People of the world! It is I, Hieronymus Mangler, World Leader (Not Pretend).

'A very evil man —' unflattering pictures of Hades in unguarded moments with expressions and poses that could be read as mad, arrogant, stupid or scary '— Sir Hades Gousset, has been trying to destroy the perfect world I created for you.

'It *was* a perfect world, wasn't it. Remember how good you felt until just a few short hours ago. Well, it was Gousset who took away that good feeling.'

A few members of the public were now noticing Hades and Persephone and the Bottom Inspectors. The Goussets felt very vulnerable and exposed.

'You had everything you wanted — pants, pants, pants and more pants. You didn't even have to pay for them.'

'It was a world without free will,' muttered Hades.

'First this man used his position of unlimited power and influence to infest the world with his Omnipants in a misbegotten attempt to claim even more unlimited power and influence. And you know what happened — chaos, death!' Cut to images of mayhem as the Omnipants went on the rampage.

Hades shuddered.

'Happily, I was able to intervene and save the world.'

Hades shuddered again.

'Justice was swift, certain but merciful.' Images of Hades' humiliation and his dumping in the landfill.

'But this man went from that pile of refuse to this Tudor pile —' cut to Pile House '— where he plotted his revenge and further crimes against civilisation and the people of this world. His chief scientist Dr Edwin Pickles —' images of Pickles in a suspiciously affectionate embrace with a pig '— devised fiendish ways of manipulating the DNA of my trees to breed a hideous mutation —' scary closeups of enraged Überunderpants bushes attacking the camera lens '— an abomination of nature. All the while he was directing his own daughter —' Images of the Wicked Witch of the West from The Wizard of Oz.

'Kill her! Kill her!' shouted someone in the crowd to a small murmur of agreement.

'— who had infiltrated my own home, my sanctum, Sacred Mountain —' views of a quaint old cottage with a quaint old lady watering the roses in the front garden '— to spread the Gousset evil here.' The roses ate the old lady. There was booing from the crowd.

'Today Victoria Gousset hijacked my good ship HMS Adamant and has sprayed poison all over the world killing all of you horribly!'

'Shame on her! Shame on her!' bellowed the crowd.

Hades thought he could hear the guns of the Bottom Inspectors being cocked again.

'Hang on,' said one voice in the crowd. 'That makes no sense at all.'

'Follow that thought through,' muttered Hades.

'If we pull together, and especially if we all go find some new, clean, uncontaminated pants to wear — I suggest the stock rooms of the stores near you, where the new clothes will be sealed in nice branded plastic wrapping and protected against contamination — we can —'

The picture broke up in wavy lines, the sound went fizzy and crackly.

'We interrupt this broadcast,' said a voice that sounded very much like Hilda, 'to bring you the truth.'

The crowd, under the spell of Mangler's narrative and convinced that a new calumny was being perpetrated by the enemy of civilisation, booed loudly.

'We don't interrupt this broadcast at all!' boomed Mangler fizzing and popping back into view, his technicians grappling to maintain control of the airwaves.

'Oh, yes we do!' countered Hilda.

'Oh, no we don't!' insisted Mangler.

'Oh, yes we do!'

'Oh, no we don't!'

'Oh, yes we do!'

'Oh, no we don't!' the crowd suggested, helping Mangler along.

'Oh, yes we do!'

'Oh, no we don't!'

'Oh, yes we do!'

'Oh, no we don't!'

'Oh, please!' interjected Persephone, which seemed to do the trick as Hilda's burqa leapt back into frame and stayed there.

'Boo!' rejoined the crowd. 'Gerroff!' 'We're not listening!' 'Bring back our Mangler!' and 'If I was a tomato, I'd throw myself at you!'

'Mangler! Mangler!'

Hilda tore off the hood of her burqa and a golden light streamed down on the crowd from the rooftop screens.

Hades averted his eyes. Even though the image of Hilda was filtered through lenses, the airwaves and LED screens he heard the boing and ouch! of thousands of men suffering injuries.

The glow stopped as she put the hood back on again and there was sigh in Leicester Square that was half relief and half despair.

'Now that I have your attention,' started Hilda, 'I'll prove to you that Mangler is lying and deceiving, that everything he says is a crock of mouldy old bananas.'

'Not possible,' shouted someone in the crowd, 'Mangler's … Mangler's … Mangler's — well Mangler just is, inne. Mangler's Mangler.' The crowd cheered in response to these wise words.

'So you know who we are, where we stand, who we stand with — full disclosure — my name is Hilda Titanium, personal assistant to the underpants magnate Hades Gousset, and joining me in the studio tonight is Hades' own daughter, Victoria Gousset, and also with us is this big blue monster, Timothy Adonis — no please don't say anything Timmy.

Thanks. Victoria is at this moment at the controls of the good ship HMS Adamant, from whose bridge we are broadcasting, and which is coming to a sky near you any moment now.'

A shadow fell across the square as the ship overhead blotted out the sun. It waved its tail before whooshing off to make an appearance over Paris, then Rome, and on round the world while the ladies were speaking.

'Yes, Victoria and Timmy hijacked the ship from Dr Mangler's own base, Sacred Mountain earlier today.'

Victoria took up the story. 'We would like to apologise for nicking this fantastic ship but we can't. It was the only way we could combat Mangler.'

'Leave him alone, you bullies!' jeered the crowd in Leicester Square.

'What's he ever done to you?' they asked.

'To explain all this, we have to go back to the beginning,' Victoria went on. 'After Dr Mangler launched his tree-grown pants, my father needed a product to compete. He came up with the Omnipants, which you will remember well because they nearly destroyed the world.'

Hilda continued. 'But why did the creation of this master underpants maker malfunction so badly? Surely a man of Hades' skill, built through a lifetime of inventing innovative underpants, could not have made such a disastrous error. No, he didn't because the pants were hacked and a virus, a berserker programme, was installed which caused chaos.'

'Well, you would say that!' exclaimed the crowd.

'I would like you to meet two important people in this story: Jeremy Maul —' the image accompanying Maul's introduction drew howls of disgust and vomiting sounds from the crowd in Leicester Square '— and Davinia Flay —' a shocked silence. Maul and Flay are small-time fixers and thugs who teamed up with Mangler in an elaborate plot to discredit Hades and seize power.

A new image appeared on the screens. This one moved and showed Maul, Flay and Mangler in a cell of rock and ice at the bottom of the world. 'And, tell me again, do you think that was sufficient reason to bring her to the heart of my

Antarctic lair, right under my artificially climate-controlled underpants plantation, and thereby expose the fact that you, Flay and I are in cahoots, and few of the calamitous events preceding this point in time were quite what they seemed to be?' said Mangler in the video.

'That image was captured just as the three people you see were discussing how to kill Victoria Gousset after she was kidnapped by Maul, and after she discovered their schemes.' explained Hilda.

Hades exploded. 'Kill Victoria? The bastards! I'll —'

'Yes, we're doing that now, dear,' said Persephone. 'Now shut up and listen!'

The screens cut to another part of the same conversation between Mangler, Maul and Flay: 'I'm not keen on keeping her here,' said Mangler. 'She would continue to be a complication, another thing to think about. How about taking her for a trip in the adamantine airship to a very remote and wet part of the planet where there are deep oceanic trenches, like the southern Indian Ocean, for example, lashing her to something not known for buoyancy, like a piano or anvil, and just drop her off?'

'That would work,' said Flay.

'Oooh!' said the people in Leicester Square.

'He wouldn't want her bumped off if he didn't have something to hide,' pointed out a voice in the crowd.

'Absolutely, that man there!' bellowed Hades, before the Bottom Inspectors could jab him in the back with their guns to shut him up.

'The person who introduced that berserker virus into the system was Davinia Flay —' the screens flashed up mug shots of Flay herself.

'You expect us to believe that?' The early evening air of London was filled with hoots of derision and catcalls.

'No, I don't expect you to take my word for it. Hearing is believing, and we have all this from Maul's own mouth. Flay was incarcerated in a cryopod in Hades' Pants Down HQ, where she found she could hack into the intranet. See website for full details.'

The big screens cut again to the ice dungeon where Maul was sharpening his carving knife and gloating about Victoria ending up as his dinner.

'Well,' said Maul on the rooftops, 'if she wasn't getting out soon, she was going to make damn sure Hades was going to suffer properly. She spent her time from then on constructing a wrecking programme right there inside Hades' own systems, with wormholes in his firewall and everything so that she could access it any time she wanted from the outside world, as well as from her locked inside world, hedging her bets, like. She didn't know what was going to happen, but she figured a vicious little friend on the inside would be handy one day.'

'And so,' said Victoria, 'Mangler triggered the zombie apocalypse to bring down Hades and fake his role as saviour of the world.'

The crowd responded with 'Yar boo!' but with less conviction than before.

'You remember that hideous laugh and that revolting voice that went with the zombie chaos? On the screen now you see analyses of two voices.' On the screens were two jagged graphs, sonograms, computer representations of sound. 'The one on the left is the voice from the underpants. The one of the right is Maul. You don't have to be an expert to see the two voiceprints are identical.'

Hilda elaborated. 'Flay and Mangler copied Maul's personality to the berserker programme raising its levels of destruction and capacity to offend many times over.'

'Ooh! Nice pubes!' said Maul's voice on the video

'It was me,' explained Victoria, 'that triggered the kill command from Mangler's headquarters, putting an end to the zombie apocalypse.'

The people of the world were yet to be convinced. 'Nah! Naff orff!' and 'No way!' they said.

'And we happen to have a recording of that too as Victoria happened to be filming herself at the moment she hit that button.' The screens continued with shots of Mangler's command centre, the minions laughing at the live feeds and

Victoria's hand darting into shot to hit the kill switch, throwing at the same time more doubt into the crowd.

'Computer graphics!' someone ventured.

'Photoshop!'

'Actors!'

'Just like the moon landings!'

But the crowd was not unanimous. 'Hang on! Just listen to what they are saying!' said one alert soul.

'This makes too much sense this does. Remember the voice, that laugh? It was horrible it was,' said another.

'With Hades out of the way,' said Hilda, 'Mangler was free to force the population of the world into his own pants. Unknown to you, these Überunderpants were genetically engineered to secrete a tranquiliser that put you under his control. Yes, there were tranks in your pants.'

'Rubbish!'

'He was then able to abuse his new position as World Leader (Not Pretend) to genetically cleanse humanity and use slave labour to plant and harvest his trees. Anyone who failed to fit Mangler's narrow vision of a pants wearer was rounded up and exiled to places like Camp Sunny Happy Days.

The screen showed a satellite image of verdant jungle, a very healthy living green, and a black gash through the middle. The camera zoomed so that the black gash became a fuming patch of hell, filled with Mangler trees and bemused listless workers.

'Slaves, ladies and gentlemen; slaves labouring to bring Mangler's product to market.'

'Well, stands to reason, dunnit. Slaves are cheap. A vast multi-national corporation has to make a profit, or what's the point?' insisted the dwindling number of Mangler fans in the crowd.

'Mangler kept up a free and plentiful supply of those pants, didn't he. He made sure everyone in the world was wearing them. He then suddenly hit you up with this huge underpants tax and you were all working madly to pay that. But you didn't notice how stupid the situation was because Mangler had bamboozled the whole world. And then people started to disappear. People that didn't fit Mangler's image of purity were lifted from the street by the Bottom Inspectors and whisked away.

'People like you, plucked from their lives so that Mangler can enforce a vision of what he thinks you should be like. People like Muriel Thingerbottom, from Gloucester, a semi employed barn hygiene operative with an eating disorder, plucked from the streets and incarcerated here. Her crime? She didn't make her Manglers look good.'

Muriel was broadcast live from the bridge of the adamantine airship: 'We were kept drugged and docile and lived in sheds. We worked 16 hours a day, our only payment being more of the drugged pants that kept us soppy. We didn't know what we were doing.

'And then this ship appeared and rescued me and I'm here to tell my story so it don't happen to you too.'

'It's a fit up!' someone in the crowd insisted.

'Shhhhhhh!' insisted several other people.

'Just think,' said Muriel, leaning in close to the camera, 'Just think how you felt when you was wearing the Überunderpants, and then think how you feel now. Can you even remember the time wearing those things?' She let her words echo over the major cities of the world on a suddenly silent and reflective population.

'She's got a point,' muttered the world.

To underline it, there was another video clip, this time of a recent dinner in Pile House, over which Mangler presided.

'My underpants,' exclaimed Mangler 'are beautiful. No one accuses my underpants of being dangerous. My underpants are simply conducting their task — ordained by destiny of cleansing the planet of the impure and spreading peace and harmony.'

'Cleansing the planet of the impure? These are just ordinary people suffering like this. There's nothing impure about them!'

'Impure! Impure! Impure! There is a reaction between certain unworthy individuals and the Überunderpants. The impure may be physically or mentally unsuited to the

Überunderpants. For these individuals, proximity to the Überunderpants can be transformative in a number of ways. This process is entirely right and completely separate from your various acts of terrorism.'

'And what kind of peace and harmony is it that is enforced by chemicals in your underpants?'

'A very manageable peace and harmony, Lady Persephone.'

'Where did they get these recordings?' wondered Persephone. 'There weren't any cameras in the room that I could see. And the camera angles are all very odd, very oddly low.'

'I think I know,' said Hades quietly. 'And so do you, if you think about it.'

'Why, the clever young vixens,' said Persephone as realisation dawned on her with a rosy glow of pride.

'Yes, transformative,' echoed Hilda. Now the onscreen images showed animations of rotating strings of molecules. 'This is where it gets very technical, so see the website for details, but these images are of the fibres of the Überunderpants. Like all genetically engineered material they are basically unstable.' The fibres started to writhe and change shape. 'Weird stuff happens when they start to change.' One fibre bit another in half.

'Over to Mangler's chief scientist, Dr Merkwürdigliebe — sorry, *late* chief scientist, who admitted to Victoria that the Überunderpants were mutating dangerously.'

'I tried to tell Doctor Mangler, but he was convinced the technology was ready. He wouldn't wait. What could go wrong, he wanted to know. It's just trees and underpants. The technology was a perfection of scruffy nature. He was convinced of that. So we didn't stop to find about the long-term affects of these organisms in the environment. Now we are finding out … How can he admit his extensions have mutated hideously and started eating people? No, he is in deep denial. He is in a profound state of delusion. This isn't happening. If he even acknowledges that his creation is destroying the world, he will claim it is sabotage. Or that the

283

plants were created by someone else to discredit him, that his plants are a, are a … plant. No, he can only see what he imagines to be perfection. If we try to do anything, he may even try to defend his little monsters. There would be a bloodbath.'

There was a monstrous fizz and pop from the many big screens as Mangler broke back into the broadcast.

'Get back in your pants! Get back in your pants! I tell you, now! You are not allowed out of your pants. Go! Now! Move! Scurry! Scurry! Scurry! You are monsters, all of you. My pants are beautiful! Only my pants are beautiful and we are going to have a perfect pants world whether you like it or not!'

Mangler's green and red face filled the screen as he leaned into the camera. He did not look the model of sane.

'Hades is a monster who stood in my way. I had to deal with him.'

Shadows of foliage waved around Mangler as he screamed his message.

'Yes, the pants tranquilised you. So what? You were happy and productive. Maybe not productive, you kept forgetting what you were doing. But you were docile — happy and docile. Now look at you. Your bottoms are hanging out, your hair is a mess, you have no idea how to live!

'Get back in your pants now! Only I can tell you how to live. Only I can tell you what to think. Obey! Believe! Buy pants!

'Ein Volk, ein Reich, ein Maker of Underpants!

'I will not be denied! Your enemy is Hades —'

There was a crunchy, splattery sound.

'Oh!' said Mangler.

Then his underpants reared, all teeth and thrashing, a hideous green jabberwocky, and moments later Mangler was a puddle of juice and offal on the floor.

'Oh,' said the population of the world. 'That'll be that then.'

70

The Bottom Inspectors put away their guns.

'Looks like you were right, then.'

'I feel a bit silly now,' said another.

The masses of people thronging the streets of the world's major cities looked at each other in a wellwhatdoyouthinkofthatthen? sort of way, or in another way that said wotdoyerreckon? And then as one burst into cheers and the cheers became revelry and the revelry became a global party that would go on for a week.

Hades and Persephone hugged mightily.

'Quite a daughter, you have there,' said one of the Bottom Inspectors.

'Quite a team,' added another.

'We know! We know!' cheered Hades and Persephone together.

The same thought seemed to catch in the crowd and spread fast, as mob thoughts tend to do.

Moments later everyone was chanting 'Victoria! Victoria! Victoria! Victoria!' The chorus rose in Leicester Square and swelled across London, and from there to every corner of the country in one fast-moving wave of ecstasy and delirium. The wave travelled the Channel and the North Sea and the Atlantic, and it travelled with the speed of revelation to Ulan Bator, to Timbuktu, to Kalamazoo and to a lot of other places with less comic names, and soon the whole world was chanting 'Victoria! Victoria! Victoria!' and the world's dog was barking along too.

In the clamour, a new refrain: 'Victoria for World Leader (Not Pretend)!'

'Yes! Yes! Yes!' cried other voices seizing on the idea.

'Yes! Yes! Yes! Yes! Yes! Yes!' said yet more.

Then the world was chanting as one, 'Victoria for World Leader (Not Pretend)! Victoria for World Leader (Not Pretend)! Victoria for World Leader (Not Pretend)! Victoria for World Leader (Not Pretend)!' For the first time in history the entire globe found harmony, unity, and common purpose without wearing mind-altering underpants, which is when Victoria decided to put her foot down.

The adamantine airship powered back into the sky above London like a thought from another dimension.

The underpants heir came back on the airwaves, peering down on humanity from the tops of thousands of buildings around the world. 'Thank you! Thank you! But I must say no, a very clear and absolute no.'

'Awwwww!' wailed the population of the planet together. 'Please!'

'I'm sorry, I can't.'

'Why not?'

'Well,' said Victoria, 'because we've had enough of power and its abuses. Look what happened last time you had a World Leader (Not Pretend).'

'Fair point,' said the world.

'And remember, overcoming Mangler was not a one-person show. Lots of people fought Mangler. Many suffered for it. Don't forget that in the end you all overthrew Mangler. Once you were free of his embrace and given the facts, you all revolted against him. That certainly wasn't a thing one person could do by herself.'

'Another fair point,' the world conceded suddenly feeling a bit chuffed at itself.

'I urge you, turn away from world leaders, not pretend or otherwise, and find your own way so that this abuse cannot happen again.'

'Oh, all right,' said the world.

'Here, hang on a minute,' said a lone voice in the middle of Leicester Square. 'It's very commendable you pitching in against Mangler and being instrumental in liberating humanity from his under-yoke of oppression and all that, but how did you get those recordings of him and his crew incriminating themselves?'

'Ooh! Good question! How did you get those recordings?' the world wanted to know.

Hilda and Victoria held up to the camera two pairs of very stylish underpants. 'We call them iPants,' they said. 'The latest thing in wearables.'

Hades flushed.

'The fibres of these pants are a complex carbon matrix that carries the computing power of any high performance machine, and is studded with nano sensors that can record images and sound. With links to the cell network, we are always online. Wherever we went, whenever we encountered Mangler or his people, we were able to capture sound and vision, we were able to record everything that went on. It was no problem to upload to a remote server and then show you the highlights.'

'Ooooh!' said the world.

'But you've probably had enough of underpants now, haven't you,' guessed Victoria.

'Not so sure about that, not since you showed us yours,' said the world. 'Where can we buy some?'

'Shall we come back to that later?' suggested Hilda. 'Right now I think there's a lot of rebuilding to be getting on with.'

'And before that, a very big party to be had,' said Victoria.

Epilogue

The two pairs of Überunderpants shook the faint traces of itching powder off their leaves. It had hurt them, turned their foliage a bit yellow round the edges, but there hadn't been much of it.

Trapped in this basement here, insufficient had penetrated to do them any real harm. They were OK, despite being unable to escape. The door was wedged shut by the debris of the ruined building above, a building shattered by some arbitrary act of violence in the general Überunderpants apocalypse and now for the time being overlooked by the humans, who had more urgent repairs to tackle.

Yet there was enough light for photosynthesis. It was getting in through the dramatic holes in the ruins above. A broken main somewhere was supplying water direct to the floor. Even better, there was this little humanoid creature that looked entirely like a root vegetable or a nut and who kept bringing them nutrition in the form of jelly and assorted uncooked meat products.

No, they were in no immediate danger and where other plants might have found this environment inhospitable, their DNA was sufficiently bonkers to stroll through.

However, they did have rather a lot of time on their hands — or on their fronds. This they decided to fill by cross pollinating. By breeding. By having sex. Plant sex. Lots of it. In all the plant positions they could think of. And they still had enough time and randiness to think up some new plant positions. They had a new career waiting

288

for them if they ever got out: they could publish a whole book on vegetable sex.

In no time at all, Überunderpants seedlings were squirming all over the floor, and soon these would be shagging each other to make more. Yes, these trapped Überunderpants were going to make themselves a jungle; their own personal jungle.

As the days passed, the two Überunderpants became more and more expert in their flornication. And as those same days passed, the sounds of the city outside the basement — not that the Überunderpants were paying attention — were changing. The grinding, thumping and clanging of the reconstruction was getting louder as the work drew closer. Before long, the jelly brought by the wizened nut-man was wobbling not so much with the vegetable passion as the rebuilding going on outside.

Soon, the basement would be once again opened to the world.

ALSO BY CHRIS PAGE

King of the Undies World

Victoria Gousset, rich, beautiful, daft, and heir to an improbably massive fortune, has been kidnapped.
Her father, mercurial underwear magnate Sir Hades Gousset, sees a way to make capital from the kidnap of his daughter and sets his own cunning plan in motion.
Persephone Gousset, volcanic wife of Hades, discovers her husband's ruse to exploit his daughter's predicament and hatches her own plot to teach her scheming husband a lesson.
The farcical collision of these events propels Victoria on a misadventure that takes her across continents and beyond, while catapulting the Goussets, their friends and enemies into a series of catastrophes that eventually threaten the destruction of the planet.

And all because of some pants.

King of the Undies World is the first volume of the *Underpants of Fire* trilogy in which Sir Hades, Victoria and Persephone pursue adventures in underwear.

Weed

In his professional and personal life Bob, aka Robert D Weed, is deemed totally useless — or, perhaps, he is the smart one and everyone around him is terminally daft.

Bob is a human weed who is tugged and pulled by a world that wants to uproot him but which discovers that he cannot be so easily tossed on the compost.

"... it's really witty and very strong ... I would compare the writing to Robert Rankin, or a really satirically biting Tom Sharpe, and will say […] that I'm really impressed by it." — A London publisher

"… Weed … is a tale that somehow manages to combine the frustrations of modern urban Mclife and blancmange abuse in the same story... a tale that is likely to feel sheepishly familiar yet feverishly alien... depending on your views about the uses of sticky puddings." — Kyoto After Dark

"Weed is a brilliantly written comedic novel while at the same time a harsh criticism of modern consumerist society. The lyrically attractive writing style spoke to me and does a good job of creating a vision of this fictitious yet very real world and company. It reminded me of Terry Gilliam's movie *Brazil* ... If you, like the protagonist, sometimes find yourself drowning in the rat race for conformity and mediocrity, this book is for you." — Amazon review

"It's so funny I weed myself. Geddit?" — The author made up this quote himself.

Un-Tall Tales

Un-Tall Tales is a collection of short fiction, poetry, flash fiction and odds and ends.

In 'The Freebie', musical wannabe Billy Freeb's fifteen minutes are upon him. Will he survive?

The poems explore underpants, teeth, chickens, and tombstones. Will literary sensibility survive?

'Cats Die' relates how our hero decides to combat the crisis of middle age by having an affair with a teenage girl. Will he survive?

The hero of 'Dumb Novel' achieves literary fame for a book he didn't write. Will he survive?

'Escapology' — on a whim, the hero has himself chained, locked in a box and dropped through a hole drilled in the Arctic ice cap. Will he survive?

Bog is a bloggy rumination on sausages and twigs. Will the human attention span survive?

Links

http://weedthenovel.com
http://untalltales.com
http://chris-page.com
www.psipook.com

www.ingramcontent.com/pod-product-compliance
Lightning Source LLC
Chambersburg PA
CBHW071255170626
46809CB00001B/232